The Trials of Marcus Clemens

James E. Anderson

ISBN 978-1-7379692-1-1 (paperback)

After many years of toying with the idea of trying my hand at storytelling, well, here goes. Thank you to all my family members, past and present, for the love and support you have lent.

A special thank you to my daughter Angela for providing me the motivation to sit down and see this through to the end. A heartfelt thank you to April P. for the simple breakroom conversations that inspired the confidence this could be done.

Table of Contents

Heading Home

As he stood on the bank, bamboo pole in hand, Marcus gazed across the nearly one-mile-wide expanse of the mighty Mississippi River flowing before him. Just as his father, and his father before him, had stood in the same location in anticipation of landing the sublimely delicious blue catfish, Marcus knew the odds were low and he would be lucky to nail a flathead or more likely the common channel catfish. Lacking that, he most certainly would be carrying home a ten-pound crappie. It was nearly April of 1963, but the weather had remained quite cool. Not the ideal time to haul in a twenty-to-thirty-pound trophy cat.

The breeze was beginning to pick up as the skies became more ominous. A late spring rain was forecast for overnight, and a slight chill trailed down Marcus' spine. Gripping the pole patiently, Marcus began to allow his mind to drift. He silently wondered how it had been in years past when his father and grandfather had fished from this same bank. His father Elijah Clemens had worked the rock quarry on the Illinois side of the river, near Quincy, for almost fifteen years. Growing up in Lewis

1

County, Missouri only about forty miles north of Hannibal, Elijah had always wondered, but could never learn, if he was related to the famous author from Hannibal, Samuel Clemens. Being raised near the levees entrusted with containing the powerful Mississippi, Elijah had a keen interest in the river and was enthralled by the tales of Tom Sawyer and Huckleberry Finn. These accounts spun by Samuel Clemens, more commonly known as Mark Twain, deeply aroused the impressionable young adventurous mind of Elijah. He was so deeply enchanted by the stories that he had named his only son Marcus Twain Clemens. And, of course, Marcus was known as Marc Twain to his friends.

Marcus wondered how much his father had been able to replicate the adventures of young Tom and Huck as he had maneuvered his adolescent years. He recalled his father's claims of driving a '32 Ford coupe across a frozen over Mississippi River at the age of 15, but Marcus questioned the validity of that anecdote. A few Halloween pranks as a teenager, but not much more to remember of his father's youth. Unfortunately, Elijah had been tragically killed in a quarry accident when the bulldozer he was operating lost traction and toppled some eighty feet into a rock pit. Four years had now passed, but Marcus, at 11 years of age, was still quite shell-shocked. Coupled with the fact that his mother had passed from brain cancer when he was but two, Marcus was left in a somewhat fragile state. A likely explanation for the solace he found in fishing, thinking, reminiscing.

Not that Marcus was alone. He lived with his stepmother Margaret in the Westside La Grange Apartments. As stepmothers go, Marcus was more or less grateful she was there. She cared for him deeply, had always treated him as her own. Although to his friends he referred to her as the "Wicked Witch of the West" because of her strict and unwavering manner, Marcus loved her and had always referred to her as Mama. In Margaret's world, tomfoolery and undisciplined behavior would not to be tolerated. Good manners, good hygiene, reverence, respect, and punctuality were the traits that Margaret had diligently endeavored to instill in Marcus. Failure to abide by these ideals was met by swift and sometimes harsh retribution. Depending upon her mood, punishment could range from being grounded, being sent to bed without dinner, or in the more extreme situations the fly swatter handle or a switch. However, so long as rules were followed, life could be comfortable.

Breaking Marcus from his thoughts, the cork on his line began to bob in the current. He tightened his grip and jerked on the pole attempting to set the hook. Alas, unsuccessfully. Dejectedly, Marcus realized it was going to be another fruitless afternoon. Gathering his tackle, bait, and small thermos bottle, he began to prepare for his trek home. Looking at the cloudy and overcast sky, he realized dusk was beginning to fall. That meant part of the almost one hour walk home would be in the dark, and mosquitoes could still be a problem at this time of year near the water.

Crossing North 4th Street and turning right to head down White Street, a devastating thought occurred to Marcus. The time change had been last night. Daylight Saving Time had arrived. And with it, longer days. Which meant it was nearly dusk, but it was an hour later than he had realized. Dinner was at 7:00 p.m. sharp, not 7:10 or even 7:05. Washed up and at the table at 7:00 p.m. By the amount of darkness beginning to engulf the streets, Marcus estimated it was likely nearing 6:30. Oh, how he did not want to face an angry, irate stepmother. He began to jog down White Street, but it had been a long day and Marcus was tired. And he was also a bit overweight, which limited his ability to sustain the effort. It seemed he had already been running for a good hour when he saw Porter's Funeral Home looming ahead. Darkness was settling all around him and Marcus was growing more uneasy by the minute. As he passed the funeral home, an unnerving yet plausible thought entered his mind. Forest Park Cemetery was just past the funeral home. Now, Forest Park was not something he particularly feared. After all, both of his parents rested there, and he visited them often. In the daylight. But from all those visits, Marcus was very knowing of the roads and paths that lay within. He was keenly aware that he could take advantage of shortcuts that could possibly get him home ten to fifteen minutes sooner, and if he were truly lucky, avoid punishment for being late. Upon reaching the cemetery, mustering all his courage, and praying for God's protection, Marcus squeezed through a gap in the chained gate used by cemetery landscapers and began a lonely walk through the maze of tombstones and markers.

It was now almost fully dark, there was no moonlight, and no stars were visible due to the heavy cloud cover. Even though Marcus had been

3

in this cemetery countless times and knew it almost like the back of his hand, in the practically total darkness, it seemed unfamiliar and wretchedly, wretchedly scary. There was little light available from the sparsely spaced gaslights that appeared near the entrances to the various gardens – Garden of Peace, Garden of Tranquility, Garden of Spirituality, etc. As he was passing the mausoleum, Marcus felt relief because he knew he was well beyond the halfway point of this frightful journey. Although he really made every effort to convince himself he was not scared (his parents were there to protect him after all), deep inside Marcus had never felt this frightened and leery in his life. Every acorn he stepped on, every twig that snapped startled him and made him wonder if it was him or some creature that had made the noise. The wind rustling through the trees, the rare but occasional hoot of an owl all complicated the situation.

Just as it seemed it could not be any more frightful, there came a clap of thunder and flash of lightening......and a voice softly behind him......."Marc". Marcus stopped dead in his tracks. He listened but didn't hear another sound. It must be my imagination, he thought. There's no one here but me. Marcus picked up the pace a bit but kept his senses on alert. Perhaps a minute passed before......."Marc". Surely one of his buddies had spotted him walking home or entering the cemetery and thought it would be jolly to try to scare him. He stopped and turned. But there was no one there. At least no one he could see. Marcus peered intently into the darkness, straining to see someone, anyone ... human. Nothing, no one. Just darkness. "Ten more minutes", Marcus said aloud, knowing he was that close to breaking free of the grasp of the cemetery. "Marc....... Marc....... Marc", unmistakably close behind. Marcus dropped all his equipment and began to run. But the voice stayed with him, right behind, calling "Marc....... Marc....... Marc....... Marc".

Fearing he would be overtaken and possibly devoured, Marcus sought refuge behind a large tombstone. Sitting on the cold damp ground, shivering with fright, tears silently began rolling toward his chin. Glancing up, and despite the looming darkness, Marcus managed to notice the name on the tombstone. Harold Lee Clemens. How strange, thought Marcus. Aside from himself, his parents and Margaret, Marcus had never seen or heard the Clemens name in Lewis County and could not help but wonder if this revelation was some form of premonition. Is this some sort of premonition? He closed his eyes and attempted to calm himself but had barely drawn a breath when the gentle and serene sounding voice behind the tombstone softly said....... "Marc". Trembling with fear, Marcus turned to confront the inevitable. Eerily, a face slowly emerged from behind the tombstone. With head cocked to one side and revealing what appeared as a rather demented smile, it seemed to whisper, "Marc".

Marcus began to laugh uncontrollably, if not somewhat hysterically, as he realized he had frantically been attempting to escape from....... a harelipped dog.

James E. Anderson

The Dog

Marcus' head pounded as the hammer ricocheted between the twin bells on the Westclox alarm clock. Fumbling to silence the incessant racket, Marcus realized his mouth was dry and the goo on the roof of his mouth was more than grotesque. "Dummy, that's what you get for sleeping with your pie hole open", Marcus mumbled as he trapsed into the bathroom. Last night's tuna casserole wasn't doing much to help with the vulgar tastes swirling around his tongue either. Marcus knew that while a rinse of Listerine would certainly help, he was going to have to proceed with a thorough scrubbing with the baking soda. Why, he wondered, won't Margaret spring the few cents more for Colgate? Most of his friends had been brought into the twentieth century and actually used toothpaste. But not old Marcus. Baking soda was good enough for Margaret growing up, so it would suffice for Marcus as well.

With his mouth somewhat refreshed, Marcus turned his attention to the bathtub. As it began to fill with lukewarm water (Margaret would chastise for the wasteful use of hot water - "electricity doesn't grow on trees, Marcus!"), thoughts of the events of yesterday and last night began emerging from his memory. Nothing doing at the river. Fish weren't biting, it was chilly…. Forest Park Cemetery. My God, it wasn't just a dream. "I was scared shitless", Marcus uttered aloud. He had run halfway through the cemetery thinking he was being chased by someone calling his name. My how the mind can play tricks when a person is truly frightened, and make no mistake, Marcus was truly frightened. Only to then realize it was nothing but a mangy dog in search of attention. Poor thing meant no harm and actually was friendly in a quiet, subtle way. After a hearty laugh and a ruffling of the ears, the mutt had wandered away. And Marcus had made it home just in time for dinner.

* * * *

The 3:30 bell rang at last, and the Monday school day had mercifully come to an end. Marcus gathered his 3-ring binder and math book and raced from classroom to the front door of Roosevelt Elementary, hoping to catch a glimpse of Cassie Worthington as she descended the steps and made her way to her bus. In Marcus' opinion she was the most beautiful girl in all the fifth grade. Granted there were only 32 girls in the fifth grade, but that still meant she was prettier than 31 others. Cassie had strawberry blonde hair worn in pigtails. The freckles on her naturally rosy cheeks and classic Greek nose coupled with the dimples that appeared with her smile, were in perfect combination with her innocent sky-blue eyes. Marcus didn't have an abundance of opportunity to see her at school because she was in Miss Hawthorne's class (where the smartest kids were placed) while he was in the "B" class with Mrs. Lawrence. Occasionally, he would spot her at Franklin's Five and Dime or Dempsey's Grocery, but she was almost always with her mother. Besides, she was far too pretty for a kid like Marcus. He was conspicuously conscious of his weight and far too insecure to approach her. But he could certainly admire from afar.

On the way home (yes, he was a walker), Marcus found himself thinking again about the events of last night. That was a dog following him. How could he possibly have imagined that a dog was calling to him? He had noticed in the dim light some type of deformity with the dog's mouth that had made it appear to have been smiling, but what would that have to do with anything? Marcus had asked friends and even Mr. Lupka, the janitor, if they knew of any deformities that could occur in dogs but had learned nothing useful. Perhaps the Encyclopedia Britannica that Margaret so prized would hold a clue.

Upon arriving home and conducting minimal research, Marcus learned of a human condition called a cleft lip or harelip. He decided that this affliction was apparently what this dog was demonstrating. A phone call placed to the receptionist for the local Lewis County veterinarian (one Dr. James Harwick) had confirmed that dogs could indeed be born with a cleft lip and/or palate. That would explain the strange "smile" Marcus had seen, but certainly not the eerie calling of his name. Of course, a cleft lip could result in a speech impediment in a person, but a dog? That seemed a highly unlikely possibility, but Marcus refused to believe that his imagination had conjured up his name being spoken in Forest Park.

* * * *

When the bell rang on Tuesday afternoon, and after witnessing Cassie board her bus, Marcus began to amble his way homeward. The weather had improved and warmed considerately, the sun shone brightly, it was remarkably beautiful outdoors. As he walked, Marcus decided it would be a lovely day to visit his parents. And it was daylight, so he felt pretty safe from any potential doom. He was a big kid now, had never before been the least bit nervous in the cemetery. As Marcus set a course for Forest Park, he couldn't help but think about the events of Sunday evening. A horrific experience for sure, and certainly enough to keep Marcus from ever visiting the cemetery after sundown for as long as he lived. As he approached the entry to Forest Park, Marcus felt a twinge of trepidation. Surely nothing unusual will happen, he thought. He was quite positive he had been through enough on Sunday to last for a good long time.

As he made his way along the roadway and past the Garden of Peace, Marcus played his usual game of reading the years of birth and death on the tombstones and calculating the ages of the departed. Marcus always enjoyed arithmetic and was quite proficient with mathematical calculations. It was science and geography that were his bugaboo in school. Marcus broke from the road, bore to his right, and began to walk down the pathway leading in the direction of his parents' graves. It was calm, warm, a genuinely peaceful day that was hauntingly disrupted when a soft quiet voice said …. "Marc". No, not again, he thought. I am not imagining this. I just heard my name very clearly. "Please don't let this

9

be happening again", Marcus prayed aloud. He turned, half expecting to see nothing, but standing behind him on the path perhaps one hundred feet away... the harelipped dog.

The dog stood as if it was not sure whether to approach Marcus. An agonizing minute passed as Marcus waited to see what was going to unfold. In a slow, deliberate pace the dog walked toward Marcus, then sat on its haunches about a foot in front of him. The dog tilted its head to the right and looked Marcus in the eye. Marcus was flabbergasted, not knowing just what to do. He was a little scared and a lot of nervous. It was broad daylight, and someone or something had spoken his name. He stared back at the dog and chokingly said, "You called my name. But you're just a mangy dog. I may be a stupid kid, but I know you can't talk." The dog did nothing but stare at him. Marcus was dumbfounded, but a calm seemed to come over him. He studied the dog, searching the mournful eyes for a clue or sign to gain insight into this mystery. Marcus tentatively reached out, placing his hand on the top of the dog's head, and gently rubbed with his thumb. The dog remained still, with not so much as a blink. He rubbed behind the right ear and then the left and then withdrew his hand. Marcus smiled a nervous and uncertain smile, but his eyes did not leave the mysterious dog. They remained looking at one another for perhaps a half minute. The dog stood, cocked its head to the left, and seemed to take in one long, studious and final look at Marcus. It was almost as if it was straining to remember or recognize the boy who stood before it. Finally, the gaze broke and the dog commenced slowly sauntering away, disappearing into the undergrowth of the neighboring forest.

Margaret

Margaret Clemens was a comely woman, although she made no real effort to enhance her looks. Following the death of Elijah, she had no interest in maintaining a social life. She was more than happy to remain a homebody. Margaret, or Mags as Elijah had been fond of calling her, stood just over five feet and weighed barely a hundred pounds. More often than not, she wore her hair in what Marcus called a schoolmarm bun. But on the occasions when she let her medium champagne hair down, it was quite lovely. Even Marcus would admit that the "Wicked Witch of the West" looked striking when she allowed herself the opportunity. Margaret enjoyed listening to the radio, and even though she'd just celebrated her 34th birthday, she was still a teenager when it came to the Everly Brothers and Elvis Presley. She had just recently mentioned to Marcus that she had heard two new groups on the radio that were quite different from one another but seemed to both have potential. One was out of California and the other from England, although she couldn't recall their names. "But," she assured Marcus, "neither holds a candle to Presley."

Tuesday was a day off from her parttime waitressing job at River's Edge Diner and Margaret sat watching The Guiding Light on the 17" black and white Philco Predicta that Elijah had given her for an

11

anniversary gift just days before his accident. She prayed that television would never break down because it was one of her most sentimental reminders of Elijah. Prior to their third anniversary they did not have a television, which made the Philco that much more special. Margaret loved to watch Ben Casey, Dr. Kildare and Gunsmoke. She and Marcus would together watch lighter fare such as The Beverly Hillbillies, The Red Skelton Show, and The Lucy Show.

Near the end of The Guiding Light episode, and during a conversation between Dr. Johnny Fletcher and George Hayes, Margaret's attention was interrupted by loud and ceaseless barking just outside the front door. After a few minutes of the unwelcome racket, Margaret rose from the couch, blurting, "What in God's name is going on out there?" She strode purposefully to the front door and flung it open to see what was causing the commotion, but to her surprise, there wasn't the slightest sign of anyone or anything. Just the faint rumble of some afternoon traffic over on Highway 81 broke the afternoon silence. "Now, what could that have been about?" Margaret wondered aloud. "That dog must have been barking for at least five minutes nonstop." Right up until the second she had opened the door – and then sudden silence. There was, however, a red handkerchief lying on the stoop. A red handkerchief with the initials E.C. embroidered on it. Margaret recognized it immediately as one that had belonged to Elijah. He had always carried one in his back pocket and now Marcus carried one of the handkerchiefs in his pocket as a reminder of, and to help him remain close to, his father. Margaret bent to pick up the handkerchief and upon touching it, noticed its slimy wetness. She knew immediately that it had been placed there by the incessantly barking dog. Marcus must have dropped it outside or perhaps lost it when fishing on Sunday.

Margaret closed the door, deposited the handkerchief in the laundry hamper, and walked to the kitchen to pour some iced tea. As she took a sip, she realized it was just past 4:00 p.m. Marcus usually got home about 4:15, unless he decided to stop at Forest Park Cemetery to pay respect to his parents, which normally added about fifteen minutes to his walk home. On days when she wasn't working, Margaret tried to have a snack and glass of milk ready for him. Marcus would have his snack, then retire to his room. He didn't often have a lot of homework, but he was particularly good about finishing it before going out to play. He was a good boy and Margaret could count upon him to be responsible enough to ensure that he would be back home in time for dinner at seven.

As expected, Marcus stepped into the apartment just before 4:30, but uncharacteristically did not verbally greet Margaret, instead going straight to his room. When he didn't emerge in a few minutes, Margaret approached his bedroom door and gently knocked.

"Marcus, are you okay? Are you feeling alright? There's a half of a peanut butter and jelly sandwich on the table for you. And a glass of milk in the Frigidaire".

After a few seconds Marcus replied, "Thank you Mama, but I'm not really hungry and I have a lot of reading to do for English."
This was not a normal response for Marcus. And it was very curious that he would not be hungry. Lunch at school was at 11:30, and Marcus rarely made it four or five hours without nourishment.

Margaret asked again, "Are you sure you're alright, Marcus?"

"I'm fine, Mama." He replied.

At five before seven, Marcus emerged from his room, ducked into the bathroom to wash his hands, and then sat at the kitchen table. Margaret was putting the finishing touches on dinner as she asked him, "Feeling better, Marcus?"

"I'm good Mama, I told you I wasn't sick or nothing," Marcus replied.

"I know you did, Sweetie, but it's not like you to turn down a peanut butter and jelly sandwich. And it's anything, not nothing. That's a double negative and is poor grammar. You need break those habits now, so you don't sound uneducated when you are grown." Margaret was not one to let a teaching moment pass unutilized.

"Yes Ma'am. Sorry. I just have a lot on my mind today. Got a big math test Friday." Marcus had a lot on his mind, but the math test was not in the inventory.

"You'll be fine, Marcus. Math is your best subject."

"I know….." Marcus paused for a few seconds before asking, "Mama, how come parrots can talk? Are there any other animals that can talk?"

"I'm not sure why they talk, Marcus. Maybe that's a question better suited for Mrs. Lawrence. I'm sure she would know far better than me. But as far as any other animals talking? I don't think so. Why do you ask? You didn't hear the hamsters you all have at the back of your classroom talking, did you?"

"No Mama. It's just that when I was walking home today, I thought I heard someone say my name, but there was nobody there. All I saw was a couple of squirrels. I looked all around, but no one was there. It was just kind of weird." Marcus immediately wished he hadn't mentioned it, but Margaret didn't seem to think anything of it.

"Well, Marcus, maybe someone was watching television, had their window open and the set turned up loud. But I assure you, the squirrels didn't call out to you. All they do is kind of chirp. Except for Alvin and the Chipmunks, which I think are the same as squirrels. They talk and sing, but nonetheless, they aren't real."

"Okay, Mama. You're probably right."

Margaret placed a plate of spaghetti in front of Marcus and another on her placemat. Spooning the sauce over the noodles, Margaret said to him, "The strangest thing happened this afternoon, Marcus. I found your handkerchief on the front stoop. Did you drop it outside yesterday or this morning?"

"Not this morning because I carried the same brand new clean one yesterday and today. I might've lost it Sunday though when I was fishing. I don't remember putting it in the hamper Sunday night."

"Well, when I found it this afternoon, it was on the front stoop and it was a nasty wet." Margaret continued, "There had been a dog

14

barking outside the front door, but when I opened it there wasn't a dog in sight, but the handkerchief was there. It was almost as though the dog had found it and brought it here to return it."

"That's weird, Mama," Marcus said. "Maybe I just dropped it on the porch last night." Marcus knew perfectly well he had not dropped it last night or this morning. Perspiration began to form on his forehead and bead on his upper lip. He knew Sunday night when undressing that he didn't have the handkerchief and figured he'd probably lost it running through the cemetery.

Marcus didn't want to lie, but he could not bring himself to tell Margaret about the harelipped dog. She might think he was crazy, or at the very least accuse him of making up a story so far-fetched as a dog speaking his name. As uneasy and confused as he was already feeling, Marcus surely didn't need any added pressure.

James E. Anderson

16

Cassie

As the days passed, Marcus began to feel relief from his anxiety over the harelipped dog. It is fair to assume, though, that the first few trips back to Forest Park to visit his parents were rather trepidatious. At first, Marcus constantly was looking over his shoulder and searching the nearby hedges and grave markers, as well as the brush at the forest's edge for any sign of the mangy dog. His hearing was also on high alert, but nothing out of the ordinary took place. Whatever had happened was in the past and there didn't seem to be any sign of a reoccurrence.

The Midwest spring had arrived, and Marcus was beginning to allow thoughts of the strange dog to fade. Children seem to have relatively short attention spans and there is always something new, seemingly on a daily basis, to occupy their consciousness. Marcus was no exception, as he directed his thoughts to the spring baseball season. He enjoyed playing but was definitely not of all-star caliber. It was a game that provided him the opportunity to spend time outdoors with his friends and as Margaret would say, burn off the pent-up energy he had accumulated over the winter months.

It was after baseball practice on the first Saturday in May that Marcus strolled into Franklin's Five and Dime with his pal Denny. They took seats at the soda counter and ordered two chocolate malts. The soda jerk's name was Ellis Compton, and he was in tenth grade at Lewis and Clark Senior High School. Marcus envied Ellis, first of all because he heard that Ellis was earning sixty-five cents an hour on his Saturdays, but more so because he was a real big shot to all the girls that came into Franklin's. He would laugh and cajole with the young teenage girls and they all seemed to think he was the cat's meow. He wore his dark brown hair slicked back in poor imitation of Elvis Presley's mane, but was barely old enough to sport minimal sideburns. It's a good thing Elvis didn't have a mustache, because Ellis was at least a year or two shy of reaching that milestone. But still, the young girls making the transition from early to middle adolescence apparently viewed him as a debonair young man and unmistakably the object of their desires.

After sucking down the last drops of their malts (complete with the obnoxious and juvenile slurping/sucking sounds of straws in the bottom of an empty glass), Marcus and Denny sauntered to the magazine rack where they began perusing the latest issues of the MAD and Cracked magazines. Marcus was a huge fan of MAD magazine, especially enjoying the Spy vs. Spy comic strips. Last summer, he had saved enough of his allowance to order a bust of Alfred E. Neuman (the mascot of Mad magazine) with Neuman's motto, "What, Me Worry?" engraved on the base. The purchase had set him back $3, and even though the bust turned out to be only about four inches tall, seemed well worth the investment to an avid fan. As he read the "The Lighter Side of…." feature, a giggling voice behind him said, "Hi, Marcus".

Marcus lowered the magazine and pivoted to his right to see Cassie Worthington smile and blink as she nervously swiveled her hips from side to side. "I was kind of hoping you might be here. Denny told me you and him might come to Franklin's after practice."

"Uh…. yeah." Marcus timidly responded. He turned back to sneer at Denny, but he was nowhere to be found. The rat fink Denny had set him up and right now he didn't know whether to be mad at Denny or thank him.

18

"Marcus, I hope I'm not being too forward, but Denny told me that you kind of liked me. But he said you were too shy to talk to me. I started noticing you back around Halloween and I always kind of hoped you would say something to me." Cassie smiled again, and Marcus melted inside.

"I...I guess he's right Cassie. I do like you. I been liking you since third grade when we had Mrs. Glover." Marcus suddenly became a shoegazer, and his cheeks flushed with embarrassment. "I just never figured you would even talk to me."

"Well, you should have tried Marcus. You would've been surprised."

"Gosh, I'm sorry Cassie. Want me to buy you a soda.... or a malt?" Marcus asked hesitantly. He knew he had fifty-two cents in his pocket. A soda was ten cents, and that would leave him enough for the thirty-five cent Mad that he'd planned on buying. But the extra twenty cents for a malt would leave him short.

"No thanks, Marcus. I have to get back to Dempsey's. My mom is grocery shopping. I just ran over here to get a copy of 16 magazine."

Marcus felt relieved that he didn't have to part with any more of his allowance (plus he could still get his Mad magazine). "Okay, Cassie." Marcus paused, then asked "Do you want me to walk you back to Dempsey's?"

"That would be really nice, Marcus."

Cassie and Marcus headed to the cash register where she handed the cashier exactly thirty-six cents for the 16 magazine and Marcus did the same for his Mad. They proceeded the two blocks to Dempsey's without saying much except to comment on what a two-face Denny was behind Marcus' back. He didn't admit it to Cassie, but Denny turned out to be the best friend a guy could have.

When they got to the grocery, Cassie turned to Marcus and said, "Since you're my boyfriend now, on Monday are you going to come to Miss Hawthorne's class after school and walk me to my bus?"

19

Marcus wasn't expecting Cassie to be so bold as to name him her "boyfriend", but it did sound good and made him feel proud. "Sure, Cassie.

That would be swell."

* * * *

For the next three weeks, Marcus dutifully waited for Cassie outside Miss Hawthorne's door and then walked with her to Lewis County School District bus #32. It only took a few days for fellow students to realize they were an "item". They would sit together on a playground bench during afternoon recess and at least once or twice hear the refrain, "Marcus and Cassie, sittin' in a tree......" Finally, on May 24, the last day of school arrived. Marcus walked Cassie to the bus, and as she prepared to board, Marcus asked, "Cassie, am I going to see you before September?" Cassie slipped him a note that she had already prepared, smiled and climbed onto the bus.

Marcus pocketed the note, sighed and began his walk home. Passing by Mueller's Pharmacy, he decided it was time to see what Cassie had written. He sat on a wicker chair outside the pharmacy and unfolded the note. From Cassie's immaculate handwriting he read,

Dear Marcus,
It has been a really good time since you became my boyfriend. You are very nice and I like you a lot. Will you call me tomorrow? My telephone number is Fairview 7-6964. I was hoping maybe some days this summer we could meet at Randolph Park and go to the playground or go to the lake and watch the ducks.
Bye,
Cassie

Marcus couldn't contain his smile. He started walking toward home with the smile still embedded on his mug when worry started to come over him. He hadn't told Margaret about Cassie. How was he going to be able to go see her without Margaret knowing? Or should he just tell Margaret that he has a girlfriend? How will she react? What will she say? Will she be okay with it? Will she tell him he's too young for a girlfriend? Should he even be worrying about it? He was going into sixth grade, only one year shy of junior high. Surely, he was old enough to do as he pleased. Right?

James E. Anderson

Randolph Park

Marcus wasted no time acting upon Cassie's request as he dialed her up bright and early Saturday morning. It was only ten past eight when Mrs. Worthington woke Cassie to inform her that she had a phone call from a boy. She instinctively knew it was Marcus and hurried to the parlor to answer. Cassie didn't even say hello or wait to hear the caller's voice, she immediately said, "Hello Marcus." He was surprised that she knew it was him, although he shouldn't have been. She had, after all, asked him to call her on Saturday. Margaret was working the 6:00-2:00 shift at the diner, covering breakfast and lunch, so Marcus had no need to explain being on the telephone so early. "Hi, Cassie," he replied. "I thought I'd call to see if you wanted to come to meet me at Randolph Park this morning. I have a game there at 10:30 if you'd like to come watch and maybe go to the lake after the game."

"Oh, I can't Marcus. I have to go shopping with my mom this morning. She's getting me a new pair of Keds and then we're going to

Dempsey's. But do you think we could meet up there after lunchtime?" Cassie was hopeful that she hadn't disappointed Marcus and that he would agree to an afternoon rendezvous.

Marcus did some mental calculations and decided he could finish his baseball game, run home for a sandwich and get back to Randolph Park by 2:00 p.m. and suggested meeting Cassie then.

"Okie dokie, Marcus. That's a good time. I'll meet you at the gazebo at 2:00." Cassie hung up the phone with a grin that was a mile wide.

"Someone looks like they found a shiny new dime, Cassandra," Mrs. Worthington said as she dusted the knick knack shelf in the parlor. Cassie had not seen her enter the room and was a little embarrassed that her mother had been eavesdropping. "That must have been Marcus."

"Yes mother, it was." Cassie's rosy, red cheeks turned another brighter shade of rouge. She had never really had a discussion with her mother concerning a boy, except to confide that there was a classmate named Marcus that she thought liked her. "He is really nice and he's really good at arithmetic!" Cassie felt that a couple of redeeming qualities would help to qualify her endearment to Marcus.

"Well, that's good darling. Perhaps being a genteel math whiz at 10 or 12 will project him to be a promising husband and breadwinner in another ten years." Mrs. Worthington chuckled. "If you're going to the park after lunch, have fun but don't be late for supper."

* * * *

Marcus' Giants lost to the Dodgers 14-3. Marcus didn't have any hits, and to be honest neither his heart nor head were into the game. At its conclusion, he raced back home, wolfed down a peanut butter and jelly sandwich, downed two glasses of grape Kool-Aid and changed into a clean pair of jeans and white tee shirt. Being eleven years old, there really was no need for a bath until tonight. He left a note for Margaret explaining he'd be spending the afternoon at Randolph Park, but would be back home before dinner. Marcus slipped on his Converse All-Stars and headed back to the park, arriving at the gazebo just before 2:00.

24

Marcus' timing was fairly accurate. He knew his apartment was just about a mile south from Randolph Park, and that it was roughly a twenty-minute walk. He really did not know where Cassie lived, but since she rode a bus, it had to be more than two miles from Roosevelt Elementary. Roosevelt was just over a mile and a half southeast of Westside LaGrange Apartments, which was the reason there was no bus service. There was talk that was going to change in the fall, simply due to the large number of students that were forced to walk to school from the complex. It had become a safety issue and even though the two-mile criteria was not met, an exception was probably going to be made.

Cassie got there about fifteen minutes after Marcus had arrived. Following a bit of awkward small talk about Marcus' big game, the youngsters headed off to explore the playground. Marcus was impressed to learn that Cassie was a bit of a tomboy. She was able to get as high as the crossmember on the swing set, traversed the monkey bars quicker than Marcus could, and despite her weight disadvantage was able to handle her end of the see saw quite nimbly (as long as Marcus sat on the inside of the handle, nearer to the fulcrum of the see saw, with his back toward Cassie). Cassie was also a fast runner and easily beat Marcus in a race from home plate at the ball field to the flagpole in center field. After about an hour of testing out the various playground apparatuses, running races and generally doing things neither of them had done in about a year (they were freshly out of fifth grade, and practically teenagers after all), Marcus and Cassie found themselves back at the gazebo.

Marcus asked Cassie just where she lived, since she was able to walk to Randolph Park but had to ride a bus to school. "I live about a half mile east of here. It only takes about ten or fifteen minutes to get here from my house. Me and my folks live over in Forest Park Estates. You know, about three or four blocks from the cemetery, on the other side of the woods off old highway 457. I guess I'm lucky I'm far enough away to ride the bus. It would really be scary to have to walk by that creepy old cemetery every day."

"That cemetery isn't so bad Cassie. A lot of nice people live there. As a matter of fact, it's so popular that people are dying to get in!" Marcus beamed with pride at his ingenious impromptu joke, but his pride was short-lived.

"Oh Marcus! That's not even funny! People dying is nothing to laugh about," Cassie admonished him. "My grandma died last summer, and I still miss her. You'll feel the same way some day when you lose somebody close to you."

"I'm sorry, Cassie. I didn't mean to say anything bad; I was just trying to make you laugh," Marcus said, trying to soothe any hurt feelings. "If it makes you feel any better, I do know how you feel. My dad died four years ago, and I really miss him a lot. And I don't even remember my real mother because she died when I was just a baby, I guess. I was so young; I don't even remember her."

"Oh no, Marcus. I didn't know any of that. I feel so bad for you. Who do you live with, your grandparents?" Cassie asked earnestly concerned.

"No," Marcus sighed. "They are all gone, too. I live with my stepmother. Her name is Margaret. My dad married her when I was three or four, so she's the only mother I've ever known."

"Marcus, that is so sad."

"Ah gee whiz, Cassie. It's not all that bad. I try not to be sad about it. My parents are buried in the Forest Park Cemetery, and I go to see them all the time. I talk to them like they are still alive and listening. It's just that it's like they nod their heads and just don't say anything back, that's all," Marcus explained. He didn't want Cassie to feel sorry for him. He didn't need sympathy. He knew that they were in a better place and that one day he would see them again.

"Well Marcus, it's still sad," Cassie offered. Trying to lighten the mood she said, "and cemeteries are still spooky."

Marcus had an idea. "I'll tell you what, Cassie. What time do you have to be home for dinner?"

"6 o'clock, why Marcus?"

"Okay. How about we walk down to the cemetery and go to my parents' graves. I'll introduce you to them, you can say hi and then I'll walk you home to your house. I'll show you there is nothing to be afraid of. I'll be right there with you and I promise nothing will happen."

"I don't think so Marcus." Cassie was clearly afraid.

"I promise, Cassie. Nothing will happen. Period. I go all the time."

"Are you sure, Marcus?"

"I'm sure."

"Okay, I trust you, Marcus."

They left Randolph Park and headed south, turning left onto White Street. As they approached the entrance to Forest Park, Cassie was obviously apprehensive. She stopped when they reached the gate. "I don't want to Marcus."

"Cassie, do you ever visit your grandmother's grave?" Marcus asked. "Are you this nervous when you do?"

"No, I guess not," she timidly replied.

"Well, these are my parents, so don't be nervous around them either."

"What about all these other people that are buried here?" Cassie asked.

"I'll tell you what Mama, my stepmother Margaret, told me a long time ago. 'It's not dead people that can hurt you, it's the ones still alive'," Marcus sagely advised.

He took Cassie's hand, and they entered the gate. In less than ten minutes they had broken off the main road, turned right and headed down the pathway to the Garden of Faith. Within another two minutes, Marcus looked to his left and said, "Here we are Cassie". It was a simple marker.

On the left was inscribed: and on the right:

  Betty Jo Clemens   Elijah David Clemens
    1929-1954   1928-1959

Marcus handled the introductions, "Cassie, this my mother Betty and my dad Elijah. Mom, Dad this is my girlfriend. Her name is Cassie Worthington, and she is a swell girl. If you were here to really meet her, you would really like her. I think she'll be my girl for the rest of my life."

Cassie was moved by Marcus' introduction. It was the most touching thing she'd ever heard and was truly impressed with Marcus' sincerity. And with her eyes beginning to well up with emotion, Cassie said, "It is a real pleasure to meet you Mr. and Mrs. Clemens. Your son, Marcus, is a really special person you should really be proud of."

They stood for a couple of moments in silence before Marcus said, "We better be going so you get home on time. Thanks for coming with me Cassie."

"You're welcome Marcus. I enjoyed coming here with you."

"I know a shortcut to get out of here, but you might get your Keds a little dirty," Marcus warned.

"That's okay," Cassie responded. "I'm all about adventure and new experiences today."

They cut across a hundred yards of uncut grass in an area not yet developed, and then entered some knee-high brush. Cassie could see a fence line a few hundred yards in the distance. There were a few oak trees and several maples scattered through the thick underbrush. Marcus held her hand as they high stepped through the worst of it. Suddenly, and out of nowhere someone started yelling loudly, as if in warning, "Marc! Marc! Marc! Marc! Marc!" They froze, Cassie's eyes as big as saucers and Marcus with a thousand thoughts running through his head. The dog? The dog? Again? It's been what, two months? And where is it, and why, and why so loud? It had been so quiet and soft before. Marcus could see the brush rustling to his left, like a wave through a wheat field and rushing toward him. As it ran past him and onto the path he and Cassie had been pursuing, Marcus recognized the harelipped dog. It suddenly stopped no more than thirty feet in front of them and stood growling for five or six seconds before diving forward, snapping and pawing at something. It was as if the dog was attacking whatever was the object of its attention. This went on for perhaps ten to fifteen seconds and suddenly stopped. The dog stood softly growling and looking at the ground in front of it.

The harelipped dog turned around and walked toward Marcus and Cassie. It dropped onto its haunches in front of them. There was blood around its mouth, on its snout and Marcus could see at least one puncture wound on its black nose. The dog did not tilt its head as before but did look him in the eye. He then turned slightly and looked into Cassie's still saucer-sized eyes before returning his gaze to Marcus. Marcus was not a hundred per cent sure until he later asked and received confirmation from Cassie. But it sounded like the dog had said "It's okay Marc," before turning and going back in the direction from which it had come.

Marcus told Cassie to wait while he went a few feet ahead. He slowly made his way forward, carefully watching where he was stepping. When he reached the spot where the dog had been growling and snapping, he nearly lost his lunch. He was looking at something he had heard about but never seen. Marcus was gazing down at a rotted and hollowed out log that contained the tattered and torn remains of at least a half dozen copperhead snakes. Had the dog not intervened and he and Cassie had continued another ten yards or so they would have stumbled upon the den of venomous copperheads. They would never had seen it in the thick brush. He would no doubt have joined, and Cassie would really have met, his parents.

James E. Anderson

The Truth

Marcus and Cassie sat on the concrete foundation of the gas pump island outside of Walt's Tire and Auto Repair on White Street, about a quarter of a mile east of Forest Park. Old highway 457 was another block further east of them. Walt McMurphy had just closed up shop and left, and the Bardahl Oil clock hanging on the wall inside the window showed the time to be almost quarter past five. They would walk down to old highway 457 and then head north to reach Forest Park Estates and it shouldn't take any more than twenty minutes to get to Cassie's house. Marcus was confident she would be home in time for dinner. The timing worked out perfectly for Marcus as he should have no trouble at all finding his way home well in advance of 7:00 p.m.

In light of what Marcus had witnessed on the shortcut through the cemetery, he had opted to return to the certainty of the paths and roads of Forest Park to exit the property. He and Cassie had not spoken, not even after reaching the relative safety and comfort of White Street. As they sat at Walt's, it became apparent that Cassie's inquisitiveness could no longer be subdued. "Marcus, what did you see when you walked ahead just before we left? You had a really worried look on your face and was acting kind of strange."

Marcus struggled to frame his answer. He had so desperately wanted Cassie to be unafraid and somewhat comfortable in the cemetery, and now he was worried if he told her what he'd seen she would never go there with him again. But he also did not want to lie to her or try to cover up the truth. He decided to be forthright and said, "Cassie, it was a bunch of dead snakes."

"What kind of snakes?"

"I think they were copperheads. I'm pretty sure. I've seen a couple in my life, but I ain't never seen a den where they lived. There was an old log, and I think it was their den," Marcus stopped talking and looked at Cassie's face, searching for a sign of fear or perhaps revulsion. He saw neither.

"I wish you'd of told me, Marcus. I'd have liked to have seen it, too. I've never seen a snake den either," Cassie's response was not what Marcus was expecting. This girl was definitely not just an ordinary girl. "But I have seen a copperhead before. My dad killed one in the backyard the summer after third grade. Chopped it's head off with a shovel. And you know what Marcus, that snake's jaws were still moving like it was trying to bite somebody. So, my dad buried the head."

Marcus was quite astonished with Cassie's matter-of-fact recitation of her experience with a copperhead. "I always heard that no matter how you kill a snake it won't die until after sundown," Marcus offered.

"That's right," Cassie agreed. "When my dad killed that one, he buried the head, but left the rest of it in the yard and the next morning, it was gone. Crawled away, I guess."

"Wow. I've never killed one, so I don't know," Marcus admitted.

They stood and started moving on down White Street toward old highway 457. Just after exiting White and starting up 457, Cassie said, "Okay, Marcus. Now I want to know what's up with that dog that killed those snakes. Is that your dog?"

Marcus sure didn't have to fib about that, but somehow felt the need to. "Nope, never seen it before."

"You know, Marcus, you're not a very good liar. That dog seemed to know you awfully well." Cassie theorized.

Marcus was taken aback. "What do you mean?"

"Marcus, there was nobody in the field anywhere around us, right?"

"Yeah," he agreed.

"Then who in the heck was calling your name?" Cassie was beginning to raise her voice. She was definitely showing irritation as her face reddened. "I know nobody was there, you know nobody was there. But I'm positive that I heard someone calling your name, and loudly, like a warning. Like somebody yelling 'don't touch that hot burner' loud. Something really weird happened in that cemetery, Marcus. And you know that I'm right."

Marcus stood, staring at Cassie. It all came flooding back. The voice chasing him through the cemetery, calling his name. And then again two days later. Telling the dog "I know you can't talk," and the dog just looking at him, mysteriously. Cassie would think him a lunatic if he were to tell her the outlandish story. But she said that she too had heard the dog yelling his name.
Situations like this are what gave birth to the old saying between a rock and a hard place.

"You heard the dog calling the word Marc?" he asked Cassie.

"Yes, I did Marcus. It doesn't make any sense, but unless you have a better explanation that you're keeping from me, I don't know what else to believe," Cassie said with a hint of disappointment.

Marcus thought for a moment, took both of Cassie's hands in his and said, "I don't have an explanation. But I have a question. Please don't think I'm crazy, Cassie, but did that dog say anything else?"

"Yes, Marcus, it did. The dog said, 'it's okay Marc' before it left."

The rest of the stroll to Cassie's house could not be described as leisurely. It was made in silence, and one could almost smell smoke with the amount of wood being burned in the minds of the young sleuths as they each attempted to unravel the mystery that faced them. As they approached 218 Fernwood Drive, Marcus made a decision. "Cassie. I didn't tell you the whole truth. I have seen that dog before."

With that, Marcus came clean with Cassie, telling her the whole spooky story of being followed and called out to in the cemetery two months ago. And of having the dog call to him again a couple of days later. And of losing his father's red embroidered handkerchief in the cemetery on Sunday only to have it incomprehensively appear on his front porch on Tuesday, at the same time he was being confronted by the dog in the cemetery that afternoon. He also informed her of the physical malady that the dog suffered. She had not noticed the cleft lip on the dog, what with the degree of surprise with which the entire situation had developed. That was something new to think about. She knew what a cleft lip was, but certainly had never heard of such a thing on a dog.

It was nearing 6:00, Cassie had to get into the house, and Marcus needed to get his tail home as well.

"What are you doing tomorrow, Marcus? After church, we usually go to LaGrange and have Sunday dinner at the Red Roof Lodge. We get home about 1:30 or so. Maybe we can spend a couple of hours trying to solve the mystery of your furry friend." Cassie was not a very shy young lady and was quite direct in expressing herself.

"I usually go fishing at the river on Sunday afternoons," Marcus replied. "Do you like to fish, Cassie?"

"I've never gone fishing Marcus. Do you think you could teach me how?"

"I can try," laughed Marcus.

"Okay, Marcus. Why don't you come and get me at 1:30 and we'll go a-fishin', yee haw!" Cassie giggled and went in the house.

As he started toward home, Marcus marveled at how fortunate he was that Cassie had approached him at Franklin's. He would never have had the nerve to talk to her. The better he got to know her, the more he learned of her outgoing and amazing personality, the happier he was that Denny had set them up. And he sure did like her. A lot.

James E. Anderson

Sunday Begins

Marcus was up at 6:00 a.m. on Sunday morning. Margaret had prepared his breakfast, which on Sunday was always his favorite – two eggs, sunny side up, with four slices of bacon and two slices of toasted bread slathered in melted butter. He had always, for as long as he remembered, preferred this tasty combination to any other breakfast alternative, probably because it was his father's favorite choice. Just as he loved a green salad with olive oil and vinegar. Marcus didn't care for french, blue cheese or ranch dressings with his salad. Elijah had loved a simple salad with vinegar and oil, and probably in view of that preference, and perhaps to curry favor from his father, Marcus had always indulged in the same. Weekdays, especially during the school year, called for a quicker and easier breakfast, usually Corn Flakes or Wheaties (the breakfast of champions). Fruit Loops were one of the newest fads, and for some reason were the logical, more carefree choice for Saturdays.

Following breakfast and bathing, Marcus donned his black slacks, best white shirt and a bowtie, and along with Margaret strolled to Old Hills Baptist Church just off highway 16, about a mile and a quarter from their front door. Sunday School convened at 9:00 a.m., followed by worship at 10:15. It was going to be a long two and a half hours for Marcus. He was anticipating an enjoyable afternoon with Cassie and was painfully aware that the time would drag until he could get back home.

He was oh so right. Sunday School seemed to last for an eternity and Marcus could not force himself to feign interest in the topic "I am the Vine, You are the Branches", based upon the passage from John 15:1-5. Even though they got to use Play Dough to simulate the creation of vines and branches - and were instructed on how God prunes the vines to discard the useless branches and create new ones – Marcus just could not concentrate. Following a seemingly endless sermon delivered by Reverend Jackson in the sanctuary, the subject of which Marcus could not recall just after its conclusion, the small congregation began filing down the front steps. Each in turn paused to shake hands with the Reverend and compliment him on the inspiring message he had delivered.

As they were making their way home, Margaret asked Marcus if he had plans for later in the day. "I ask because Mrs. Dougherty invited us for cupcakes and Kool-Aid around three this afternoon. She is such a lonely old widow, and I think she really does enjoy the company. I know you like to fish on Sundays, but it would be a nice gesture to come along, don't you think?" Here we go, thought Marcus. A rock and a hard place. He was in a quandary and was going to have to open up to Margaret.

Marcus cleared his throat and apologetically offered, "I'm sorry, Mama, but I can't go to Mrs. Dougherty's today. I do have plans this afternoon. I hope that's okay."

"Really, Marcus? Your fishing is that important that you cannot help to soothe the existence of a poor old lady? Your callousness is quite upsetting Marcus. I can't describe the disappointment I am feeling right now."

Marcus thought long and hard as he struggled with what to do. He did not want to disappoint Cassie, but at the same time was upset with the reality of failing the expectations of Margaret. "Okay Mama, I'll cancel my plans and I'll go with you to see Mrs. Dougherty." Marcus was stuck. A rock and a hard place.

Reaching the apartment, Marcus went to his room where he began mentally constructing how to tell Cassie that he could not teach her to fish today. He figured he could call her just after 1:30, when he expected she would get back from lunch. He and Margaret wouldn't leave home to see Mrs. Dougherty until about 2:30, so he had plenty of time to break the news and try to smooth things over. However, he was preparing himself to face the backlash he fully expected from Cassie.

A quick Sunday lunch consisted of a bologna sandwich with mustard and Kas Potato Chips. As a special treat, Margaret removed the caps from two orange Vess sodas. A Vess soda was generally a once a week treat and represented a large step up from the usual milk or Kool-Aid. As Marcus finished his last bite of the sandwich and prepared to take his plate to the sink, he said to Margaret, "Mama, I have something I need to tell you."

"What is it, Marcus?" Margaret answered, looking up to Marcus as he scraped his crumbs into the trash and deposited his plate in the sink.

"Mama, I was supposed to go fishing with someone this afternoon."

"Oh? Who were you going with Marcus, Denny?" she asked.

"No, Mama. It was a girl. Her name is Cassie, Cassie Worthington. She lives over in Forest Park Estates. She's my really good friend. I was going to teach her how to fish today."

Margaret studied Marcus' face and could sense his dismay at having to cancel his plans. "Well, Marcus, how do you intend to tell this…Cassie, that you're not going fishing with her. Were you just going to not show up? If so, I can tell you right now that no girl wants to be stood up by a boy. That is one of the most disrespectful things you could do Marcus."

"Oh, no ma'am. I have her telephone number. I was going to call her. That's why I'm telling you about her now. She was going to church and then to lunch down in LaGrange and is supposed to get home about 1:30. So I need to ask your permission so I can call her then to tell her I can't go today," Marcus explained.

"I see," said Margaret. "And how long have you known this girl? I've never heard her name before."

"Well, I first knew her in Mrs. Glover's class in third grade, but we never talked to each other until we met at Franklin's about the time baseball practice started. But I've seen her at school a lot. We were in different classes, she's in the 'A' class – she's really smart and pretty. And now she's my girlfriend…. I mean friend. She's my friend, but she's a girl," Marcus blushed at his unintended confession.

"Forest Park Estates, eh?" Margaret mused. "That's a pretty stylish neighborhood. And a long way. How long would it take you to walk there, Marcus?"

"I haven't gone from here to her house yet, only from the cemetery to there. But I think that I can get there in about forty minutes or so."

"So, you already have been to her house, Marcus? That's a little disconcerting." Margaret's expression indicated a bit of concern. Marcus was a little young to be galivanting around with some young girl. "Why, may I ask, were you at her house and when. And where was I?"

Marcus was beginning to worry. This was not the way he had intended for this conversation to go. "It was yesterday, Mama. Remember, I left you a note? After my game, I went back to Randolph Park and met Cassie there. We messed around at the park and ….."

Margaret interjected, "You what at the park?"

"We just messed around, you know? Rode the swings, the seesaw, the jungle gym. Cassie is a real tomboy. She even beat me in a race. She's a really fast runner, especially for a girl."

"Okay, Marcus….so continue. What after the park. When and why did you go to her house?" Margaret wanted to know everything. But Marcus could not tell her everything.

"Well, she said she didn't like the cemetery and I wanted to show her there was nothing to be afraid of, so I took her there. We went to mom and dad's graves, and I think she was okay with it and then I wanted to be nice, so I walked her home."

"I guess that was nice, Marcus. Certainly, the gentlemanly thing to do. Maybe I am raising you right, after all." Margaret looked up at the clock on the kitchen wall and smiled. "Marcus, it's ten minutes to one o'clock. If you change quickly, you just might make it to the Worthington's by 1:30. I doubt Mrs. Dougherty will be terribly disappointed if you don't accompany me today."

"Thanks, Mama. I love you," Marcus exclaimed as he hugged his Mama.

James E. Anderson

Sunday Midday

Marcus changed into jeans and tee shirt in a flash, raced to the kitchen and filled his small thermos with cherry Kool-Aid and then high-tailed to the back porch where he retrieved two 8' bamboo poles, his tackle box and a small spade to be used to dig up worms. Back through the apartment and out the front door, calling over his shoulder, "Thanks, Mama. I'll be home before dinner."

Knowing time was short, Marcus ran until he could hardly get his breath, then slowed to a walk. He stopped at the gazebo when he reached Randolph Park and sat to regain his composure. He was so happy that Margaret had relented, and he could go fishing with Cassie. Mrs. Dougherty was a very nice old lady, and she did bake some really good cupcakes, but Marcus had visited her before, and it was an honestly boring time. Being in the company of Cassie was such a tremendous alternative.

After just a moment or two's respite, Marcus plodded onward. As he neared Forest Park Estates, he began to be overwhelmed by feelings of nervousness. He was no doubt going to be required to meet Mr. and Mrs. Worthington. How would they respond to him? Will they be overprotective of their daughter? Will they react as Margaret initially had? Will they trust him to accompany their daughter anywhere, much less the banks of the mighty Mississippi River? All these thoughts flooded his mind as Marcus turned onto Fernwood Drive. As luck would have it, Marcus saw a car turning into the Worthington's driveway about a half block ahead. As he approached, he recognized it as an Oldsmobile F-85 Jetfire, red with chrome trim and a white roof. A nice vehicle. Although Margaret did not own a car, Marcus was certainly planning to in a few years.

From a distance he saw the family piling out. Mr. and Mrs. Worthington, Cassie, and what must have been a younger brother, a little boy probably no more than four years old. Marcus must have been easy to spot with all the equipment he was carrying, as Cassie began waving and walking toward him. The rest of the family waited by the car as Cassie approached Marcus and insisted on taking the thermos and spade. He resisted at first, but Cassie was persistent, and he gave in, handing the items over, but maintaining possession of the poles and tackle box. As they approached the car, Mr. Worthington stepped forward and reached out removing the bamboo poles from Marcus' grasp. "Let me have those son, I'll lean them against the carport. You're probably pretty tired of carrying them all this way."

Cassie's mother stepped forward and offering her gloved hand said, "Hello, Marcus. I'm Debbie Worthington and that is my husband, Jack."

Mr. Worthington took the few steps back from the carport and stuck out his large right hand. Marcus' hand was engulfed by Mr. Worthington's. "Nice to meet you, Marcus."

"It's a pleasure to meet you, Mr. Worthington, Mrs. Worthington."

"And you, Marcus." Mr. Worthington continued, "Cassie has nice things to say about you. Says you're a fine upstanding young man. And says you're a math whiz to boot."

"Well sir, I don't know about all that, but I do like math and am pretty good at it."

"I can appreciate that, Marcus. I work as an accountant up in Keokuk, so I like math as well. You know where Keokuk is Marcus, in Iowa?"

"Yes sir, I think it's about thirty miles or so right up highway 61, isn't it?"

"That's right Marcus. You're pretty knowledgeable about geography too, aren't you?"

"I guess so Mr. Worthington," Marcus shyly responded.

Mrs. Worthington interrupted, "I hate to break in on the man talk, but why don't we go indoors to continue. Cassie can get out of her dress and into something suitable for fishing, and Marcus can sit down with a glass of iced tea and relax. And you two can continue your conversation."

"Good idea, Debbie. Come on Marcus, let's get you that glass of tea." With that, Mr. Worthington open the front door for Mrs. Worthington, Cassie and Marcus. Cassie headed straight for her bedroom, Debbie Worthington to the kitchen, and Marcus and Jack Worthington to the living room. Marcus took a seat on the couch while Cassie's father collapsed into his easy chair. The little boy came running in and jumped onto his father's lap, laughing. "Daddy, Cassie says she's going fishing. Can I go, too?" Jack Worthington smiled and in his very meek attempt to sound like Porky Pig said, "D-d-d-don't think so folks!" After giggling at the Porky Pig voice, the boy asked, "Why not Daddy?"

"Because you're too little. That big ol' catfish might mistake you for bait and swallow you up Charlie! Then who would I have to cut my grass some day when I get old and feeble!"

"Okay, Daddy." Charlie slid off his lap and ran off to his bedroom.

Mrs. Worthington came into the living room carrying a tray containing three ice filled glasses and set it on the coffee table. She placed three wooden coasters on the coffee table and as she proceeded to place the glasses on them said, "Here's some of the sweetest southern iced tea you'll ever taste, Marcus."

"Thank you, Mrs. Worthington," Marcus said as he reached for his glass. His first sip was heavenly. He wasn't used to drinking tea, Margaret's specialty was Kool-Aid. "Wow, this really is good," he exclaimed.

"Thanks for the compliment, Marcus. I seeped it last night, sweetened it and left it in the refrigerator all night, knowing it would be perfect for this warm afternoon." Mrs. Worthington seemed proud of her accomplishment.

"So," said Mr. Worthington, "where are you two going fishing today? Is there a pond nearby?"

"No sir," Marcus replied, "I always go to the river and fish off the bank. Been doing it all my life. Sometimes I get some nice catfish. Almost always hook a crappie, but I always throw them back."

"Sounds like you're an experienced angler, son. I hope you'll take care of Cassie. She's not used to being around the river, and I'm sure the currents are dangerous......"

"Jack, are you sure Cassie will be safe?" Mrs. Worthington asked.

"I think so, Debbie. She has a good head on her shoulders, and if she trusts Marcus to look after her, we probably should, too."

Marcus was relieved to know Mr. Worthington had faith in him.

"Don't worry, Mrs. Worthington," Marcus explained, "Where we are going there are trees and stuff at the water's edge. The catfish like to feed around the logs and reeds that grow there, so there really isn't any current to worry about."

Before any more questions could be raised, Cassie entered the living room. "Ready, Marcus?" she quizzed. "You bet Cassie." Marcus was quite ready.

As they headed to the front door, Mrs. Worthington reminded them that dinner was at 6:00 p.m., and not to be late.

"We'll be back, Mrs. Worthington, I promise," Marcus intoned. "And thanks again for the tea, it was really good."

James E. Anderson

Sunday Ends

Marcus and Cassie picked up all of the gear and began making their way out of the development. "I hope my parents didn't give you too much of the third-degree Marcus. Sometimes I feel like they think they are Joe Friday and Bill Gannon from Dragnet," Cassie quipped, "Just the facts ma'am." She laughed heartily. Marcus loved her laugh.

As they strode toward the river, Marcus and Cassie began discussing the mysterious dog. How did it know that those snakes were just ahead in the direction they were going? Why did it follow Marcus through the cemetery that first night ostensibly calling his name? Maybe Marcus was hearing things. Maybe it was Denny or one of his other friends playing tricks on him. But if so, why again two days later? Why the red embroidered handkerchief on the stoop? Was it even the dog that placed it there? How could it have been when the dog was with him in the cemetery? And why yesterday the yelling of "Marc" over and over as if in warning? All these things questionable and possibly within the realm of possibility. But the one thing that stands out, the one thing that is indisputable is that they both distinctly heard the harelipped dog speak the words "It's okay, Marc," in plain English. No one else said it, one of them did not imagine it. They both heard it and they both heard it very plainly. The dog, beyond the shadow of doubt, said it.

They finally arrived at the rocky bank of the muddy Mississippi River and it was time to get down to the business of fishing for catfish. The two of them walked south a couple of hundred feet to reach a tree line. Marcus explained to Cassie that catfish liked to feed along the shoreline where reeds grew freely and there were downed tree limbs and small logs in the shallow water. He took one of the bamboo cane poles and began to instruct Cassie on how to rig it. "First Cassie, you take a roll of Dacron" (similar to thread, a polyester developed about twenty years ago) "and tie a knot about two feet from the handle of the pole. Then wrap it in spirals around the pole all the way to the tip. Cut it and tie a knot like this," Marcus demonstrated, "and then put a loop in it."

"Okay, got it," Cassie said. Marcus continued, "Then take about ten feet of monofilament" (fishing line) "and tie a loop in one end. Make a loop-to-loop connection and your fishing line is ready." He reached into the tackle box for more goodies. "Tie an Aberdeen hook to the end of your line." Marcus completed this step. "Be careful not to hook yourself, Cassie. Come up a few inches from the hook and tie a split shot weight so the hook and bait will sink. And about a foot above that tie your cork bobber to the line and you're all set."

Cassie confidently smiled. "That seems easy enough."

"Okay then." Marcus was anxious to find how well Cassie listened and had learned. "Now you rig the second pole while I go dig us up some bait." Marcus took the spade and a small paper bag and headed to a clearing fifty feet or so away. By the time he returned with about a half dozen worms in the bag, Cassie was in the process of tying the weight and cork to the line. When she'd finished, Marcus examined her handiwork and determined she had done quite well. The knots seemed sturdy, she had spiraled the Dacron correctly and the hook, weight and cork were all attached correctly.

The only thing left was to bait the hook. Marcus showed her how to run the hook through the worm near the tail, fold the worm and hook it again in the middle, and then once more near the head. "You don't want the worm to get off the hook, and you don't want the fish to nibble it off either. You want him to bite down on the whole thing so you can hook him."

Cassie grabbed a worm. Marcus warned her, "He's slippery. Mind what you're doing and don't stick yourself with the hook. You see the point of the hook? Right behind it is that little piece that points back to the 'U' of the hook. That is the barb, and when the fish bites and the hook sticks him, the barb is what keeps the hook from coming out. If it sticks in your hand, it can be hard to get out of there, too. So be careful."

Cassie took her time, was careful and did a fine job of baiting the hook. She wasn't at all squeamish about handling the worm.

"Great job, Cassie!" Marcus congratulated her. "Now we just go over to the reeds and branches, you drop the line in the water and just walk along the bank kind of dragging it through the water until you feel a strike."

"Is that when the fish bites the hook?" Cassie asked.

"That's right," Marcus answered. "When you feel the strike, or if you see the cork bob down into the water, you've got a fish. If you see or feel that, raise the end of your pole straight up to try to set the hook in its mouth. Depending on the size of it, you can probably walk back enough to get it to shore."

They spread apart about forty feet and began to fish in earnest. After thirty minutes or so, Cassie squealed, "Marcus, I got one! I got one!" Marcus dropped his pole and went running toward her yelling, "Pull up on the pole, set the hook!" Cassie did as instructed, and the pole began bowing near the end. "Keep the end as high as you can, Cassie. And start walking backward." He ran to the edge of the water and waded in a bit. As Cassie continued to back up, the line got within Marcus' reach. He grabbed hold of it and pulled the fish out of the water. "Look at that Cassie, you got about a three pound or so channel catfish! You might want to take it to the taxidermist and get it mounted!"

"Really, is that a big one, Marcus?" Cassie asked breathlessly.

"No, I'm sorry, Cassie. I was just kidding about mounting it. But that's really good for a first-time fisherman, I mean fishergirl," Marcus laughed. Cassie echoed his laugh, then ran to him and threw her arms around him. "My first fish, Marcus. Thank you!" and kissed him square on the lips.

Marcus was red-faced and at a loss for words, but Cassie had already moved on. "Marcus, show me how to get the hook out. The poor thing probably hurts."

"Okay, Cassie. Watch carefully." And Marcus, as gently as possible removed the hook. "Do you want to take it home, Cassie? Think your mom will clean it and fry it?"

"No way, Marcus. Do you want it?" She asked.

"No, I don't think so. How about we just throw it back in Cassie? Maybe we can catch it again another time." Cassie liked Marcus' suggestion and he handed her the catfish. She walked to the river's edge, gently placed it in the water and watched it swim away.

"That was fantastic, Marcus. Thank you so much for bringing me and teaching me how to fish." Her smile was broad and genuine.

They sat for a bit on a tree stump, reflecting on the day and shared a cup of Kool-Aid from Marcus' thermos. Marcus reckoned it was about time to head back to Cassie's house. He discarded the unused worms and began removing the Dacron and monofilament line from the poles. Cassie untied the hooks, weights and corks and they repacked the tackle box. They took one last look at the wide and majestic Mississippi before picking everything up.

"Marc."

Cassie and Marcus turned to one another in utter disbelief.

Again, softly, "Marc".

They both looked to the south, the direction from which the sound emanated.

And yes, there he stood. The harelipped dog. He stood near the tree line where they had been fishing just moments before. He stared at them for a few brief seconds, then turned and slowly walked further south. Marcus and Cassie stood still, bewildered. The dog walked only a few feet, then stopped, turned and looked back at them again. For a second time he began walking away, and once again stopped and looked back at them. Cassie spoke first, "Marcus, he wants us to follow him."

"Cassie, I don't know if that's a good idea......" Cassie cut him off. "Yes, it is Marcus. That dog saved our lives yesterday. Whatever he needs us for, we need to help him."

The harelipped dog waited for them to catch up and then continued along the tree line another one hundred and fifty feet or so beyond the area where they had been fishing among the reeds and branches. He proceeded to a huge felled oak tree and stopped. Marcus had never seen a tree so gigantic. Even though it was lying on the ground, the diameter was so large Marcus could not see over it. The diameter had to be at least between four and five feet. He could see the base about thirty feet to his right. When it had fallen, it had ripped the roots right out of the ground. Marcus and Cassie walked toward the base of the trunk. The diameter here was even more outstanding, probably six to seven feet. They examined the base and were amazed by how shallow the root system was. For a tree so tall and majestic, the root system was likely less than two feet into the ground.

The harelipped dog walked around the base and roots and stood on the other side, looking in the direction of the river. With Cassie leading the way, she and Marcus followed the dog to the other side of the tree. The dog began slowly walking toward the river. When it reached the first branches, it stopped.

And it growled. And then it whined. Almost as if emitting emotion. A canine version of anger and of sorrow. While the dog remained still, they climbed over and through several of the branches before spotting what the dog had brought them to see. The mutilated corpse of a young woman.

James E. Anderson

The Aftermath

Marcus and Cassie shared the backseat of the Jetfire with Charlie as Mr. Worthington drove and Mrs. Worthington occupied the front passenger seat. The entire fifteen-minute excursion, from police station to the Westside LaGrange Apartments, was spent in utter silence. Mr. Worthington had visions racing through his head of the shock and revulsion that Cassie must have experienced with the morbid discovery. Mrs. Worthington also remained speechless and was visibly distraught over the horrific circumstances her daughter had been drawn into.

* * * *

Marcus had been the first to vomit. The mangled snakes had been disgusting, had turned his stomach and nearly brought up his lunch. But the sight of this young woman, probably no more than a teenager as the police officer had later theorized, was far worse and he could not control the overwhelming urge. Marcus had hurled until there was nothing more to expel. The horrid taste of bile was enough to make him start again, had there been anything left. Cassie was fortunate to have had Marcus in front of her, shielding her from a full view of the scene. She had been spared from seeing the damage inflicted upon the young girl's face. But she was close enough to see and hear Marcus, and the sounds of his violent retching were enough to cause her to follow suit. As quickly as they could compose themselves, they made their way to North Frost Street and then on to Main Street and a pay phone outside of the long-abandoned Phillips 66 gas station. Marcus dialed "0", and when the operator came on, asked to be connected to the Lewis County Sheriff's Department. A quick description of their discovery brought immediate urgency to the police receptionist, and she instructed Marcus to stay nearby the phone and a deputy would be there shortly.

They had to wait only ten minutes for an officer to arrive at the pay phone in front of the gas station. The officer identified himself as Deputy Mitch Daniels of the Lewis County Sheriff's Department. He withdrew a pad and pencil from his uniform breast pocket and proceeded to notate all the pertinent details the youngsters had to relate. Marcus and Cassie explained how they had been fishing and noticed the huge fallen tree. They had decided to explore and that was when they had made the grotesque discovery. The officer asked Marcus if he could take him to where they had seen the body. When Marcus said he could, the officer asked Cassie to wait in the back seat of his car until they returned.

Marcus took him to the fallen tree and as they started around the base of the trunk, the officer instructed him to wait there. "You don't need to see this again, son," said Deputy Daniels. He proceeded toward the branches Marcus and Cassie had climbed on and through. Moments later Marcus heard the static of the radio and clearly heard Deputy Daniels say, "Sadie, we got us a homicide. Victim appears to be a Caucasian female, most likely a teenager."

Within minutes of Deputy Daniels and Marcus arriving back at the police cruiser, a hearse from Porter's Funeral Home pulled up. Just moments later a white Ford Fairlane arrived. The driver placed a placard on his windshield, below the wiper. The placard read Lewis County Coroner. In a few minutes, another patrol car parked. A female officer stepped out and headed straight toward Marcus and Cassie. She introduced her herself, "I'm Deputy Wilcox. You must be Marcus Clemens and Cassandra Worthington." They nodded simultaneously.

She walked them to her patrol car and opened the back driver's side door. "We are going to ride down to the station. We'll call your parents, let them know what's going on, and that you're alright. Then we'll get statements from you, ask you a few questions, and by then you'll be able to go home. Sound good?"

"Yes, ma'am," they answered in unison.

After their arrival at the station, they both were asked for the names and telephone numbers of their parents. Marcus and Cassie were then separated. Cassie was taken into a room by Deputy Wilcox, Marcus to another room by an officer named Deputy Mathews. Each was given a Coco-Cola, told that their parents were being called and then asked for a detailed description of the afternoon's events.

While offering their descriptions and answering questions, another deputy was busy making telephone calls to their respective families. As might be expected, Margaret was extremely upset. After repeated assurances that Marcus was unhurt and appeared in no way overly upset, Margaret calmed. When told she could come and get Marcus shortly, she informed the deputy she had neither a car nor a driver's license. He told Margaret not to worry, that the Sheriff's Department would arrange for his transportation home.

The deputy's conversation with the Worthington's was quite similar. Mr. Worthington had answered the call and despite an abundance of worry and angst, had accepted the details with a modicum of calm. However, as he relayed information to his wife, her response bore no resemblance to calm. Debbie demanded to speak to the deputy herself. Grabbing at the receiver, she insisted that Cassie be put on the line. She felt she had to hear her voice to know Cassie was alright. Despite repeated pledges and guarantees from the deputy attesting to Cassie's well-being, Debbie Worthington would not be placated until she heard Cassie's voice with her own ears. Against his better judgement, but understanding the motherly concern, the deputy put her on hold and walked down the corridor to interview room number one.

Explaining to Deputy Wilcox the anxiety expressed by Mrs. Worthington, the interview was suspended while Cassie was taken to the telephone. Following fifteen minutes of assurances of her well-being, Cassie had convinced her mother to calm down and dry her tears. Debbie promised Cassie they would be there for her in a matter of moments, the call was ended, and Cassie was returned to the interview room.

Ten minutes or so after she had finished giving her account of the events and dutifully answering questions, Cassie was brought into a waiting area where her parents had been anxiously anticipating her arrival. Mrs. Worthington practically smothered Cassie with her hugs. "Cassie, are you sure you are alright? You're not hurt at all?"

"No, I'm not hurt at all, mother," Cassie responded while regaining the breath that had been squeezed out of her. "It was a wonderful, fun day until the very end."

"Tell us everything Cassie. The officer told us a lot, but I want to hear it from you, okay?" her father asked in a calming voice.

After retelling the day's experience to her mother and father, Cassie asked, "where is Marcus?"

"I don't know," said her father. "I guess maybe his parents picked him up already."

"No, Daddy. He doesn't have any parents, they both died."

"We're sorry to hear that, Cassie. But he lives with someone. I'm sure they came for him," her mothered offered.

"He lives with his stepmother, but she doesn't have a car," Cassie explained. "Daddy, will you take him home, please?"

"Okay, Cassie. We'll go find him and then we'll call his stepmother and let her know he's safe and we're bringing him home."

* * * *

Jack Worthington had called Margaret just after 7:30 to tell her that he and his wife would be bringing Marcus home and would be leaving the police station shortly. It was nearly 8:00 when they arrived at Marcus' building. Margaret was waiting, arms folded across her bosom, pacing the sidewalk in front of their apartment. Mr. Worthington eased into a parking space next to the sidewalk. Upon switching off the headlights and cutting the engine, Mr. Worthington turned, and resting his elbow on the seatback said, "Marcus, you did a good job taking care of Cassie this afternoon. None of what happened is your fault. Circumstances are what they are, and nothing can be changed. I don't want you to feel any guilt or remorse over any of it." Looking toward his daughter, he continued, "Cassie is a strong girl, and she will be just fine."

"Yes sir," Marcus replied. He did feel guilty about what had transpired and wished Cassie had not been forced to witness what they had seen. Mr. and Mrs. Worthington got out of the car, approached Margaret and began speaking. Cassie reached out and placed her hand on Marcus' right forearm. "My dad is right Marcus. Nothing about this is your fault. I had a wonderful day with you. You taught me to rig a line and catch a fish. We couldn't do anything about what happened to that girl. It's a good thing your dog took us to her, or she would have been there a long time before anybody else would have found her."

"You're right, Cassie. But I sure wish you hadn't of seen any of that. I should've made you wait while I looked. I'm sorry."

"It's okay, Marcus." Cassie patted his arm and smiled.

"Cassie?" Marcus looked earnestly into her eyes. "You haven't told anyone about the dog, have you? Especially not the police?"

"Of course not. Who would have believed me, anyway? They would probably think I was a raving lunatic!"

"Marcus, are you coming?" Margaret called.

"Coming, Mama." Marcus opened the door to get out, but looked back at Cassie and said, "I'll call you tomorrow, okay?"

"You better call me, mister," Cassie replied.

James E. Anderson

Back to The River

Marcus had a hard time falling asleep. He kept replaying the horror of his first sight of the young girl slumped against the massive trunk of the fallen tree. He kept remembering the bright reds, greens and yellows of the bottom portion of her dress. A thick white petticoat. Bright white, albeit blood-stained, from the waist up, red shoes, it was reminiscent of a costume of days gone by. How had she gotten there? Did someone drag her body down there or had it happened right there? When? Were he and Cassie fishing while this terrible crime was being committed? Could they have prevented it? So many questions, and a mystery far too complex for any eleven-year-old to begin to try to unravel.

Mercifully, Marcus drifted off.

However, sleep did not offer respite. Dream stages only enhanced the realm of possibilities flowing through his mind. Finally, and perhaps rightfully, his mind began focusing on the continuing mystery of his own life. The dog. Why again, the dog? Why does it keep appearing? What is the meaning? How does it know when things are happening or about to happen? How does it, how can it speak? The active moments just before awakening, the multitude of questions. The lack of answers.

Marcus had not set his alarm as he normally would. It had been a far too trying of a day and he had forgotten. He had tossed and turned all night, and despite having a fan blowing, he awoke to bed sheets soaked with perspiration. He made his way into the kitchen where he prepared the acclaimed breakfast of champions. After a bowl of Wheaties and two slices of buttered wheat toast, Marcus felt ready to face the day. It was Monday, and Margaret was again on the breakfast-lunch shift. She had departed for work at 5:00 a.m. so Marcus knew he was on his own until at least three in the afternoon.

It was nearly eleven when he remembered he had promised to call Cassie. He dialed her number and she picked up on the second ring. "Hello, is this Marcus?"

"Hello, Cassie. I overslept this morning, so I'm kind of late calling. It was a long night, and I didn't sleep well." Marcus felt a little guilty for calling so late in the morning.

"It's okay, Marcus. I didn't sleep well either. I kept seeing that girl's shoes and the colors of her dress kept swirling like a kaleidoscope in my mind. Marcus, I hope I never see anything like that again." Cassie paused and then asked, "Marcus, how did you know that girl was dead? Maybe she wasn't dead yet and we could have helped her if we had only…"

Marcus interrupted her mid-sentence, "We couldn't help her Cassie. Her eyes were staring at the sky and they weren't moving. And there were flies on her."

"Oh God, Marcus." Cassie began to sob. Marcus wasn't sure what to do or say. "I'm sorry, Cassie. I shouldn't have told you that. I'm sorry."

Cassie regained her composure and said, "It's alright. I'm just glad I didn't have to see her face." A lengthy pause and then, "Marcus, did you hear the dog too?"

"What? What do you mean Cassie? What do you mean, did I hear the dog, too? What did you hear?"

62

"Marcus, it was like a voice whispered in my ear, but no one was there. Remember when the dog said 'it's okay Marcus' at the cemetery? It was that voice, but the dog was a long way away. And it was not like he said it. It wasn't out loud," Cassie told him. "Do you know what I mean? I kept thinking of that all night. When I woke up, I thought I had dreamed it, but I didn't. I know I heard it." Cassie's intonation was emphatic.

"Cassie, this is important. What did the voice say?" Marcus knew the answer before Cassie could deliver it.

"It said, 'she's dead, call the police'."

The line was silent for a long while.

"Marcus, are you still there?"

In a few seconds, Marcus responded, "Yes, Cassie. I heard it too. I think I had forgotten until you asked if I had heard it. Cassie, it seems like he said it to you and I just kind of overheard."

"How could that be, Marcus. That is your dog. He came to you in the cemetery. Twice. I never even saw him until the day with the snakes."

"But Cassie, he only speaks when you are there. Don't you think that's strange?"

"Yes, Marcus, it is."

Marcus decided he'd had enough of this supernatural type of discussion. He was going to have to change the subject. "Cassie, I'm going to visit my parents today. Do you want to come with me?"

"I do, Marcus, but I can't."

"Why not, Cassie?"

"I'm not allowed to leave the house for a while. My parents don't think it's safe. They said they don't want me outdoors or out of their sight until whoever killed that girl is caught." Cassie explained. "I'm sorry, Marcus."

"It's okay, Cassie. I guess I understand why they would say that. I'll just go by myself and then I'll go to Denny's house. I'll call you again tomorrow, okay?"

"Okay, Marcus. Goodbye."

As Marcus cradled the receiver his mind was awash with thoughts and scenarios. A talking dog, a dead girl, a girlfriend who can't leave her house.

Mystery and the unknown. This is promising to be a long summer.

* * * *

After breakfast, Marcus bathed and dressed for the day (predictably, in jeans and white tee shirt). A quick sandwich preceded the trek to Denny's house. Denny was Marcus' best friend. He was about the same height as Marcus, but skinny as a rail, and was at least twenty pounds lighter. He played shortstop on the baseball team, could hit really well, and was fast as the wind. Denny always had his hair in a crewcut. He really had no choice. His father had been a ship's barber in the navy during World War Two and insisted on cutting Denny's hair. The only problem being that Doug Wallace only knew two ways to cut hair, just as he had done it on the ship. He always told Denny he had two options to choose from, crewcut and crewcut.

Marcus and Denny played catch for a while on Jamison Street in front of the Wallace house and then headed for the river. On the way to the river, Marcus told Denny about taking Cassie fishing the day before and bragged on how well she had done. He expected Denny to interrupt with questions about the dead girl, but as it turned out, Denny had yet to hear anything about it. When Denny didn't mention it, Marcus felt obligated to fill his friend in on the news. Denny was enthralled by the story. "Wow, Marcus. I should have been with you instead of Cassie. When we go to the river, I always feel like we are the 1960's version of

Tom Sawyer and Huckleberry Finn. That could have been the highlight of a book that somebody could write about us some day." "Yep. You're right Denny. I can see it now, The Adventures of Denny Wallace and Marcus Clemens. Number one best-selling book," Marcus laughed for the first time in at least twenty-four hours.

Arriving at the riverbank, Denny wasn't satisfied for long with throwing rocks into the water. "Marcus, how far down the bank were you guys fishing yesterday? I want to see the tree where you found the girl."

"It wasn't far, but I don't want to go there today, Denny. It's too creepy."

"Don't be a baby, Marcus. We'll both be twelve next month, we're almost teenagers now. We're not little kids anymore. Creepy is for little kids, we're practically in junior high. Come on, let's go."

Giving in to Denny's pressure, Marcus led the way to nearly a half mile downstream. "There it is," Marcus pointed to the huge oak lying prone. "She was on the other side."

"How did you know she was on the other side?" Denny asked.

Marcus wasn't about to tell Denny about the dog that had been playing havoc with his and Cassie's lives.

"We didn't, we were just exploring and decided to go around to the other side, that's all."

"Let's go," Denny said as he started toward the base of the tree.

"No. I'm staying here," Marcus felt nervous about returning to the scene. As Denny circled the base of the tree and disappeared from sight, questions began flooding Marcus' mind. What if the girl's spirit is still there? What if she felt he was being disrespectful bringing his friend there like the place where she may have died was some sort of tourist attraction? Marcus was starting to feel very leery about the possibility of paranormal activity, in view of the fact that the dog could clearly communicate with him.

"Oh, my God!" Denny shouted from the other side of the tree. "Ahhhh!!!"

Marcus immediately broke out in a sweat and ran around the base of the tree, calling to his friend, "Denny, Denny, are you alright?"

Marcus was terrified to see his friend Denny lying face down on the leaf covered ground. Despite his apprehension, he ran to his friend and knelt at his right side. Grabbing Denny's shoulder, Marcus, with tears beginning to well, attempted to turn over his limp frame and said, "Denny, please be okay."

As Marcus rolled him onto his back, Denny's eyes opened wide and he yelled, "Gotcha!" and began laughing.

River Revisited

The summer seemed to be lasting an eternity. Marcus and Cassie spoke on the telephone regularly but rarely saw one another. With law enforcement seemingly unable to connect any dots in the search for the young girl's killer, Cassie was more or less homebound. Marcus would usually visit her and have lunch with her and her mother on Wednesdays. Occasionally, Cassie would talk her mother into bringing Marcus along on their forays to the Five and Dime and grocery store on Saturdays. Mrs. Worthington felt confident enough in dropping them off at Franklin's while she did her shopping a few blocks away at Dempsey's. She knew Mr. Franklin ran a tight ship in his store and chances were slim of there being any monkey business being conducted on his watch. This at least gave them a brief taste of a normal summer. A chance for them to sift through the magazine rack, pick up a few desired issues and spend a little time at the soda counter. They both enjoyed watching Ellis Compton work his magic on the prepubescent and young teenage girls that congregated in droves on summertime Saturdays. As the summer progressed, he had become far more outgoing with the young ladies.

Ellis' confidence seemed to have soared. He had advanced his flirting prowess immensely since the spring. He had now incorporated small and simple, but deliriously effective, sleight of hand magic tricks into his repertoire and was driving the girls insane in their admiration.

Of course, Marcus still found plenty of time to hang out with his best friend Denny. Despite the cruel prank he had pulled on Marcus the day after the tragedy, Marcus had a soft spot inside for Denny. They had been best friends since first grade and many a cruel joke had been pulled on one another over that time. Many mean jokes and many downright disgusting ones, as only boys can conjure up. Their baseball team had not fared well, winning only two of their twelve contests, but they had certainly had a boatload of fun. Cassie had even convinced her father to bring her to watch Marcus play in a handful of the games, usually leaving disappointed in the outcome of the games, but always happy for the opportunity to see and talk to him.

Marcus and Cassie tried to make the most of any chance they could to be in each other's company. By July, Cassie was even successful in cajoling her parents into taking Marcus along to church (First Baptist, off of White Street) and to lunch at the Red Roof Lodge. Try as she might though, Cassie just had no luck persuading them to let her go to Randolph Park with Marcus. And there was absolutely no hope in asking to go to the river to land another catfish.

Marcus and Denny did however pull in some nice channel cat over the summer months. The largest was at least a thirty pounder which took a team effort to bring up onto the bank. Denny brought it back to his father on Jamison Street, claiming it as his own because he lived quite a bit closer than Marcus. And his father could clean and fillet it much quicker than could Marcus if he'd taken it home. With there being seven people in the Wallace household, the leftovers were gone by the next afternoon.

It was also during the summer of 1963 when Doug Wallace taught Denny and Marcus the fine art of noodling. The boys spent the early weeks of August perfecting the nuances of the sport. Their location on the river being just over a mile downstream of Lock and Dam No. 20 made it a perfect spot for noodling. The boys learned to work the shallow waters near the bank, searching beneath logs and fallen limbs for catfish dens. Upon locating a den, they would reach into the hole with one hand. If the den was occupied, invariably a catfish would endeavor to bite down on the hand in a defensive maneuver attempting to escape from the intrusion. The plan at that point is to grab the catfish behind the gill and pull it out of the hole. Of course, there are inherent risks such as getting cut and suffering a resulting infection. Or more dramatically, the chance of the hole having been abandoned by the catfish and residence being taken up by snapping turtles, beavers or muskrats. Denny and Marcus, while aware of the dangers involved in noodling were, as most youth are, impervious to the possibility of anything remotely going wrong. And so it was that they both became fairly proficient at their newly learned skill.

* * * *

For as long as he could remember, Marcus had been fascinated with Lock and Dam No. 20. He loved watching how it operated. To Marcus, it was a marvel of engineering. According to lock operators he had spoken with, the dam itself was nearly a half mile long. It was remarkable to Marcus how the gates functioned, either letting water in or out so that barges and other watercraft could make the transition from shallow to deeper water or vice versa, as they made their way up or downstream on the Mississippi River. He had learned that the river had an elevation drop of over 400 feet as it flowed more than 2,000 miles from Lake Itasca in Minnesota to the Gulf of Mexico at New Orleans. Marcus often wondered how the riverboats and steamboats in the nineteenth century, before the construction of locks and dams, had navigated the uncontrolled waterway.

School was set to begin in two days, the day after Labor Day, on September 3, 1963. Marcus was now twelve years old, and Cassie was only three weeks shy of the milestone. The entire summer had passed uneventfully in Lewis County. No more tragedy, no robberies, not even so much as a serious car accident on U.S. Highway 61, the main thoroughfare through Lewis County. And Cassie had spent essentially her entire summer vacation as a prisoner in her own home. After Sunday services, and as was customary, the Worthington family had driven to LaGrange for lunch. And, as had become more or less biweekly, they were accompanied by one Marcus Clemens. At Margaret's insistence,

Marcus had forced Mr. Worthington to accept two one-dollar bills to pay for his own ($1.75 a head) lunch. As they sat at a round table at the Red Roof Lodge feasting on a family style meal of fried chicken with all the fixings, Jack and Debbie engaged Cassie and Marcus in a conversation concerning the approach of the new school year.

"Well kids, sixth grade on Tuesday. Only one more year until junior high school. How about that!" exclaimed Cassie's father.

"You two must be excited to get back to school and see all your friends," said her mother.

"Yes ma'am, yes sir," Marcus replied.

"I'm just thankful to be able to get out of the house. I don't know how Charlie can stand being home all the time," said Cassie of her three-and-a-half-year-old brother. "It's been a really boring summer. I used to hate riding the bus, but I think it will be fun to get on the bus again."

"I'm sure it will be therapeutic for you both, to break away from the boredom and be mentally engaged again," theorized Mr. Worthington.

Dessert was ordered for all by Mr. Worthington to celebrate the new school year (warm homemade apple pie a la mode). Cassie fairly raced through finishing her dessert, as she found it impossible to hold back what she had been patiently waiting to ask, "Mom, Daddy...It has been a really long boring summer. I've been couped up all summer and nothing has happened to anybody, anywhere around here. When we get home, can I go with Marcus to the lock and dam? He promised me in May, he would show it to me, and now it's September."

"Now Cassie, I.... I just don't know. I mean.... Jack, honey, what do you think?" asked Cassie's mother.

"I don't know either, Cassie. I mean I wasn't anticipating the question. It has been quiet all summer..."

"I don't mean to interrupt, Mr. Worthington," said Marcus (as he interrupted), "but there are people working at the lock and dam. It's not like we'll be there alone like if we were fishing."

Cassie's mother and father looked at one another in silence, as if communicating telepathically. After what seemed an eternity, Mr. Worthington said, "I'll tell you what. On the way home, we'll take you to the damned dam and drop you off. We'll go home, put Charlie down for a nap and I'll come back, pick you up at five. How does that sound?"

"That sounds great, Daddy. Thank you!" a relieved and excited Cassie could barely contain herself as she squeezed the wrist of a smiling Marcus.

"Just be careful, Cassie," her mother intoned, "that is still a raging river and nature is nothing to be taken for granted."

"Here Marcus," said Mr. Worthington as he handed Marcus a coin, "take this dime and run up to the pay phone and call your stepmother so she knows where you'll be and when you'll be home."

Marcus strolled to the lobby, dropped his dime and dialed his home phone number. The line was busy, so Marcus waited about five minutes and tried again. On the third ring Margaret answered, "Hello?"

"Hi Mama, it's me, Marcus."

"Marcus, are you alright?" she asked.

"Yes Mama, I'm fine. I'm still in LaGrange with Cassie's family. I just called to let you know that Cassie's dad is dropping us at the dam so I can show it to Cassie. He's coming to get us at 5:00, and then I'll be home. Okay?" Marcus was a little bit apprehensive about clearing this final hurdle.

"That's fine, Marcus. As long as you're here for dinner."

"Oh, I will be Mama." He was a little surprised at how agreeable Margaret sounded. She seemed in an unusually pleasant mood. "I'll see

71

you when I get home, Mama," Marcus said. As he started to pull the receiver from his ear and was about to hang up the telephone, he heard Margaret call his name.

"Marcus…. Marcus," she said.

"Yes, Mama."

"I just got off the phone a few minutes ago. There will be a surprise waiting when you get home." The line clicked off and there was nothing but a dial tone.

* * * *

As they pulled into the parking lot at Lock and Dam No. 20, Jack Worthington checked his watch. "Well, it's quarter of two. I'll be back at five o'clock. You kids have fun and stay out of trouble, okay?"

"Yes sir," said Marcus as he opened the left back door and stepped out.

"We will, Daddy, bye. Bye, Mom." Cassie said as she gleefully bounced out of the back seat.

The Jetfire sped away as Marcus and Cassie headed toward the walkway leading to the guide wall from which they would safely be able to watch the lock operation. As they walked, Marcus asked Cassie, "How come you've never been here Cassie? I thought everyone around would have been to old No. 20, but you said you never even heard of it."

"I don't know, Marcus. We just moved here when second grade was about over. I guess it was spring of '60," Cassie tried to calculate the timeline. "We just never came over to the river. If it wasn't for you, I wouldn't even have ever seen it."

"Well, that's not true, Cassie. You go to LaGrange every week," Marcus noted, "You can't drive from here to LaGrange on highway 61 without seeing the river."

Cassie had an epiphany, "You're right, Marcus! I do see it all the time. I just never realized that was the Mississippi River. Even when we were fishing, I didn't know that was the same river I see in LaGrange. Wow!"

"Cassie, you need to read about Tom Sawyer and Huckleberry Finn and learn more about this river."

"Is that the book that guy Mark Twain wrote?" she asked.

"Yep. Matter of fact I was named after him. My middle name is Twain. Marcus Twain Clemens," Marcus said with a touch of pride. "Haven't you ever noticed some of my friends calling me Marc Twain?"

"No, Marcus. I haven't," Cassie responded honestly. "Why did your parents give you that middle name?"

"Cassie, are you sure you're in the 'A' class?" Marcus teased. "My last name is Clemens."

"So what?"

"So what? Are you kidding me?" Marcus wasn't believing this. "Cassie, Mark Twain's real name was Samuel Langhorne Clemens. He was from Hannibal, probably less than forty miles from right here."
"Really?"

"Yes. My dad once told me he always wondered if we were related to Samuel Clemens since we had the same last name. But he never found out."

"Wow, Marcus. That's pretty neato." Cassie thought and said, "It would be really cool if you were related to a famous author."

"Sure would be." Marcus acknowledged.

They had arrived at the guide wall. As they gazed over the water into Illinois on the opposite bank and waited for a barge or boat to near the locks, Marcus thought he would continue educating Cassie by giving her some of the history of Lock and Dam No. 20, at least as he knew it.

"Cassie, if you look behind us, that used to be a town called Tully, Missouri. Way before the Civil War it was an important port on the river and was a busy little town. But, about 1850 or so, there was a big flood, and it was pretty much destroyed. What was left was nothing more than a ghost town."

"That's sad Marcus. Did a lot of people die?" she asked.

"I don't know, nobody ever told me that," Marcus answered. "But when they started building the dam in 1932, they tore down whatever was left of Tully. It took three years to finish building the dam and locks and it opened in 1935."

"Wow, it's been here almost thirty years already." Cassie was actually interested in what Marcus was telling her. "My dad was just a kid when they built this!"

"And guess how much it cost to build, Cassie?"

"I don't know, probably a lot," she ventured.

"Yeah, four million dollars. Do you know how much that would be today? I bet President Kennedy doesn't even have that much money!" Marcus laughed and Cassie joined him.

They walked a little further up the guide wall so they could get a better view of the river north of the dam. "Cassie, did you notice how the water was pouring through the dam like a waterfall and dropping about eight or ten feet?" Marcus asked her.

"Yes. What was that about?" Before Marcus could respond, Cassie said, "Wait a minute. I get it. Look at how much higher the river is on this side of the dam. They do that to control how much water flows downstream, don't they?"

"That's right, Cassie." Marcus was impressed. Girls weren't supposed to comprehend things like that.

"Okay, Marcus. So, when a boat comes, they open a gate to let the boat in and the water level in the 'lock' – right – is the same as where they came from. Then they close that gate and then they let water in – or – out a little at a time until the level is the same as the side they are going to. When it is, they open the gate and the boat goes on its way, right?" The wheels were spinning in high gear inside Cassie's head.

"You pretty much got it, Cassie," Marcus was truly proud of her.

They waited a bit more to see the real thing occur, but there just wasn't any river traffic today. Maybe because of the looming holiday businesses weren't moving product up or down the river. Perhaps the recreational boaters were waiting until tomorrow. Marcus checked his new Timex wristwatch – a birthday gift from Margaret – and saw it was just past 4:30 and knew they had only thirty minutes to get to the parking lot. Mr. Worthington had trusted them, and Marcus didn't want to betray that trust. Better to be early and wait than to be late. And plus, he might be early. "Cassie," Marcus called, but Cassie seemed enamored with her newly found passion. "Cassie," Marcus called again, "We need to head back to the parking lot."

"Okay, Marcus. Let's go." Cassie came skipping toward him. Marcus was so glad Cassie's parents had allowed her to come with him. They walked back down the guide wall, turned onto the walkway and headed for the parking lot. Cassie was really happy, in a splendid mood, and Marcus was elated to see the joy on her face when she suddenly stopped and all of her joyful facial features abruptly drooped. Standing before them on the walkway was the harelipped dog, with something in its mouth. Instructing Cassie to wait, and consumed with dread, Marcus approached the dog. When he got within a few feet of his mangy friend, the dog growled and seemed to moan. He then dropped what he had held in his mouth, turned and walked off into the overgrowth south of the walkway. Marcus cautiously approached the object and saw that it was a red ski mask. He tentatively picked it up and immediately noticed that the nose and mouth were sewn shut. There were dark splotches that appeared to be randomly splattered on the face of the mask. As Marcus was studying the mask, Cassie stepped around him and picked up another item. "Marcus, what is this do you think?" Looking at what she was holding in her hands, Marcus knew exactly what it was. A red handkerchief with darker red blotches. And the embroidered letters E.C.

Cousin Judy

Mr. Worthington pulled into the lot at ten of five and was somewhat surprised to see Marcus and Cassie already waiting, sitting on a pair of large stones. As they climbed into the backseat, Cassie's father could sense that something was amiss. There was no laughter and both faces reflected a tone of somberness. He studied his daughter for a moment before asking, "What is it, Cassie? Something is bothering you. I can see it in both your faces. Did something happen? Tell me, now."

Cassie looked at Marcus, trying to wordlessly relay to him that they had to be cautious about how and what they divulged to her father. Marcus broke the uneasy silence. "Mr. Worthington, we found something on the walkway as we were leaving. I think maybe you might want to give it to the police."

"What? What do you mean give it to the police? What the hell did you find?"

"Don't be upset, Daddy. It's probably nothing. Here you decide." Cassie removed the ski mask from her shoulder bag and handed it to her impatient father.

Jack Worthington held the mask up to take additional advantage of the brilliant late afternoon sunlight as he examined it thoroughly. He spent several minutes carefully handling this possible piece of evidence, turning it inside out to check the inside, running his fingers along the inside ridges of the sewn closed mouth and nose holes, examining the eyeholes, and finally staring at the front of the mask. Eventually, he looked back at Cassie and Marcus and said, "Kids, I don't want to alarm you, but this ski mask looks like it may have dried blood on it. You may be right. I think we'll swing by the police station and turn this over to them." Cassie's father dropped the ski mask onto the passenger side of the front seat and drove to the police station.

Upon arrival, Jack Worthington instructed Cassie and Marcus to wait in the car while he ran inside. Approaching the duty officer at the front desk, he held the ski mask at arm's length and said, "Your detectives may be interested in this."

The officer looked up from his Outdoor Life magazine quizzically and seeing the object being offered asked, "And what, pray tell, is that?"

"Well, it appears to be a ski mask, doesn't it?" Jack said with a touch of sarcasm. "Look officer, my daughter found it over at the dam. It appears to have what looks to me like dried blood on it. Whether it is or not, you fellows can figure out. I just found it rather strange. If you recall, there was a murder just a mile or two from the dam back in the spring."

The duty officer took the mask from him and began his own examination. "Yes sir, you're right Mr. ......?"

"Worthington, Jack Worthington. My daughter Cassandra and her friend Marcus Clemens were the ones that found the girl's body back in May, just before Memorial Day. And today she found this." He nodded toward the ski mask.

"I'll see that this gets into the right hands Mr. Worthington. All the big shots will be back tomorrow and I'm sure they will be interested in checking this out."

* * * *

Marcus stood on the sidewalk in front of his apartment and watched Cassie and her father drive off to Forest Park Estates. With his right hand he reached into his back pocket and pulled out his reasonably clean red handkerchief. His left hand went into his left front pocket and retrieved the handkerchief they had found on the walkway. He held both of them in front of him. They were identical, save for the apparent dried blood on the one in his left hand. There was no doubt it was his handkerchief. He had only been left with just six of his father's embroidered handkerchiefs and he had lost one in the cemetery in March. It had turned up on his front porch, apparently left by the mysterious dog only a few days later. And then only about a month after that he had lost another (or perhaps the same one, who could know). That was on the Saturday that Cassie had approached him at Franklin's. After walking her to Dempsey's Grocery, he had reached for his handkerchief to blow his nose and realized it was gone. Figuring he had dropped it on the way from Franklin's, he had retraced his steps back to the Five and Dime looking for it. Upon re-entering the store, he had checked around the magazine rack to no avail and then asked Ellis at the soda counter if perhaps he had left or accidently dropped it there. Ellis had just laughed and said, "Ain't seen it kid, but old man Franklin sells a bunch of handkerchiefs over there." Ellis had pointed to his left and said, "They'll hold snot and boogers better than your old one did anyway, kid." Marcus' last avenue was the lost and found, but Beverley the cashier had checked and come up empty handed. Marcus felt terrible about losing his father's handkerchief. But here he stood, months later, with it firmly in his grasp. The new question being, with whose blood was it stained?

Marcus headed to the front door, but then remembered noticing a strange car parked out front where Mr. Worthington normally parked to pick him up and drop him off. He turned back to take another look at what appeared to be a car at first, but on closer examination turned out to be an El Camino pick-up. It was powder blue and extremely unique. The front half looked like a standard sedan automobile while the rear half consisted of a low-slung pick-up truck type bed equipped with fins. Marcus assumed the owner of that vehicle definitely had some panache.

As Marcus entered the front door, he could see Margaret at the kitchen table with her hands cradling a cup of coffee. It was very unusual for Margaret to be drinking coffee at quarter after six in the evening. "Mama, I'm home. I'm sorry I'm a little late, I…."

"It's okay, Marcus. Remember I told you there would be a surprise when you got home? Well, here he is. Do you remember Cousin Judy?"

Marcus was confused. Here *he* is, Cousin Judy?

A fairly tall and quite tan gentleman came into view. He had apparently been on the other side of the table, across from Margaret and out of Marcus' line of sight. Marcus did not recognize the man at all. He was probably about six feet tall with short and prematurely gray hair, although his eyebrows and five o'clock shadow were still youthfully dark. "How are you doing Marcus? I haven't seen you since you were a tot. Probably what, about four years old?"

"I'm sorry sir," Marcus confessed. "But I don't think I remember you."

"I didn't know if you would or not, Marcus." Margaret went on to explain, "This is your father's cousin. His name is Jude Allensworth, but he's always been known to everyone as Judy. Your father always referred to him as Cousin Judy."

"Mags is right, Marcus." Cousin Judy verified. "Been called Judy all my life. My mother and your father's father, your Grandpa John Clemens, were brother and sister."

Wow, this is pretty cool, thought Marcus. He had not known there were any living relatives on either of his parents' sides of the family. He only knew of Margaret, and while she had family, the closest relatives were in Texas. She had even mentioned the possibility a couple of years ago of moving to Texas but had decided against it.

"Anyway, I live in Savannah, Georgia." Cousin Judy explained. "But I've got a business deal going and have to be in Chicago for a series of meetings. I have this thing about flying, so I thought I'd take an extra week or so and drive up to Chicago. And since I have plenty of time, I thought I'd swing by and see what little bit of family I still have around here. I was born in Monticello, which isn't too far from here, maybe fifteen miles or less."

"Cousin Judy, do you know much about my family?" Marcus was steeping with curiosity. "I remember some stuff that my dad told me, but not very much."

"Well, I was only around until I was eighteen." Cousin Judy offered Marcus his background story. "Enlisted in the army in '43. Spent some time in France and got back in the fall of '45. By the next spring I was on my way to Georgia. An old buddy of mine from the army, his family had a textile mill outside of Savannah, and he talked his dad into hiring a brash young hick out of Missouri to drive a truck for him. And next thing you know I'm the southeast sales manager."

"So, most of what I know came from the teenage years. Let's see, when I went into the army your dad wasn't but fifteen if I recall. I never met your mother. Hell, I'd have never met you and your stepmom except for that I came to your dad and Mags wedding back in…. what year was it, Margaret?"

"1956, Judy," Margaret answered from the kitchen, where she was preparing a chipped beef and gravy dinner.

"Yeah, yeah. That was it '56," confirmed Cousin Judy.

"Cousin Judy, I guess what I was wondering is if I would have any cousins or anything." Marcus was desperate to learn if there wasn't anyone left from his father's family. "Did my dad have any brothers or sisters? Am I the last one in the Clemens family?"

"I'm sorry to say, Marcus, but as far I can recollect you are the last surviving member of the Clemens family," Cousin Judy hated to let Marcus down. "There should have been more, you should have had cousins. Elijah had a brother; did he ever mention him?"

"No, never. Where does he live?" Marcus asked.

81

"He doesn't Marcus," replied Jude. "You see, Marcus, Harold passed away when he was three years old."

"Was he sick or something?" Marcus wondered.

"No, he was healthy as a buck. Your grandfather John Clemens had taken Elijah and Harold with him to hook some catfish for dinner. Elijah was about six years old, and Harold was three. Elijah was playing in the rocks on the bank while your grandfather was fishing, and Harold had wandered off towards the tall weeds further up on the bank." The story was difficult for Cousin Judy to relate, but Marcus really needed to know things about his family. He continued, "Your grandfather was frustrated at not having caught anything and with trying to keep up with two young boys. He later said he asked Elijah repeatedly to check on Harold, but he continued fiddling with the rocks. Finally, an angry John Clemens threw down his pole and went up to get Harold. When he found him, it was too late. He had stumbled upon a den of copperhead snakes and been bitten by seven or eight of them."

Marcus broke out in a cold sweat and felt nauseous.

Cousin Judy furthered the story. "Harold didn't die right away. It took about two days. Your grandparents were in absolute agony. The guilt hung on Elijah like a shroud. I doubt he was ever able to forgive himself for the death of his baby brother. He told me once when he was about your age that he would have given anything to have traded places with Harold. When he thought of him it was always 'if only I had kept up with Harold'. In reality though, it was if he'd only been able to understand what his father had told him."

"My mother and I rode over in the carriage so my mother could try to help in any way she could. She was one of the few who could totally understand your grandfather. But anyway, Marcus, that is the story of your Uncle Harold."

"That's a terrible story Cousin Judy. I feel so bad for my dad. He probably carried that guilt all of his life. I wonder why he never told me about Uncle Harold?"

"Because of the guilt probably, Marcus. From what I have heard, he never talked about Harold."

"Cousin Judy," Marcus sought more understanding. "I'm confused. What did you mean when you said my dad didn't understand what grandpa had told him?"

"Marcus, Judy, dinner is ready," Margaret called from the kitchen.

"Okay Mags. Marcus and I are going to wash up and we'll be right there," Judy responded.

Cousin Judy stood to go to the bathroom to wash up when Marcus said, "Wait, Cousin Judy. You didn't answer my question. You said my dad didn't understand what grandpa had told him and you said your mother was the only one who understood grandpa. What do you mean?"

"Marcus, didn't your father tell you anything about your family? Your grandpa wasn't the first in the Clemens family, but I certainly hope he was the last. He had a bad speech impediment. Poor man had a cleft palate. He was a harelip."

James E. Anderson

Dinner Topics

Upon arriving home, Cassie had gone to her bedroom, ostensibly to read. Jack had made a beeline for the liquor cabinet where he had prepared two gin and tonics, one for himself and one for his wife. With drinks in hand, he had proceeded to the kitchen where Debbie was busy preparing a light dinner of ham and cheese omelets. Omelets and buttered toast were the traditional Sunday evening fare, since no one was ever starving following the large family style lunch feasted upon after church. Noticing the drinks in his hand, Debbie asked, "What are we celebrating Jack?" Rarely was alcohol consumed on Sundays in the Worthington household and the sight of the gin and tonics piqued her curiosity.

"Something happened with Cassie at the river today, Debbie," Jack began.

"Is she hurt? Where is she, Jack?" Debbie demanded.

"No, no, no, she's fine. Relax, Debbie. Cassie's in her room reading The Hardy Boys or something. Here, take that off the burner and sit down for a minute." Jack set the drinks on the kitchen table and pulled out a chair for Debbie.

She sat, took a sip and looked at her husband expectantly.

"Sweetheart, Cassie and Marcus found something today when they were leaving the dam and walking to the parking lot. It's probably nothing and not a big deal at all, but you never really know."

"What do you mean? What did they find, Jack?" she asked.

"They found a ski mask. I'm sure it's noth…."

"A ski mask?" Debbie interjected and then softly, but nervously laughed. "Who wears a ski mask during Indian Summer? It's far too warm for something like that."

"Agreed. That was my first thought as well. But there was somethi…."

Again, Debbie broke in, "Jack, that's what a robber or a kidnapper would wear. You don't think somebody was stalking Cassie, do you? Oh my God, do you think she is in danger?"

"Honey, you need to relax. Have another sip and calm down a little bit. I looked at it very carefully. Nobody had been wearing it. It was dirty, you could tell it had obviously been out in the weather for a long time." Jack wanted to ease his wife's concerns, but at the same time did not want to gloss over the reality of the situation. "The only thing that troubles me is something that I noticed on the face of the mask." He paused to finish his gin and tonic.

"What, what Jack?" Debbie asked as he downed his drink. Her anxiety had not diminished.

"Debbie, it looked like it had dried blood on it. Like if at some point it had been, I don't know, like when you smack the palm of your hand into dishwater, and it splashes into your face. You understand what I'm trying to describe?"

"Yes Jack, I do. But that's a disgusting way to explain it." Then Debbie had a thought, "Maybe somebody lost it last winter. You know, maybe they were rabbit hunting, and it was cold, and they were cleaning the rabbit, you know? I can remember my dad and uncle rabbit and squirrel hunting and cleaning them. I'm pretty sure they had blood on their clothes from doing that, right? Maybe that's what happened is all."

Jack sensed she was trying her best to avoid what he was quite certain was the true explanation. "Debbie. I know you haven't forgotten the girl Cassie and Marcus found in May, have you? I have a suspicion it has a connection to that."

"You think so, Jack?"

"I do. That's why I took it to the police. I've got a feeling they can look it over and maybe use it as evidence against someone eventually." Jack said with an air of confidence.

"Perhaps you're right, dear. I hope you are. Nothing would make me feel better than to see the man that did that to that poor girl get his comeuppance."

* * * *

Margaret was clearing the dishes from the table as Cousin Judy rolled himself a cigarette loaded with Prince Albert tobacco. Lighting the cigarette, inhaling deeply, and sending tiny smoke rings filtering across the kitchen, Cousin Judy turned his attention to Marcus and his day at the river. "So, Marcus, Mags tells me you took your new girl over to the dam to show her the sights today. How did it go?"

"Oh, it was fine. Wasn't much to see, though. Wasn't nothing going on, no boat traffic at all," he explained.

"Well then, how'd you pass the time?" Judy put the back of his hand to the side of his face to shield Margaret from seeing him wink at Marcus. It took a few seconds for Marcus' innocent mind to decipher what he was inferring.

"I just explained to her how the lock and dam operated and why they built it in the first place. You know, just kind of told her a little bit of the history behind it." Marcus was curious if Cousin Judy shared his father's interest in the river. "Did you used to do a lot of fishing when you were young Cousin Judy?"

"Yes, I did. Quite a bit I suppose. And drop the 'Cousin' would you? I never really cared for it when Elijah called me that as we were growing up. Just call me Judy, okay Marcus?" Judy tousled Marcus' hair and smiled. It was probably just his imagination, but Marcus couldn't help but think that Judy reminded him of how his fading memories framed his father. The haircut, physical stature, facial features, and even the smile. "Yeah, Marcus, biggest difference being I did most of my fishing in ponds around Monticello. Didn't get over here to the river too often. Wasn't exactly walking distance, you know?"

"I know, Cousin Judy. I... I mean Judy," Marcus stammered. "It's a long enough walk from here."

"Speaking of the river," Judy redirected the conversation, "Mags tells me you had a bit of adventure this spring. Said you came across the body of a young lady over on the bank. That must have been a growing up moment for you."

"Yes sir, it was. I ain't never seen a dead body. Well, not since my daddy's funeral, I guess. But it's not the same seeing one out in the real world like that. It sure is something I'll never forget." Marcus suppressed a shudder at the memory. Thoughts of the horror of that day reminded him there was a lot of information about this mystery that he was not about to share with anyone, least of all Margaret and Cousin Judy.

"I was sure it would scar him for life," said Margaret. "He had nightmares for a month afterward."

"Did not, Mama, you're exaggerating," said Marcus. "For a couple of nights, but that's all."

"Perfectly normal, Marcus. That could happen to an adult as well," Judy intoned. "You were caught totally off guard; not like you were provided a warning that anything out of the ordinary was about to happen. Mags says as far she can tell, the police still don't have a clue about what happened, or who did it."

"That's right," Margaret said, "According to the Lewis County Tribune, there was no evidence that could be collected. Nothing was left behind. They may never have even identified her except for the clothes she was wearing."

"I knew it!" exclaimed Marcus. "I knew that dress she was wearing was a costume or something, wasn't it Mama?"

"That's right. It was a dress style commonly worn by Polish Polka dancers. After a couple of weeks, that is how they were able to identify the girl. It turned out she had belonged to a polka dance club of some type that met every week at a Holiday Inn up by Alexandria," explained Margaret. "As luck would have it, one of the Lewis County cops remembered there had been an article about the club in the Clark County Courier and they were able to put two and two together."

"You mean that even though that is only about twenty miles north of here," Judy asked, "it took an article in a Clark County newspaper about the polka dance club for somebody to realize the connection between the club and the girl? That's crazy. By the time a week or so passed, word should have been spread that a girl was missing from that club, wouldn't you think?"

Margaret mulled over the question and said, "You are right, Judy. Somebody had to know right away that she was missing and probably reported it. All of the local police agencies should have been notified of a missing woman, and Lewis County should have suspected immediately that it was her."

Marcus weighed this new information that he had not previously known. He had not even been aware that the girl had been identified, much less anything else Margaret had detailed. The point that kept coming to his mind was the fact that no evidence had been left behind nor collected at the scene. If that was true, it became even more mysterious to him why the dog brought the ski mask to him and Cassie. If it indeed was an article of evidence in the girl's murder, how and why did the dog possess it? How long had he been holding on to it? Why didn't he just leave it there for the police to find? And why did he bring the red handkerchief? Why was it blood-stained and did that mean it was there at the time of the crime? What is the connection between the ski mask, the handkerchief and the girl?

Just the Facts

Marcus tossed and turned all through the night. Margaret had offered Marcus' bed to Judy for the night, and thus he found himself on the couch. Perhaps that was partly to blame for his fitful sleep. But more likely it was the thoughts and visions of the girl's corpse that haunted him so severely. He kept seeing her brightly colored dress – red, green and yellow - and the pristine white upper half marred by her very own blood. Every time Marcus awoke the scene was as fresh in his mind as the day when he witnessed it. And every time he would fall back to sleep, he would find himself standing amongst the tree branches and discovering her body yet again.

In his waking moments, he saw the mournful look in the harelipped dog's eyes as it stood with the ski mask and handkerchief in its mouth. What is the connection with the dog? Marcus couldn't shake the memories from the cemetery. From the very first confrontation, everything seemed surreal. He was sure someone was calling his name. He kept hearing 'Marc'. No one ever called him that unless it was followed by 'Twain'. "Hey, Marc Twain", he was used to hearing on the playground. But no one called him just Marc. Everyone said Marcus.

Eventually Marcus must have cleared his mind of the dreadful thoughts and memories, for he awoke feeling somewhat refreshed to the pleasant smell and sizzling sound of bacon frying in the kitchen. He could barely detect the muffled sound of conversation from his make-shift bed in the living room. With it normally being just himself and Margaret in the apartment, Marcus was unaccustomed to there being any conversation that he was not a part of. As he stretched and shook off the cobwebs, Marcus remembered Cousin Judy.

Glancing up from his coffee, Judy was the first to notice him in the archway separating the two rooms. "Good morning sleepy head!" he boomed. Margaret turned away from the stove to face Marcus and said, "Well, it's about time, I thought you were going to sleep all day. I'm glad you decided to join us for breakfast, Marcus."

"What time is it, Mama?" asked Marcus. "It sure feels awfully early."

"It's just past 8:30," Judy informed Marcus. "Here, pull up a chair, Marcus. What would be your pleasure? Cup of coffee? Glass of milk?"

"A glass of milk, please. I'm not old enough for coffee yet, Cousin Judy,"

"Marcus, it's just Judy, remember?" Judy reminded him. "You know, if I remember correctly, I started my coffee addiction at about 9 years old. Probably a good thing you haven't started drinking it yet. Between coffee and these cigarettes, my teeth have really yellowed through the years. Next thing you know, they'll figure out that coffee causes cancer!" he said, laughing heartily before taking a drag on his self-rolled smoke.

Margaret served up a fine breakfast of fried eggs (sunny side up for Marcus), bacon and toast. Marcus' favorite breakfast. But today, in honor of Cousin Judy, Margaret had gone above and beyond by frying homemade hash browns to perfection. Marcus was delighted by the meal, and for at least a little while, cleared his mind of the nightmarish thoughts that had consumed his sleeping hours. After breakfast, while Margaret cleared the table and began the chores of washing dishes and cleaning up the kitchen, Marcus and Judy stepped out onto the front porch and took seats in the two Adirondack chairs that Elijah had built for himself and Marcus' mother just after they had wed. Margaret had always respected Marcus' mother and never felt any jealousy or resentment over any possessions or relics that remained from her and Elijah's short time together.

As they sat absorbing the sunlight on an unseasonably warm early September morning, Judy turned toward Marcus and said, "You know, there are a few other things I probably should tell you about your family, Marc. Do you mind if I call you Marc? I notice Mags calls you Marcus, but that just seems kind of formal, doesn't it? I mean, we're just a couple of guys, you know? You could call me by my given name, Jude, but that just seems…formal. I prefer Judy, more informal, you know what I mean Marc?"

"Yeah, that would be swell, Judy," Marcus replied with a smile. Nobody called him Marc, but if Judy did, they would share a special bond. Especially so since Judy was the only living relative that Marcus had.

"Well good then, Marc. I'm going to be leaving in a couple of hours, so I figured I should fill you in on some of what your dad apparently never got around to. I don't know when, or even if I'll get back to Missouri again, so here goes with more family history for you."

"Now, I've already told you about your Uncle Harold. Harold Lee Clemens was his full name. He passed in 1934. Your grandparents were John Stuart Clemens and Anna Claire Clemens. I'm reasonably sure her maiden name was Smith, and I think she was from somewhere in Iowa."

"That's pretty cool Cous…. I mean Judy. I never even knew what their names were." Marcus was more than happy to learn about his ancestors.

Judy smiled and said; "I wish I didn't have to be the one telling you this stuff, Marc, but I guess I'm glad that I am. My mother's name was

93

Mary Elizabeth Allensworth, and my dad was Jude Lawton Allensworth. Neither of them lived to be fifty years old."

"So, Judy, you were named after your dad? That makes you a junior then, right?" Marcus asked.

"No. I actually have a different middle name from my father. His was Lawton, mine is Urban. And I have always hated it," explained Judy.

Marcus couldn't contain a smile. "It is a funny kind of name."

Judy wasn't amused, but continued, "Okay, to get back to your grandparents. Since you were at the dam yesterday, and seem to know a little of its history, here is some more for you. Your grandfather was a carpenter and worked on the dam when it was being built."

"Wow, I wouldn't have known that if you hadn't of told me."

"Yeah, Marc, but here's the sad part. I told you, your grandfather had a harelip and could not speak well," Judy went on with his history lesson. "As a result of his speech problems, nobody wanted to work with him or around him. Everybody kind of saw him as a freak or something. He really made people around him feel uncomfortable. So, they had him building temporary wooden handrails to keep people from falling into the river. It was December of 1934, not even six months after Harold had passed. John was working on the handrail, alone, and who knows, maybe he was thinking about Harold. I mean he never forgave himself for Harold dying, always thought it was his fault." Judy stopped and gathered his thoughts, while Marcus waited patiently for what he almost was certain was coming.

"Anyway, it was something like twenty degrees that day, the river water was freezing, and no man could survive a fall into that water." Judy paused again for a few seconds before continuing, "They think that he fell, but you know what, Marc? I'm not convinced that Uncle John didn't jump. He was awfully depressed."

"Oh no, Judy. Do you think grandpa killed himself?"

"I guess we'll never know, Marc. His body was carried away by the current and never recovered. But you know the damnedest thing about it, Marc? Your grandfather was only thirty-one years old when he died. And do you know how old Elijah, your dad, was? Thirty-one. Ain't that some coincidence?"

Marcus let it all settle in his mind. During the silence, Judy rolled himself another cigarette. As he lit it and took a deep draw, Marcus came out of his trance and asked solemnly, "Judy, do you think my dad might have been thinking about Uncle Harold and wasn't paying attention when his bulldozer turned over?"

"Naw, I doubt it, Marc. Your dad was very conscious about his surroundings and what he was doing when he was working. He knew that what he did was a dangerous job, and he had to be safe and alert at all times. No, no. No chance. It was just purely an accident." Judy tried his best to be convincing.

They both had sat in silence for a few moments when Margaret stepped onto the porch and said, "Marcus, the telephone is for you. It's Cassie."

"Hello, Cassie. How are you doing today?" Marcus asked casually. After learning so much about his family, his mind had temporarily turned the page on the ski mask, the dog and the dead girl.

"Marcus, I'm troubled. My dad is certain that ski mask was worn by whoever killed that poor girl." Marcus couldn't recall the tone of Cassie's voice sounding this distraught. "Marcus, that was her blood on that ski mask."

Marcus was surprised Cassie's father had been so blunt as to tell her that. "Are you serious, Cassie? Your father told you something that bold? How would he know that anyway?"

"No, Marcus. You've seen enough of my dad to know he would never tell me something like that," Cassie was rather surprised that Marcus would even consider that her dad had told her what he suspected concerning the ski mask.

95

"If he didn't tell you, then how do you know what he thinks about the mask?"

Cassie decided it best to slow down and start at the beginning. "When we got home, after dropping you off, I went to my room. I told my dad I was going to read until dinner was ready. I went to the bathroom, and when I came out to go into my bedroom, I saw my dad making drinks. You know, like martinis or something. Anyway, my parents never drink alcohol on Sundays unless there is something major going on. So, I snuck out of my room and eavesdropped while they were talking at the kitchen table. And that's when I heard my dad telling my mom what he suspected."

Marcus couldn't argue with Mr. Worthington's assessment. "Well, to be honest, Cassie, that's what I thought, too. I couldn't hardly sleep last night thinking about all this stuff."

"Me neither." Cassie agreed and then asked, "Marcus, what are you doing today? Is your stepmother working today?"

"Yeah, I think she leaves about one o'clock to go to work. She has the dinner shift from 2:00 until 9:00." Marcus then added, "And I don't know what I'm doing. Judy is leaving in a little while."

Cassie was puzzled, "Judy? Who is she?"

Marcus forgot that Cassie didn't know that Judy existed. "Oh, I didn't get a chance to tell you. My father's cousin Judy is here. He is on his way to Chicago and stopped to see us."

Now Cassie was really confused, "Wait Marcus. Are you saying Judy is a man? Something doesn't sound right."

Marcus had to laugh. He could understand Cassie's confusion, as he had been in the same situation just last night. "It does sound odd, doesn't it? My father's cousin's name is Jude, but everyone calls him Judy. He is from around here, but he lives in Georgia, now."

"Oh, okay. I understand now," she said and then added, "Marcus, if you don't have any plans; I mean if you're not going to Denny's or going fishing or anything, my parents are having a Labor Day barbeque this afternoon if you'd like to come. They have a couple of neighbors coming over, but there are no kids my age, and I am going to be lonely and bored. Will your stepmother let you come; do you think?"

"Give me a minute, Cassie, and I'll go ask," and Marcus laid the receiver down. He went to the front porch where Margaret and Judy were sipping iced tea. He explained Cassie's invitation and added a "Please, Mama." At length, Margaret relented, telling Marcus to be home by seven even though she would not be there until later.

"I've got an idea for you both," said Judy. "Since I'm leaving anyway, how about I drop you off, Marc, at Cassie's house and then I'll take Mags to the diner. Two birds with one stone you might say."

"Thanks Judy! I'll go tell Cassie I'll be there around one." Marcus literally ran back to the phone.

* * * *

As promised, Judy's El Camino, with Marcus in the middle and Margaret manning the passenger seat, pulled up to the Worthington's red brick home on Fernwood Drive precisely five minutes before one o'clock. Margaret stepped out to allow Marcus to exit. After reminding him to be home by seven, and as she often did, threatening (idly) to call from the diner to make sure he was there, Margaret hopped back in. Marcus leaned into the open passenger side window and once again told Judy goodbye. He couldn't be sure if he would ever see him again, but it was nice to now know for certain that he had at least one blood relative.

As he turned to start up the sidewalk, Marcus was mildly surprised to see Cassie already walking toward him. Still at least ten feet from him, Cassie could not contain herself, "I'm so glad you are here, Marcus. This is driving me crazy."

Marcus was caught off guard. "What do you mean, Cassie? Don't you like your neighbors?"

"No…. I guess I mean yes, I like them fine. But no, they're not what I was talking about. It's this whole situation with the girl and the dog and everything. That's why I needed you to be here today. I can't stop thinking about things and I need you to talk to about it." Cassie was almost pleading.

Granted, Marcus hadn't known her for long, but he had never seen her this distraught. "I'm right here Cassie. I'm here for you, whatever you need."

Cassie barreled forth, "Marcus, did you know that girl's name was Zofia Wozniak. She was only nineteen years old. Her parents are Polish immigrants. They just came from Poland a few years ago and they have a farm over by Wayland."

"No, I didn't know what her name was," Marcus responded. "All I know is she belonged to a polka club up in Alexandria. That's why she had that colorful dress on."

"Alexandria? That's not even big enough to call a town. Why would there be a polka club there?"

"Don't know. Judy and Mama were talking about it last night. There's a Holiday Inn there on highway 61. That's where they have meetings or dances or whatever they do." Marcus told Cassie what little he knew.

"I know where that is. We have been there for lunch a couple of times in the summer," said Cassie. "It is on my dad's way home from work and not far from Keokuk. I have gone to my dad's office with him a few times and we've gone there for lunch. You know, they have those 'take your kid to work' days."

Marcus wondered, "Cassie, how did you learn all that stuff about the girl?"

"From eavesdropping. Remember I told you on the phone. My dad knows a lot about that girl. I guess he talks to a lot of people that

98

have information. Or maybe he's been talking to the police. I don't know."

"Come on, Marcus. Let's go in the house. Everybody is in the back yard. We can go in the living room and watch television while we talk." Cassie turned and headed to the front door with Marcus in tow.

After grabbing two Coca-Colas from the fridge and settling in front of the television, Cassie and Marcus continued their conversation. Cassie reiterated what she had told Marcus on the phone, "My dad says that was blood on that ski mask. And it had been out in the weather for a while. So, I think he's right. Whoever killed that girl probably wore that mask."

"Well, if that's true, the police should be able to get fingerprints off of it," Marcus offered.

"I hope you're right, Marcus. But you know, it has my fingerprints on it, and yours, too." Cassie remembered handing it to her father. "And my dad's. His are all over it. He was all turning it inside out and stuff."

"Well, that's okay Cassie," Marcus reasoned. "They know none of us did it. So, whoever else's fingerprints are on it is the killer."

Cassie had another concern. "Marcus, why did that weirdo dog have your handkerchief along with the ski mask. And why did it have blood on it?"

"I can't answer that, Cassie. That handkerchief has been missing since the day we met at Franklin's." Marcus told her.

"But here's what I want to figure out. What is going on with that dog? You said something that one day that I just remembered last night when I had trouble sleeping. Do you remember what you said, Cassie?" Marcus asked.

"No, Marcus. What did I say?"

"You said it was like the dog talked right into your ear, but not out loud. That's what it seemed like to me, too. But the only thing he has said to me, when you weren't around, was 'Marc'. At the time I thought he was saying it out loud, but now I'm not so sure. And besides, that would be physically impossible. But maybe it is some type of telepathy. Maybe that dog has the power to put words directly into our heads. Maybe he doesn't have a voice and doesn't really speak at all. What do you think?"

Back to School

The hammer rocked the bells on his trusty old alarm clock to let Marcus know another school day had arrived. It was Tuesday, September 3 and the first day of the last year of elementary school. The sixth grade beckoned him, and Marcus was more than a little bit anxious to learn who his new teacher would be. His hopes, along with those of just about every boy entering sixth grade, was that he would find his name on the roster headed by the lovely Miss Dorothy Cameron. As far as any boy at Roosevelt could ascertain, Miss Cameron was far and away the most beautiful teacher in all of Lewis County. More than one young lad in the upper elementary grades had been verbally reprimanded for penning naughty notes or poems, or for drawing semi-lewd pictures involving this popular teacher. Fifth and sixth grade boys are approaching the age where sexual tension is beginning to take root, and sometimes misplaced and premature desire can yield unsavory results. But, while he found Miss Cameron attractive, Marcus was not overwhelmed by the desire to be in her class. Undoubtably, he would enjoy being in her presence daily, but he was pragmatic enough to realize she was at least fifteen years his senior.

And besides, he was the one kid at Roosevelt that could point to the prettiest girl in the entire school and boast that she was his girlfriend.

So it was that Marcus had set his alarm to sound fifteen minutes earlier than he had in previous years. He wanted to be sure to arrive at school plenty early in order to be waiting when Cassie's bus arrived. He wanted to be her knight in shining armor, ready and willing to walk her to her new classroom.

Margaret had left early to work the breakfast/lunch shift, but she knew she could trust Marcus to wake up, bathe, feed himself breakfast and leave in plenty of time to get to school before the bell would ring. She could feel even more confident this year, for she knew the level of dedication Marcus had developed toward Cassie. She knew he could not allow himself to let Cassie down by not being there waiting when she stepped off the bus at school.

The talk of adding a bus route to handle the continually growing number of students at the Westside La Grange Apartments had finally come to fruition. If Marcus had chosen to ride the bus (which was not a requirement), he could most likely have rewarded himself with an additional forty-five minutes of sleep in the morning. However, he actually enjoyed walking to and from school, and was aware that moving into seventh grade next year would require attending Woodrow Wilson Junior High School. Wilson JHS was located nearly five miles from his apartments and Marcus had no intention whatsoever of walking that far. His days of freedom would become more controlled, but when the time came, there really would be no alternative to taking the bus.

As he journeyed the quietest stretch of country road along the route to Roosevelt, Marcus thought he heard breathing. It was hard to discern, what with the chirping of crickets in the nearby wheat field. Through his few years of walking these roads adjoined by nearby wheat, alfalfa and soybean fields, Marcus had become attuned to the sounds of insects. Chirps are the signifying sounds of crickets. They are short pure-toned sounds separated by interludes of silence. Whereas katydids display a variety of sounds such as lisps, lispy trills or rattles. These can range across a spectrum of long raspy continuous syllables, short staccato sounds, and the rattle being produced by many katydids and consisting of long, raspy notes strung together.

As he continued walking and the chirping diminished, Marcus drew the unmistakable conclusion that what he had thought was breathing was sounding more like gentle panting. Like that of a dog. He turned to see his mangy old harelipped friend following about eight to ten feet behind. "Well, hello fella. How have you been?" Marcus knelt, allowing the dog to approach. The dog stood quietly, allowing Marcus to gently stroke the top of his head and down to his shoulders. After accepting about thirty seconds of Marcus' attention, the dog abruptly turned and headed back in the direction from which he had come.

"You are one strange little animal," Marcus had barely spoken the words when a logging truck loaded with timber came speeding by the dog, and just after passing Marcus, a loud explosive sound bellowed as the right front tire blew forcing the truck to suddenly swerve to the right and off the road. The force of the sudden swerve broke the restraining straps that secured the timber, and logs immediately flooded the highway and its adjacent shoulder. The truck driver did an amazing job of regaining control of the runaway rig and gradually brought it to a stop.

After just a few seconds, the driver jumped down from the cab and began surveying the catastrophe that bestrewed the road and immediate surroundings. Marcus ran toward the man to make sure he was alright, but it was Marcus that the truck driver was concerned about. "Are you alright boy?" he shouted.

"Yes sir, I'm fine. I wanted to see that you were okay. I was really worried you were going to flip the truck over," Marcus said trying to catch his breath.

"Yeah, no problem here except for this mess. Man, I felt that tire giving way, I seen you walking on the side of the road...... I thought sure I was going to hit you. You were real lucky I got past you before I lost control." The truck driver put his hand on Marcus' shoulder. "Real lucky. I couldn't have lived with myself if I'd have killed you, son. It's a damn good thing you wasn't twenty or thirty feet further down the road, you'd of been a goner. You had an angel sitting on your shoulder this morning, boy."

Marcus turned and looked back up the road, but there was no sign of the harelipped dog.

* * * *

Deputy Mitch Daniels dropped Marcus off at Roosevelt Elementary. A passing motorist had called the police from a pay phone to report the accident and resulting road blockage. Deputy Daniels had been the second officer to arrive and sensing that Marcus was in jeopardy of being late to school had given him a lift. They both had recognized the other from the scene at the riverbank.

As Marcus was exiting the cruiser, Deputy Daniels told him, "Best be careful young man. It seems to me you're traveling in some menacing circles this year."

Marcus had already missed the arrival of Cassie's bus. He ran to the sixth-grade classrooms and began searching the rosters for his name. He found Marcus Clemens on Mrs. Wolfe's roster and entered room 14b. He went straight to her desk and stood at attention. Mrs. Wolfe looked up at him and said, "You must be Marcus Clemens. Why are you late on the first day of school, Marcus? A detention would not look good on your record on the very first day of school in the 'A' class now, would it?"

"No ma'am, Mrs. Wolfe, it wouldn't. But I have a note from Deputy Daniels, ma'am. I was a witness to an accident on Foster Road this morning." Marcus handed her the note and crossed his fingers.

After studying the note front and back (although nothing was written on the back), Mrs. Wolfe said, "Okay, Marcus, excuse accepted. We are seated alphabetically, but since you weren't here this morning everyone moved up one desk. You'll have to sit in the back next to Miss Worthington." Marcus turned to face the class and spotted Cassie struggling to suppress a grin. He hurried to take his seat before Mrs. Wolfe changed her mind.

It seemed an eternity, but morning recess finally arrived, and the class retired to the playground. Marcus and Cassie found a bench and Marcus began detailing the events of the morning. After pouring through a condensed version of the story, Marcus said, "Cassie, that dog saved my life. If he had not been there to delay me just those few minutes, I would

104

have been further down the road and that truck or those logs would have killed me."

"I told you Marcus, there's something really strange about that dog. Did he speak to you?" Cassie asked.

"No, he didn't Cassie. I don't know what it is, but he only speaks when you are there."

The whistle sounded marking the end of recess and everyone lined up to march toward the restrooms and water fountains. They returned to classroom 14b and began a lesson on the Civil War. With so much on their minds, Cassie and Marcus both had difficulty focusing on Mrs. Wolfe's boring presentation. Mercifully, the long history lesson was finally halted by the lunch whistle.

Cassie, followed by Marcus, collected her tray and portion of spaghetti and meatballs, dried bread and carton of milk. They found seats with a bit of separation from other students and began pecking at their food while further delving into the mysteries surrounding the harelipped dog. Suddenly, Cassie put down her fork and looked at her boyfriend. "Marcus, I noticed something strange yesterday. Maybe you can explain it for me."

"Maybe Cassie, what is it?"
"Marcus, when you came to my house yesterday, I saw your stepmother get out of the car to let you out, right?"

"Right Cassie, she had to, I was sitting in the middle," explained Marcus.

"Okay then, next question. Who was driving the car, Marcus? Was that Cousin Judy?" she asked.

"Yes, of course. Why do you ask?"

"Just wanted to be sure. Where did you say he lived Marcus?"

"I told you, Cassie. He lives in Georgia. He was on his way to Chicago and stopped to visit with us." Marcus was totally lost with Cassie's line of questioning.

"Are you absolutely sure, Marcus? How can you be sure?"

"Because he said so, Cassie. He's my dad's only cousin. He doesn't have any reason to lie to me or Mama." Marcus felt defensive. So far, he had never had any reason to feel on edge with Cassie. She and he were like soulmates, they thought alike, liked the same things, had never had an unkind word for one another. But this conversation was bothering him.

"Aside from his word, do you have any other proof, Marcus?"

"Yes, as a matter of fact, I do Cassie. When you and your father dropped me off at my apartment Sunday evening, I didn't even know Judy was there until I went inside. But before I did, I noticed a strange car out front. The same blue El Camino that Judy drove to bring me to your house. You know how good I am with numbers. It had a Georgia license plate. I-G-54713."

"Well, Marcus, I'm good with numbers too. When he dropped you at my house that same blue El Camino had an Illinois license plate. JR9705."

The Mausoleum

The first four weeks of sixth grade were essentially uneventful for Marcus and Cassie. The subject matter had been a bit more challenging than what either of them had encountered thus far in elementary school. Perhaps it was more challenging, perhaps it was merely the methodology of the indomitable Mrs. Louise Wolfe. She was responsible for the preparation of the brightest sixth graders enrolled at Roosevelt Elementary, and was thusly determined to send an accomplished group of disciplined and productive young adolescents on to Woodrow Wilson Junior High School. She was a demanding, but fair taskmaster who demanded and generally received exemplary results. She could be gruff on occasion, but was nonetheless liked and respected.

Cassie, herself being extremely competent in every subject imaginable, a very well-rounded student, had been sailing through the first quarter. Marcus, having been placed for the only time since first grade in the 'A' level class, found the going a bit more adverse. His math skills remained top drawer, he enjoyed history and social studies, but still faced difficulties with science. By and large, it was his aptitude in math and improvement in social studies and geography that had prompted his

107

promotion from the 'B' class to the 'A' level. He was oh so glad for it to have happened. It was wonderful being in the same class with Cassie. And he was ever so thankful that fate had caused him to be late for the first day of school, prompting the revised seating arrangement that had resulted in his sitting right next to Cassie.

A quarter of the way through the first semester, it had been announced that a debate club would be formed. Meetings and debate practice would be an extracurricular activity held in the school library. The announcement came on Wednesday and interested parties had until the following Wednesday to sign up. The meetings would be held weekly on Friday afternoons for one hour. While Cassie was interested in getting involved, she was concerned because there was no bus service being provided for club members. Those seeking to join would be required to secure their own transportation home after meetings. With her family owning just the one car, Cassie had no form of transportation to rely upon. She discussed this with Marcus at lunch, just after learning about the club being formed. Marcus was very sympathetic to her plight but could offer no real solution. They both asked around during recess to see if they could find anyone who lived near Forest Park Estates and that was also considering joining the debate club. Unfortunately, anyone who did indicate an interest either was a walker or was in the same situation as Cassie. Several kids told them that they wanted to join but had no way to get home from the meetings, either. Back in class, and just prior to the final bell, Marcus furiously scribbled a note, reached over and tossed it onto Cassie's desk. When the bell rang, they made a beeline for Cassie's bus. After navigating the five crowded steps leading from building to sidewalk, Cassie stepped over onto the grass and unfolded the note Marcus had scribbled. She smiled and said, "Good idea, Marcus, I'll ask." Marcus felt a small sense of accomplishment as he watched Cassie board her bus and take a seat in the second row.

Marcus was sitting at the kitchen table, struggling with the concept of cell structure when he was relieved to be interrupted by a ringing telephone. He assumed it was Margaret, on her break at the diner, checking in on him. But he was surprised by the voice on the other end of the line. "Hello, Marcus. This is Debbie Worthington, Cassie's mother."

"Oh, hello Mrs. Worthington. How are you this afternoon?" Marcus attempted to be as polite as possible.

"I'm fine, Marcus, thank you. It's very gentlemanly of you to ask. I wanted to call and talk to you and possibly to Mrs. Clemens afterward, as well."

"I'm sorry, Mrs. Worthington, but Mama is at work right now. She should be back about nine-thirty or ten o'clock, depending on if she gets a ride home with either the cook or the dishwasher or has to walk." Marcus immediately wished he had not elaborated on Margaret's uncertain transportation situation. He hoped he didn't make himself and Margaret appear to be poor. He could not wait until he was old enough to start earning some money. He desperately wanted Margaret to have a car of her own.

"That's not a problem, dear. If you would just ask her to call me at her convenience. I'll be up late tonight watching television, so that won't be a problem. But in the meantime, Cassie tells me that she would dearly love to
join the debate club at school. And I certainly don't have a problem with her doing so. However, Jack and I have only the one car, and therefore Cassie would have no way of getting home after the meetings. Cassie seems to have that figured out, and that is why I wanted to talk to you, Marcus."

"Yes, ma'am." Marcus knew where he thought this conversation was going but did not know if Cassie had revealed to her mother the contents of the note that he had given her.

"Marcus, Cassie has suggested to me that since you were already signed up for the club, that you had offered to walk Cassie home after the meetings. Is that right, Marcus? Did you offer?" Cassie's mother asked.

"Yes, Mrs. Worthington, I did. I'm sure Cassie has told you that I walk to and from school every day. I don't mind at all walking Cassie to your house. I mean, it is only one day a week. It's not a problem for me at all." Marcus was right about the intent of the call, and he had to smile. Yes, he had in his note to her, offered to walk her home, but he did not mention having any intention of joining the debate club. He had rather just planned to hang out or do homework while she attended the meetings.

"One more question then. Have you asked your stepmother's permission for this? It will make you quite late arriving home from school on Fridays, you know. I want to know from Mrs. Clemens that she approves of this arrangement, and then I'll discuss it with Jack tomorrow evening."

"Yes ma'am. I will ask Mama when she gets in tonight and then I will have her call you." Mrs. Worthington certainly sounded agreeable to the proposal, and Marcus was almost certain that Margaret would give her blessing. The only roadblock that he foresaw was approval from Cassie's father.

* * * *

The next day, Cassie practically bounded off the bus, quite the jump in her step. "You sure look happy this morning," observed Marcus as he met Cassie on the sidewalk. "I guess your mother told you that Mama said it was okay for me to walk you home."

"Yes, as soon as I woke up this morning. She could have told me last night because I was still awake when your stepmother called. It's funny, she could have told me right then, except she thought I was asleep. I went to bed at nine o'clock but couldn't fall asleep. But it doesn't really matter. I already knew anyway." Cassie was rambling with excitement.

"What do you mean you already knew? How did you know?" Marcus asked.

"Eavesdropping, Marcus. I have become like a secret agent, sneaking around listening to conversations," Cassie laughed heartily. "Come on, before we're late." They jogged up the steps and stepped into the hallway.

"Oh yeah, Marcus. My mom really likes you. She says you are very responsible for your age and you have a good head on your shoulders."

110

Cassie felt good relaying the compliments that her mother had conferred to her.

"That was nice of her to say, Cassie. Now, I hope your dad likes me as much and agrees with Mama and your mom when he gets home tonight," said Marcus hopefully.

"I'm sure he will, Marcus. He likes you, too."

"How come your mother couldn't ask him last night, Cassie," Marcus asked.

"Oh, he had to go to Mt, Pleasant, Iowa yesterday. When he has to make that drive, he doesn't get back to Keokuk until late, so he just stays there in a motel by the office," Cassie explained. "He'll be back tonight, and my mom will ask him. He'll say yes because he always does. If anyone says no it is always my mom. She's the worrier. I'll call you tonight and let you know what he says."

True to her word, Cassie called just before seven with the good news. "Marcus, I think we should celebrate Saturday. Let's go to Randolph Park and have some fun!"

"We'll make it a date, Cassie. I'll pick you up at ten Saturday morning and we'll walk there together," Marcus was happy that Mr. and Mrs. Worthington had faith and trust in him.

Saturday morning could not come fast enough for Cassie and Marcus. They had had their fill of school for the week. They had both gotten signed up for the debate club and were already anxious for the first meeting the next Friday. Cassie was super excited. She seemed to already know that she wanted to run for class president in the seventh grade and thought the debate club would be the place to learn about public speaking and arguing political views. Marcus, on the other hand, was not really looking forward to speaking in public and wasn't really sure he had the mental quickness that would allow him to think on his feet and come up with spontaneous answers. But, for Cassie, he was willing to give it a go. He had talked Denny into signing up also, hoping that having him there as well would help him develop some courage.

Marcus was a little early arriving at Cassie's house on Saturday morning, but she was looking forward to going to the park and was ready to go when he arrived. On the way to the park, they discussed the debate club and just what they were expecting it to be like. Cassie repeated to Marcus how much her parents were beginning to like and trust him. The confidence they were showing meant a lot to him and he vowed to Cassie that he would always look out for her and she could always feel safe with him.

They arrived at the park and spent an hour or so on the playground apparatuses before moving on to the lake. Rather surprisingly, the ducks had not yet left for warmer climates. Normally migration had begun by late September, but it was now mid-October, and they were still swarming the lake. The days had remained unseasonably warm, but cooler weather was just around the corner. Marcus and Cassie sat on a bench at the south end of the kidney shaped lake, enjoying the playfulness of the beautiful birds.

As Marcus and Cassie took in the activities of the waterfowls, they were unaware that they themselves were being observed. Predatory eyes peered from the thick marsh at the northeast side of the lake. In heavy camouflage, they could never have been seen from where the ducks were splashing at the south end. But they were watching.

Before long, boredom began to set in for Marcus and Cassie. "What else can we do, Marcus?" Cassie had become restless.
"Want to go by the cemetery? You haven't been there with me for a while. We could swing through there before going to the A&W for lunch like we had planned," Marcus suggested.

"That sounds good," Cassie said and then asked, "Is the path you made on the shortcut still cleared?"

"Yes, I just used it last week. I go through it at least once a week to keep it beaten down and make sure there are no more surprises," Marcus knew Cassie was still a little hesitant about finding more snakes. "And I haven't seen the dog since the first day of school, so there shouldn't be any problems."

They took the shortcut into the cemetery. The path was still beaten down as Marcus had promised and it was an uneventful trip. They stopped at the Garden of Faith so Marcus could commune with the spirits of his parents and Cassie offered up a prayer for their peacefulness. After the brief stop, they continued down the road toward the front entrance. It was a peaceful, quiet fall day, temperature in the upper 60's. They were discussing the merits of onions on the coney island dogs they were planning on for lunch, when Cassie noticed something that had escaped her attention previously. "Marcus, what is that building with the big open doorway? I never noticed it before."

"I don't know how you've missed it, Cassie. It has been there since way before I was born. That's the mausoleum," Marcus told her.

"I think I've heard of a mausoleum, but I don't know exactly what it is. What is it, Marcus?"

"I guess it's kind of like a house for dead people. Instead of burying them in the ground they are in crypts. There are like doorways on the wall that have caskets behind them. Think of it like a wall full of filing cabinet drawers, except the drawers are all sealed." Marcus did his best to explain.

"Can we go in there?" Cassie wondered aloud.

"Yeah, Cassie. It's a public mausoleum. A private one you couldn't go in; they usually keep them locked up. But this one is public. It has that huge doorway and there's another one at the other end. It has nice stained-glass windows high up on the walls. There are no lights, it just has the natural light, so you can only go in the daylight. Do you want to see it inside?" Marcus asked her.

"Yes, I do Marcus. Can we?"

"Sure." Marcus took Cassie's hand, and they walked the two hundred or so feet from the road and uphill on the path to the broad

113

doorway. They stood in the doorway taking in the vast expanse of the mausoleum. It was bordered on the far end by a forest, that could be seen from where they stood, through the open doorway some fifty yards ahead. "So, are we going in?" Cassie asked. Marcus thought Cassie sure was awfully brave for a twelve-year-old girl. "Sure thing. Do you see what I mean about the light, Cassie? It has gotten a little overcast, so there's not a lot of light in here, but we can see well enough."

They took a few steps into the building and looked at the wall to their right.

Each crypt was marked with a name and relevant information, just as a tombstone would have been, identifying its occupant. The walls on each side contained vertical rows of four crypts stacked one above the other, the entire length of the building. About midway through the building, and on each side, there were alcoves containing a cross on the wall below a tall and beautiful stained-glass window. Below and facing each cross was a small pew for those who wished to offer prayer or to meditate.

Looking at the very first vertical row of crypts to their right, Marcus suggested they play the tombstone math game, calculating the age of the person within the crypt. They were about eye level with the second crypt up and it was the easiest to read, so they decided to play using the crypts in that row. They began walking along the wall on the right, trying to beat each other at figuring the age the quickest. However, the further they walked toward the center of the building the less light was present. As they neared the midway point, Cassie said, "Marcus, it's getting too hard to see. Let's go to the other wall and start back toward the door."

As they began to turn to the opposite wall, Marcus tried to speak but the words stuck in his throat. Standing before them was someone dressed totally in camouflage, holding a machete, and wearing a red ski mask with nose and mouth sewn shut. Marcus managed to reach over, push her back and yell, "Run, Cassie!" before taking a step forward. Cassie bolted for the doorway, but Marcus knew he was between a rock and a hard place. His instinct was to run, but at the same time he wanted to buy Cassie time to get as far away as possible. It turned out he did not have the opportunity to do either. From his left, and out of nowhere, a dog came streaking into view, leaped and latched onto the right arm that held the machete. As the camouflage clad figure toppled under the weight

114

and vicious bite of the dog that Marcus now recognized, the machete fell to the mausoleum floor. Marcus quickly bent, picked it up and took a few steps backward toward the doorway watching the dog continue its attack. In a matter of seconds, the figure somehow managed to throw the dog off, jump up and run to the far doorway. As the figure disappeared through the doorway and into the adjoining forest, the dog stood watching the escape. Marcus turned to the doorway through which they had entered to make sure Cassie had gotten away and was shocked by what he saw. Cassie was standing there looking at him. And next to Cassie stood the harelip dog. Marcus turned back to where the dog had just attacked the figure only to see emptiness. How could that be?

Marcus walked the sixty or more feet to the doorway, machete still in hand. As he neared Cassie, with her left hand on the head of the dog, he said to Cassie, "Are you alright?"

"Marcus, you saved me. Thank you," and threw her arms around him as he dropped the machete. Marcus took her by the shoulders, held her at arm's length and said, "No, he saved us," and nodded toward the dog - which was no longer there.

"I don't understand," exclaimed Marcus, "Where did he go? Cassie, where did he go?"

"I don't know," she replied, "I think maybe we're not supposed to know."

Marcus and Cassie began walking once again toward the main entrance. Marcus held the machete firmly in his right hand, and he and Cassie both kept a vigilant eye out for the camouflaged figure. Leaving the cemetery and walking down White Street toward the A&W, allowed them to relax their guard a bit. There was a fair amount of Saturday traffic on White Street. Small town that it was, Saturday was the day for most local families to do their weekly shopping at Dempsey's and visit other local shops on Main Street. It dawned on Marcus that he probably stood out like a sore thumb wandering down White Street with a machete in hand. As they approached Walt's Tire and Auto Repair, Marcus stashed the machete in a thick hedge next to a stack of used tires.

Fifteen minutes later, they were picking up their coney island dogs and root beers from the walk-up window and taking seats at a picnic table. Between bites, Cassie opened up to Marcus, "He spoke to me again. Did you hear him?"

"No, I didn't, Cassie. What did he say?"

"He said, 'Don't tell anybody about this. Trust Marcus, trust yourself.' I wonder what he meant?" Cassie was hoping Marcus might know.

"I don't have any idea. When did he say this?" he asked.

"As soon as I ran out of the door, I looked back and you were fighting off that, whatever it was, and the dog just appeared next to me and spoke."

"Wait, wait, wait, Cassie. What are you talking about me fighting anybody? I didn't do anything. It was the dog. I told you to run, and the next thing I knew that dog came running and jumped up and bit the guy. And then the guy got away, he ran off into the forest. I didn't do anything." Marcus couldn't believe Cassie thought he had done anything. It was the dog that had saved them, again.

"No, Marcus," Cassie insisted, "Don't try to tell me what I saw. You tackled that guy like a football player, he dropped the machete and you picked it up while he ran out the other door. The dog was standing by me the whole time. He didn't do anything until you were walking toward me, and that's when he spoke to me."

"This is crazy. I did not touch that man. It was the dog. But when I turned to look at you, the dog was standing by you. Cassie, that is not possible. That dog could not be in two places at one time." Marcus was totally confused.

"Marcus, there is something mystical about that dog. We need to find it and figure out where it lives, what it does all the time. It stays gone for weeks, but always seems to show up when something bad is about to happen."

"You're right, Cassie. We have got to solve this mystery."

* * * *

Walking home, they stopped and retrieved the machete before making the decision to revisit the mausoleum. Neither had much to say as they made their way back to the scene. Both were consumed by fear and trepidation at re-entering the mausoleum. What if the mysterious man returned? Even though he now possessed the weapon, the machete, would Marcus be able to defend Cassie if it became necessary?

According to Marcus' wristwatch it was only approaching four-thirty in the afternoon, but with the increasing cloud cover and absence of artificial light in the mausoleum, visibility was waning rapidly. With machete at the ready, Marcus led the way back to the center of the mausoleum where the mysterious figure had appeared. They stood surveying the room. Cassie pointed to the alcove to the left and said, "Marcus, that must have been where he was waiting. He was probably watching us. If we hadn't turned when we did, there's no telling what might have happened to us."

"Cassie, do you know what I just remembered? He was wearing a red ski mask. Just like the one that the dog brought to us at the dam."

"Oh my God, Marcus, you're right," Cassie exclaimed. "And Marcus, I remember now. The nose and mouth were sewn shut, exactly like the other one."

Marcus thought for a minute and said, "Cassie, we need to go a pay phone and call the police right away. We have to tell them about what happened and give them this machete."
"We can't, Marcus," Cassie said solemnly, but firmly.

"Why not?" Marcus asked.

"Because the dog said so. He said, 'Don't tell anybody about this. Trust Marcus, trust yourself.' That's why not." Cassie was firm in her commitment to the dog.

117

"But Cassie, that guy could've killed us!" he exclaimed.

"I don't care, Marcus," Cassie was adamant. "How many more times does that dog have to save our lives before you will believe in him? I believe in him now! And I trust his advice. I say we find a safe place to store that machete and try to figure this out ourselves. We're smart kids Marcus, we can do it."

"I don't know Cassie. That thing probably has fingerprints on it and they…"

"Fingerprints?" Cassie practically shouted. "Are you serious Marcus? I don't remember, but the guy was probably wearing gloves. I bet the only fingerprints on it are yours. You've been carrying it around all afternoon!"

"You are right, Cassie. I'm not sure, but I think he might have been wearing gloves." Marcus couldn't say for sure if he wore gloves, but if it was the same person that killed the young girl at the river, and the red ski mask made that seem quite possible, then it was highly likely that he would not want to leave fingerprints.

"Marcus, what's that?" Cassie asked as she pointed to the pew in the alcove to the left.

Walking to the pew, Marcus spied a red cloth on the floor. Picking it up and unfolding it, his eyes grew wide. He turned toward Cassie and said, "I don't understand. I don't understand."

"What Marcus, what is it?"

"It's mine." He held up a red handkerchief with the embroidered initials E.C.

Revelation

It was the long way to get to Cassie's house, but it had to be done by way of a detour to Marcus' apartment. Margaret was working the dinner shift, so the apartment was empty when he and Cassie entered. Marcus checked his closet first but failed to see anywhere that he could sufficiently hide a weapon that was nearly two feet long. He thought about putting it beneath his mattress, but Cassie nixed that idea. "What if your stepmother changed your sheets or decided to flip your mattress?"

He settled upon his old toy box. It was about two and a half feet long and eighteen inches wide and deep. It was filled with old toys that he would probably never touch again but held onto because most of them had been given to him by his father. He cleared almost everything out, placed the machete at the bottom and Cassie helped him heap the toys back in on top of it.

Before leaving the apartment, Marcus had to know one thing. He had one handkerchief in his back pocket, one was in the laundry, the blood-stained one was still hidden safely in his closet. There should have

119

been three when he looked in his top dresser drawer. He checked, but there were only two. In his front pocket was the one they had recovered from the mausoleum. When had it gone missing, how could he have not noticed that one was missing, and how could it have ended up in the mausoleum?

They locked up the apartment and headed back to Cassie's house. On the way, Marcus said "How are we supposed to figure anything out? We're not the police. We don't know anything. All we know is we could have been killed today."

"I don't know, Marcus. But the dog said to trust ourselves. We'll figure something out, somehow." Cassie did her best to reassure Marcus.

They made it back to Cassie's house in plenty of time for her dinner. "So, we'll pick you up at the usual time for church tomorrow, Marcus?" Cassie asked.

"Yeah, that will be swell Cassie. I'll see you in the morning." Marcus turned to walk away, but Cassie stopped him when she said, "Maybe God will speak to us at church and give us direction."

"I hope so, Cassie." Marcus smiled as Cassie waved and went in the house.

Marcus began walking home with a thousand questions dancing through his head. He could not shake the image of the dog attacking the man in the ski mask and camouflage clothing. Nor could he forget looking back at Cassie and seeing the same dog at her side. Impossible. Cassie swore it was not the dog that attacked the man, but he that had done it. And Marcus knew for a fact he had not. Why would Cassie say that when it obviously was not true?

As Marcus neared his apartment, thoughts of the dog and the excitement of the day had taken a backseat to curiosity about what Margaret had left in the refrigerator for Marcus' dinner. He hoped she had prepared something that he could heat rather quickly in the oven. After the coney island dog earlier in the day, he really did not feel like a bologna sandwich and potato chips. Turning the last corner to approach

120

the apartment, Marcus was surprised to see a familiar vehicle parked at the sidewalk. Cousin Judy's powder blue El Camino. He had wondered if he would ever see Cousin Judy again with him living so far away. As he got closer, Marcus had to check. And he had been right, Georgia license plate number I-G-54713. He could also see smoke being blown out of the open driver side window.

Marcus walked up to the open passenger side window, peered in and said, "Hi, Cousin Judy!"

"Well, hello Marc. How have you been? Long time, no see. And it's Judy, remember?"

"Yes sir, Judy, I forgot again. You're back awful quick. I figured it would be a while until I saw you again."

"Yeah, me too Marc. Things come up, sometimes you gotta be ready at a moment's notice to get up and go. That's the business world, you know. They say jump, you say 'how high', the way of the world today."

"You on your way back to Chicago again, Judy?" Marcus asked.

"Nope, not this time son. Got to be in Des Moines, Iowa Monday morning. Got a meeting to discuss a late shipment they're trying blame on us." Judy explained.

"I thought you were the southeast sales manager, Judy? Is Iowa part of the southeast?" Marcus was curious.

"Well, not technically Marc. But in this case our Midwest Division plant couldn't handle the quantity that was ordered, so southeast had to step in and make up the shortfall. It's complicated how it all works and ties together."

"But, at any rate, I'm only about four hours from Des Moines and don't have to be there until Monday, so here I am again." Marcus was glad to see Judy. Maybe he could learn a little more family history from him.

"Oh, I'm sorry Judy. Mama is working at the diner right now," said Marcus.

"Yeah, I figured that Marc. I just got here about twenty minutes ago. I thought about driving over to the diner, but then I remembered you always make sure to get home before seven. I know you're probably careful not to incur the wrath of Mags!" Judy laughed heartily.

"Tell you what, Marc. Hop in, we'll ride over to the diner and I'll treat you to dinner. We'll sit around afterward, I'll have a couple of smokes, you have an ice cream sundae or two, we'll shoot the…. I mean we'll chew the fat, and then we'll give Mags a ride home. How's that sound?" Judy's offer did sound appealing. He hardly ever ate at the diner, but Buster, the dinner cook, could fry up a delicious hamburger.

"Gosh, I don't know Judy. I think Mama already cooked something for my dinner. All I have to do is warm it in the oven." Marcus didn't want to upset Margaret by wasting the food she had prepared.

"Okay, Marc. You check to see what she left for you while I run in and use the bathroom. If you're satisfied with what Mags made, I'll just go to the diner by myself," Judy suggested.

Marcus unlocked the front door and entered the apartment followed by Cousin Judy. Marcus headed toward the kitchen while Judy went to use the facilities. When he finished in the bathroom, Judy passed through the archway, took a seat at the kitchen table and began rolling a cigarette. "So, Marc, how was your day today? Spend it with that cute little redhead, did you?" Judy asked.

"Yeah, we spent the day at the park and had lunch at the A&W."

"That sounds like a fun day for a couple of - I forget Marc, how old are you and the redheaded girl anyway?" Judy asked.

"Twelve, we're both twelve now, Judy. Cassie just had a birthday a couple of weeks ago." Marcus told him.

"Is that right? Did you get her a nice birthday gift, Marc? What did you get her?" he asked.

"A subscription to 16 Magazine. She really likes all those girly teenage magazines. It took a couple of months allowance, but Cassie's worth it. She's pretty neat, you know, for being a girl." Marcus felt his face flushing.

"Well, that was really nice of you Marc. So, what are you thinking? Did you make a decision?" Judy asked, peering into Marcus' eyes like he was trying to read his mind.

"About what, Judy?" The intense stare made Marcus felt a wee bit uncomfortable.

"About dinner, Marc. Did Mags leave you anything or do you want to go with me to the diner?" Judy smiled as he asked.

"Oh, no she didn't. All I have is bologna and potato chips, so yeah, going to the diner would be super." Marcus replied.

On the drive to the diner, Marcus thought of some things that caused him a bit of consternation. It was rather strange that Cousin Judy, who he had only met once, and did not remember meeting, at his father's and Margaret's wedding had never been around during the last seven years. And although he lived nearly a thousand miles away, had suddenly come around twice on his way to business meetings within a matter of weeks. Secondly, Marcus had now seen Georgia license plates on Judy's El Camino during both of his visits. And yet, Cassie swore that she saw an Illinois plate on his car. She was so sure that she could even recite the tag number. The third thing that stuck in Marcus' mind were the questions Judy had asked at the kitchen table. His interest in Marcus' day and the questions about the redheaded girl. He did not remember telling Judy that Cassie had red hair and he knew that Judy had never seen her.

When they arrived at the River's Edge Diner there were several empty booths. It was almost seven o'clock and most of the dinner rush had already come and gone. When Judy made eye contact with Margaret, she waved and motioned to a booth near the window for Judy and Marcus to sit at. Marcus slid into the booth and looked up in time to see Judy removing the windbreaker he had been wearing. Marcus' eyes must have registered surprise when he saw the gauze and bandage on Judy's right forearm, because Judy immediately said, "Oh it's nothing Marc. Just a scratch. Craziest thing Marc, I was coming through southern Illinois this afternoon and had a flat tire. Jacked the car, went to take the skirt off to change it and scraped my arm on a jagged piece of metal. Bled like a stuck hog for a little bit, but it turned out it wasn't a big deal at all. Didn't even need stitches." Judy rubbed his nose nonchalantly and sat down.

Coincidences

Lying on the couch with sleep eluding him, Marcus continued pondering the myriad of unanswered questions that were beginning to tax his mind. There had to be solutions that he just was unable to see. How did his father's handkerchief end up where the harelipped dog could find it at the river? Was it connected to the red ski mask? They both apparently had splattered blood on them, although by not offering the handkerchief to the police, there was no way to be certain the blood on both items came from the same source. What on earth was the involvement of the dog? He continually kept appearing at the most opportune of times. He was either saving his life or Cassie's, or he was delivering and depositing evidence. And now, unanswered questions about his own family. Marcus, as much as he liked and looked up to Judy, just did not quite know what to make of his father's cousin. How did he appear to know so much about Cassie? Who or what was the camouflaged figure in the mausoleum? And what was his, or its, intentions? With the machete in hand, it certainly appeared nothing less than threatening for himself or Cassie, or more likely both of them. Despite Judy's nonchalant demeanor and casual explanation for his

125

injured arm, Marcus could not shake the memory of the dog and the damage he must have inflicted on the camouflaged figure's arm. He found it futile to deny a modicum of suspicion surrounding his Cousin Judy. Thoughts swirled in his head like tumbleweed caught up in a dust storm on the prairie. Mercifully, sometime after midnight, Marcus finally managed to drift off.

Marcus arose on Sunday morning, bathed and brushed his teeth and was preparing to go into his room to dress for church when he realized that Cousin Judy had not yet awoken. He walked into the kitchen, wrapped in a towel, and asked Margaret to please wake up Judy so that he might be able to dress. "Marcus, I'm busy preparing breakfast. Just go knock on the door and tell Judy you need to get in there to dress for church. And tell him breakfast will be ready in five minutes."

Marcus approached his bedroom, but before he could raise his hand to knock on the door, he realized he could hear Cousin Judy's voice. It sounded muffled and somewhat slurred and disjointed, and it dawned on Marcus that Judy was talking in his sleep. Whatever he was saying sounded like incoherent gibberish, but Marcus thought he could decipher some of it. He picked out some words and partial phrases such as "put an end to it", "stop it before it gets out of hand", "you know what you have to do" and "...... no evidence behind". Apparently, Judy was dreaming about his upcoming business meeting in Des Moines. Marcus knocked and trying be heard clearly, but without startling him said, "Sorry to bother you Cousin Judy, are you awake? Mama says breakfast is about ready, and I need to come in and get dressed for church, if it's okay."

After a few coughs and the clearing of his throat. Judy responded by saying, "Okay, Junior. I hear you. I'll be there in a minute."

* * * *

After finishing his oatmeal and English muffin breakfast, Marcus ducked into the bathroom to gargle with Listerine. He then collected his $1.75 from Margaret to pay for his family style lunch and asked Judy, "Will you still be here when I get back this afternoon?"

"No Marc, I'll probably head out before lunch today. I'm pretty sure this fine breakfast that Mags was kind enough to fix for us will last me for a few hours, and I kind of wanted to get to Des Moines a little early so I can prepare for that meeting tomorrow morning."

"Oh, okay Judy. Well, it was good to see you again. And thanks for dinner last night. That was a swell hamburger, and that was really good apple pie, too. I'm going out to the front porch to wait for Cassie and her family to pick me up. Bye Judy, bye Mama, I'll see you this afternoon."

"Wait up Marc. I'll go with you to the porch. I need a smoke anyway."

Marcus led the way to the front porch where they both settled into the Adirondack chairs. Marcus looked at Judy and couldn't stop himself from asking, "Judy, when I woke you up this morning, you must have still been dreaming because you called me Junior. Do you have a son named Junior?"

"I didn't call you Junior. I said Marc, like I always do."

"No, Judy. You called me Junior plain as day. But that's okay, I was just wondering. I thought maybe I had another relative besides you, after all."

"Afraid not Marc. I never married, never had any kids," Judy reported.

"That's too bad. I wish I had a cousin of my own." Marcus lamented.

A couple of silent moments passed before Marcus had another question, "Judy, remember yesterday when you asked me some questions about Cassie? You called her 'that red-headed girl'. How did you know she had red hair?"

Judy looked surprised by the question at first, before saying, "I don't know. Lucky guess? Maybe I'm psychic."

"Come on, Judy. I'm serious, how did you know? You had never seen her before, and I don't think I had mentioned it to you."

Judy looked Marcus in the eye and said, "Marc you're not a top-notch detective, are you? Remember the day I dropped you off at her house? She was standing outside her front door on the sidewalk. She had two pigtails in her shiny red hair. I don't miss a trick, Marc," and he winked.

Just then a horn honked, and Marcus turned to see the Worthington's Pontiac Jetfire double parked next to Judy's El Camino.

"Bye Judy. Have a good trip," Marcus said as he jumped from the chair and ran down to the street. As he stood to go back into the apartment, Judy waved to the young redheaded girl who was looking at him from the back seat.

* * * *

It was a good day at church. The sermon was inspiring, the Sunday School lesson was interesting, and Marcus thought Cassie was especially glowingly pretty. Afterward they stood on the sidewalk waiting for her parents to return from collecting Charlie from the preschool nursery. Cassie said to Marcus, "It had a Georgia license plate today."

"I know," Marcus acknowledged. "I looked at it last night when we left the diner after dinner."

"Something else, Marcus," Cassie said, lowering her voice. "Your Cousin Judy's arm was bandaged just where the dog bit that camouflage man yesterday."

"Okay, Cassie, so you think Judy was the one who wanted to kill us at the cemetery?" Marcus was a little perturbed at the insinuation, although he had had the same initial reaction upon seeing Judy's bandaged arm. "And besides that, you swore that I fought off that guy. You said the dog was next to you."

"I'm really getting confused, Marcus. I'm not sure what I saw or didn't see. I know I saw you knocking him down, but then you told me that the dog jumped up and bit him and I drew a mental picture of that happening. And then I dreamt about it all night. I'm just not sure anymore."

"We'll figure it out, Cassie, I'm sure we will...."

"Shhh.... shhhh, here come my parents."

As Jack approached them carrying Charlie, and with Debbie but a step behind, he said, "Let's go kids, we need to beat the rush to the restaurant."

The car was uncharacteristically quiet on the drive to La Grange. Marcus and Cassie both were lost in their thoughts, Cassie's parents were not partaking in their normal analysis of Reverend Drummond's sermon, and even Charlie sat silently holding his teddy bear.

Arriving at the Red Roof Lodge, with tantalizing aromas wafting from the kitchen and rolling like a fog over the parking lot, everyone's mood immediately improved with the expectation of culinary delight they were about to experience. The Red Roof Lodge was just a small-town dining establishment, but the folks who prepared the food were extremely competent. No one ever stepped away from the Sunday family-style lunch feeling they had been shortchanged. Not only was the food four-star quality, but there had never been a complaint relating to the abundant quantity that was served.

There was less than a five-minute wait until 'Worthington, party of five' was called and they were escorted to a round table near the center of the dining room. Marcus and Cassie took their seats. Jack pulled out a chair for Cassie's mother and then positioned Charlie in a booster seat next to her. He then removed his suit jacket and placed it on the back of his chair before seating himself. They all scanned the menu, although everyone already knew they were ordering family-style fried chicken dinners. Cassie was sitting to the right of her father and she was the first to notice the red smudge on the right sleeve of his starched white shirt. "Daddy are you bleeding?" she asked as she pointed to his arm.

"What?" he asked as he rolled his arm to see the crimson seeping through the cloth at his forearm. "Oh, damn. I'll be right back," he said as he stood and hurried to the men's room.

Cassie looked at her mother with concern and asked, "What did Daddy do to his arm, mother? He is bleeding."

"He's alright, Cassie. He took some storage boxes filled with old musty clothes and a bunch of magazines and books to the county dump yesterday. He said he was tossing them into a pit when he tripped and fell on an old wire box spring and scraped his arm." Debbie related to her daughter. "He said it was just a scratch, I'm sure it's fine. But it does concern me a bit that it bled through the bandages like that. It's a good thing he took off his jacket before it got stained."

Marcus sat taking it all in. Of course, he could not ask now, but he wondered if Cassie realized that her father's arm was bandaged in the same place that Cousin Judy's was? Strange coincidence.

* * * *

"What time is it, Marcus?" Cassie asked.

"Almost two o'clock," Marcus responded. They sat on a wooden swing suspended from a dogwood tree by braided polyester rope in Cassie's front yard. The afternoon was cool, but the windbreaker worn by Marcus and Cassie's sweater made it comfortable. They quietly swayed to and fro on the swing.

Finally, Marcus brought up what had been on his mind. "Cassie, you acted surprised at your father's arm in the restaurant. Didn't you already know he had hurt himself yesterday?"

"No. I hadn't seen him since we left on Saturday morning until this morning. And he already had his shirt on at breakfast this morning.

He came in early, like six o'clock, and I guess he went right to the shower and got dressed. He never mentioned it."

"I don't understand. So, he went to the county dump yesterday and never came back until this morning?" Marcus thought that seemed suspicious.

"Yes, Marcus. Every third Saturday my dad has to pull security duty at his office, and he has to spend the night there. My mother hates it, she hates being left alone like that. Actually, and swear to me you'll never repeat this, sometimes I kind of think maybe she doesn't believe him." Cassie confessed.

"I swear I will never tell anyone, Cassie," Marcus took a minute to process what she had told him. "What makes you think she might not believe him?"

"Because I hear them argue sometimes. Especially early on the Sunday mornings after he's been gone. I told you, I'm pretty good at eavesdropping."

Since they had been sitting on the swing not a single car had passed by on Fernwood Drive. So, they were both mildly surprised when a dark sedan pulled up and parked in front of Cassie's house. Both front doors opened, and two men dressed in suits, one wearing a fedora, exited. They met in front of the car, where the one not wearing a hat pulled a small notebook from his jacket breast pocket, flipped it open and looked at it briefly before pointing at the house. They started up the sidewalk and noticed Cassie and Marcus on the swing. The one in the fedora turned to them and in a gentlemanly gesture removed his hat (revealing the reason for the fedora – not a single hair on top save for the sparse combover). "Do you kids live here?" he asked.
"I do," Cassie replied hesitantly.

"I'm Detective Bill Evans, I go by 'Skip'. And this is Detective Luther Marlowe. We just call him 'Sticks'. We were looking for a man by the name of Jack Worthington. Is he your dad by any chance?"

"Yes sir," Cassie said nervously, wondering for what reason two policemen would be looking for her father. "Do you want me to get him for you? He might be taking a nap."

"That would be nice of you, sweetheart. Would you mind?" asked 'Sticks' Marlowe.

"Sure, I'll just be a minute." Cassie ran to the front door.

Marcus studied the men as they spoke in hushed voices. 'Sticks' certainly had an appropriate nickname. He was probably at least six feet tall and couldn't have weighed more than 120 pounds soaking wet. He definitely didn't fill out his suit like Detective Evans, it more or less hung on him. He reminded Marcus of the scarecrow from The Wizard of Oz. Detective Evans put him in mind of Officer Gunther Toody from the television show Car 54 Where Are You?, short and stocky. If he lost his combover, he could be called 'Cueball' instead of 'Skip'. Marcus felt guilty for finding humor in these detectives. He had no idea why they were here to see Cassie's father and was hopeful that he wasn't in any kind of trouble.

Cassie's parents both came out the front door and greeted the detectives on the sidewalk. After speaking for a few minutes, Mrs. Worthington went back into the house, while Jack Worthington walked down to the sedan with the detectives. Jack leaned against the car while the two policemen stood at angles in front of him. It appeared to Marcus that 'Sticks' was asking the questions while 'Skip' was taking notes in his little notebook. He tried his best not to be obviously staring at them, but curiosity was killing him. According to Marcus' Timex wristwatch, the interview drug on for just over a half hour. At its conclusion, there was no handshaking or pleasant goodbyes. Jack walked silently back to the house, oblivious to Marcus on the swing.

Another fifteen minutes passed, and Marcus thought about going home. It had been almost an hour since Cassie had gone into the house. He wondered if she had forgotten he was there. He was close to giving up when the front door opened, and Cassie walked the fifty feet from door to swing and sat back down next to him. "Hey," said Marcus.

132

"Hey," Cassie said back. They sat in silence for a few moments before Marcus said, "I wonder what they were saying?"

"I know what they were saying, Marcus," Cassie paused and with tears beginning to well up in her eyes said, "And I'm scared."

"What? What is it, Cassie?"

"Marcus, remember the girl at the river?" She looked up into his eyes.

"Yes, of course, why?"

"Remember where the dance club met? At the Holiday Inn in Alexandria?"

"Yes, I remember," he said, "Why?"

"And do you remember that I told you my dad and I had eaten lunch there sometimes when I went to his work with him?"

"Yes, Cassie, I remember everything you tell me. What is going on?" Marcus was getting worried.

"Marcus, some people have said they saw my daddy drinking in the bar at that Holiday Inn. They claim they saw him there last night." Cassie began sobbing softly.

"Probably mistaken identity, Cassie. You said your dad was at his office last night, right?" Marcus asked.

"They say they wouldn't have been sure, but the man that was there that looked like my dad had his right arm bandaged. That's why those detectives came here. They came to ask questions, but they wanted to see if his arm was bandaged."

"Cassie, your parents told you all of this?" Marcus was incredulous.

"Of course not, Marcus. Would any sane parent tell their twelve-year-old daughter something like this?" she responded.

"I'm sorry, Cassie, of course they wouldn't have." Marcus apologized. "But how do you know all of this?"

"How else, I was eavesdropping," she admitted.

"That's not even the worst of it, Marcus," Cassie took a deep breath. "Do you remember why my dad wasn't home Wednesday night? He had to drive to Mt. Pleasant that day and stayed in a motel by Keokuk?"

Marcus nodded and looked into Cassie's demoralized face.

"Marcus, they found the body of a teenaged girl Thursday morning two miles from Keokuk. She was murdered Wednesday night." Cassie began to cry. Hard.

"Relax, Cassie. You can't let your parents see you acting like this in your front yard. You have to pull yourself together." Marcus tried to be an authoritative voice of reason as he drew her close.

"Everything will be alright. It's all just coincidence."

Research

When Marcus met Cassie at her bus on Monday morning, both wore somber expressions on their faces. Marcus had greeted Cassie with an uninspired "Hey," and she had responded in kind, "Hey, Marcus." They silently made their way into the building and down the corridor to room 14b. Once seated, the morning dragged along, seemingly forever. Every word spoken by Mrs. Wolfe seemed drawn out and the tone deep, much like a 45-rpm record played at a 33-1/3 rpm speed. Mercifully, lunch did finally arrive, and with it an opportunity for Marcus and Cassie to sit and discuss the matters they had both been contemplating all morning long.

Marcus felt obligated to initiate the conversation but was unsure where to begin. "Cassie, I have been thinking this all over and it just doesn't seem real. It's like a dream that I cannot wake up from."

"I know, Marcus," she said in a depressive tone. "I still can't believe those policemen came to the house yesterday. And I'm really upset that another girl has been killed. Marcus, you know my dad had nothing to do with it, right?"

135

"Of course not, Cassie. It's probably a case of mistaken identity. Your dad would never be involved in anything like that, I'm sure of it. I'd bet anything that he was not in that bar Saturday night, and he was nowhere near what happened to that girl on Wednesday." Marcus wanted to reassure Cassie, but in his heart, he was far from convinced that Jack Worthington was not somehow mixed up in everything. What really stumped Marcus was his bandaged arm. There is no way on earth that Jack Worthington was in that mausoleum on Saturday afternoon threatening him and Cassie, his very own daughter, with a machete.

"Marcus, after you left yesterday, I overheard my parents arguing again. My dad admitted that he does stop at that Holiday Inn occasionally for a drink but swore that he wasn't there on Saturday night. He told my mother that he was at the office on his security duty just like he always is when it's his turn. And he also swore to her that he was at the Motel 6 on the north side of Keokuk on Wednesday night," Cassie related.

"And what did your mother say?" he asked.

"She cursed him and called him a liar. She said if he would lie about going to that Holiday Inn, that she couldn't believe anything he said about anything else, and that for all she knew he was a murderer. That Holiday Inn is where that Wozniak girl met with her dance club. Marcus, my father might have seen her there, or maybe even have known her from that place. This is too much to have to think about," Cassie said, almost pleading for some type of solace.

"Your father didn't do anything, Cassie, I'm sure of it. Everything will be alright, you'll see."

Following the final bell of the day, Marcus saw Cassie to her bus and after promising to call her after dinner, watched her climb the stairs and take her seat in the second row. With his mind boggled by conflicting thoughts and a myriad of possibilities, Marcus began his walk home. There was no doubt in his mind that Cassie's father could not have been the man dressed in camouflage in the mausoleum. There was just absolutely no way that he could possibly have threatened his own daughter. And the more Marcus thought about it, he also felt quite certain

136

that the figure in the mausoleum was not as tall as Jack Worthington. Although it all happened so fast, could he be sure?

Marcus' thoughts were broken when he realized he was approaching the stretch of road where he had almost been killed by the logging truck. Prior to Saturday at the cemetery, that had been the last time he had seen the harelipped dog. The memory of the dog stopping him and preventing him from possibly being maimed or even worse, brought a whole new train of thought and mystery to mind. Where does the dog live, where does it stay when it is not performing miracles on behalf of Cassie and himself. It had become all too obvious that the dog possessed some type of unnatural power. Marcus had to find some answers and decided that on Tuesday he would visit the library and research telepathy and paranormal activity. In the meantime, Marcus felt the urgent need to bypass his apartment and continue to Cassie's house. He couldn't put his finger on a reason, but just had the uncontrollable urge to be in her presence. Something was pushing him in his mind and heart to go to her and be with her.

Cassie was surprised to see Marcus on the front porch when she answered the door. It was nearly four-thirty, and her father wouldn't be home for another hour and dinner wasn't until six o'clock. "Hi, Marcus, I thought you were going to call after dinner, I wasn't expecting to see you."

"Yeah, I don't know what it is, but something was telling me to come see you right now. Maybe it was a subconscious thing for me to check to see how long it will take us to walk here from school on Friday, after debate club." Marcus suggested.

"Well, I'm glad you're here, regardless of the reason." Cassie seemed in a much better mood than when he had last seen her boarding the bus. "I'll get us a couple of Coca Colas and meet you on the swing, okay? Be right back." Cassie headed off toward the kitchen and Marcus went to the wooden swing.

Within moments Cassie emerged from her house carrying two six-ounce Coca Colas and joined Marcus on the swing. "You seem in a better mood, Cassie," Marcus said, taking a sip.

137

"I feel a little better. I was talking to my mother. Of course, I couldn't admit I'd been eavesdropping, so she doesn't know that I know as much as I do. I just started out by asking her who those two men were that were talking to daddy yesterday. She really surprised me by telling as much as she did," Cassie reported.

"What did she tell you," Marcus couldn't wait to find out.

"Well, I was surprised that she told me they were policemen. She said there had been a crime in Keokuk and the police thought perhaps my dad might have been a witness to something critical to the case. She said there was nothing to worry about, it's not like he was a suspect or anything. She...." Cassie was suddenly interrupted.

"So, she didn't tell you anything you didn't already know?"

"No, Marcus, I guess she didn't," Cassie said with a little bit of dismay after being interrupted.

"Didn't what? What are you talking about, Cassie?" Marcus said after Cassie's curt statement.

"You asked if my mother told me anything I didn't already know, and I said I guess she didn't."

"No, I didn't," Marcus explained, "I didn't say anything."

"Yes, you did and..."

"Wait, it wasn't Marcus, it was me," Cassie realized Marcus had not spoken and looked to her left to see the harelipped dog.

"Oh, my God, Marcus, it's the dog." She began looking around frantically for any potential threats. As far as she knew, the dog only appeared when it was necessary to save them or if he had to bring their attention to something dire.

Marcus peered at what had drawn Cassie's attention and was somewhat alarmed to see the dog.

The harelipped dog moved from the side of the swing and sat facing Marcus and Cassie, about five feet in front of them. The dog had a peculiar voice that did not emanate from its mouth. It sounded to Cassie like a normally spoken voice, however it would not have registered on a decibel scale. Her brain could hear the voice, but her ears could not. Clearly, the dog was communicating with her telepathically. Marcus looked into the harelipped dog's mournful eyes, which were fixated on and whose stare seemed to penetrate Cassie's eyes, and noting the tilted position of its head, came to the conclusion that the dog was indeed talking to her in some mystical manner.

"I can only communicate through you, Cassie, so you will have to pass along anything I say to Marcus. It is important for him, or both of you, to go to the library and perform some extensive research. Study the Lewis County Journal. Research birth and death records for 1947 and 1948. Look especially hard for names you may recognize. Please be diligent. There is only so much I can do."

Before Cassie could muster a response to the request, or perhaps directive, the dog pivoted, walked to the sidewalk and sauntered down the street in the general direction of the cemetery. Cassie sat in a state of near disbelief, but there was absolutely no doubt in her mind that what she had heard the dog say had been very, very real. Marcus, sensing the tension that was so obviously thick in the air that it could have been cut with a knife, gave her a few moments to consolidate her thoughts and compose herself. He waited until her eyes met his and then asked, "He spoke to you, didn't he?"

"Yes, he did Marcus. He told me something that he said I needed to repeat to you."

"Why couldn't he just talk to me?"

"I don't know. He just said that he could only communicate with me and that I had to pass what he said on to you. You couldn't hear him, right?" Cassie asked.

"No, Cassie. But I could see that you and the dog were locked onto one another through your eyes. The stare that you both had toward each other was so intense I was expecting to see lightning bolts shooting back and forth. What did he tell you to tell me?" Marcus was preparing for the unexpected.

Cassie repeated word for word as best she could recall what the dog had said. And with her level of intelligence and amazing memory, her recitation was nearly verbatim. After absorbing the instructions Cassie had related, it took only seconds for Marcus to formulate a plan. "Cassie, I don't really want you to lie to your parents, but how about you tell them that you and I have to go to the library after school tomorrow to do research for a report that we are giving together. Tell them that I will walk you home afterward. We can make it a practice run for Fridays after debate club. We should be able to access old Lewis County Journals on microfiche, and if we are lucky, maybe we'll find what the dog was referring to."

"I hate to lie to them too, Marcus. But the dog made this sound super important. I'll ask after dinner tonight and let you know in the morning."

"Can you just call me tonight, Cassie? I need to let Mama know if I'm going to be late from school tomorrow afternoon. Tuesday is her day off and she'll be expecting me."

Cassie's call came just as Marcus was spooning in his first bite of mashed potatoes. He excused himself and jogged to the telephone. "Hello," he answered.

"Hi, Marcus, it's Cassie. They were a little nervous since that girl was killed up near Keokuk, but they decided that was a ways away, so they said okay. They were a little bit reluctant, but as long as I can get home before my dad at five-thirty we'll be okay. But we will have to hurry, that only gives us about an hour to check the microfiche."

"An hour should be good, Cassie. You take 1947 and I'll look at 1948. We'll figure out what it is we're looking for." Marcus wanted to sound confident, even though he knew they had no idea what it was that the dog was expecting them to find.

* * * *

Following the bell that announced the conclusion of Tuesday's classes, Marcus and Cassie risked the punishment of detention by running to the library. They immediately went to the microfiche cabinet under the heading of Lewis County Journal, Cassie grabbing all the rolls labeled 1947 and Marcus the ones in the file marked 1948. They went to the microfiche readers and began pouring over the pages of the Journal searching furiously for any names that might ring familiar. They were both searching feverishly and specifically for the names Worthington or Clemens. Cassie was fairly positive they would not locate the Worthington name, as her family had come mostly from central and eastern Illinois, and she and her family had moved to the Missouri side of the Mississippi River from Springfield, Illinois more than a decade after the late 1940's. Cassie ran across a few isolated stories containing the Clemens name, but almost all referred to people living well outside the Lewis County area. After twenty minutes or so, Cassie ran across something that garnered her interest. She read the beginning of the announcement and then asked, "Marcus, is your Cousin Judy's real name Jude by any chance? I just found that name and it is an unusual name, the first time I've seen it so far today."

"Yeah, Cassie, it is Jude. What is the last name in the story?" Marcus asked her.

"Allensworth. Jude Urban Allensworth." Cassie read.

"Are you kidding me?" Marcus was taken quite by surprise and almost shouted his response. "Yes, that is Cousin Judy's full name. What does it say about him?"

"Relax a little bit, cowboy. It can't be your Cousin Judy. It is a birth announcement. If it was your Cousin Judy, he would only be sixteen years old, and even though I haven't seen him up close, I'm quite sure he's older than that," Cassie said trying to calm Marcus.

"That's really strange, Cassie. I can't believe there could be another person in Lewis County with the exact same name."

"Wait a minute, Marcus," Cassie read more of the announcement and then exclaimed, "Marcus, the father's name is Jude Urban Allensworth, too. The baby is a junior!"

"What?" Marcus was beside himself. "I don't get it at all. Judy told me he never got married and never had any kids. But that story you're looking at says he was married and did have a son."

"Not exactly, Marcus. The mother of the baby doesn't look like she was married to him. Her name is Paula Sue Schaeffer, a 1946 graduate of Lamar High School in Quincy, Illinois," Cassie read from the microfiche reader. She went on to read to Marcus that "Mr. Allensworth is employed by the Montgomery Boat Works of Hannibal, Missouri, where he has been employed as a diesel mechanic since January of 1942."

"What date was the baby born, Cassie?" Marcus asked.

"The birth announcement says Tuesday, June 3, 1947. That would make the baby 16 years old right now," Cassie answered.

Marcus was at a loss. "Cassie, if that really is Cousin Judy's son, it means everything he told me was a lie. He said he went into the army in 1943 when he was eighteen, but that says he started working at the boat works in 1942. In January, right? In January of 1942, he wasn't even seventeen yet. He said he got back from the army in 1945 and moved to Georgia in 1946."

"And the baby was born in June of 1947. That's a year after he supposedly moved to Georgia. Plus, it says here that he is currently employed at the Hannibal Boat Works in Hannibal. Marcus, what he told you doesn't make sense." Cassie felt sorry for Marcus being broadsided with such devastating news.

"You are one hundred per cent right, Cassie. He flat out lied to me about all of it. I don't know whether to believe anything that he has told me about my dad or my family." Marcus was clearly desolate. "On

142

the bright side, Cassie, that means I have a cousin out there somewhere. Since you found that in 1947, I need to keep going through 1948. Maybe there is more to young Jude in 1948."

Cassie continued pouring over news stories from 1947 while Marcus even more diligently perused the pages from 1948, especially with a specific name to search for. Fifteen minutes into his quest, Marcus settled upon a story. "Cassie, what did you say the baby's mother's name was?" he asked, already certain that he clearly remembered her name.

Cassie checked the notes she had jotted down, to be sure her response was correct. "Paula Sue Schaeffer."

"Oh brother. Cassie, I don't like where this is going."

"What is it, Marcus? What did you find?" Cassie dreaded the answer Marcus would give.

Marcus read from the microfiche reader, "A positive identification of the decomposing female body found on the banks of the Mississippi River near La Grange on Sunday, May 23, has been made. The woman is identified as Paula Sue Schaeffer, aged twenty years, of the 3300 block of DeMarco Street in Quincy, Illinois. Cause of death, as previously reported, was blunt trauma to the head. Miss Schaeffer had been reported missing by her mother, Gladys Schaeffer, on Saturday, May 15. Miss Schaeffer is survived by her only offspring, Jude Allensworth, age one year. Young Allensworth has been under the care of the state since the disappearance of his mother. The elderly Mrs. Schaeffer is disabled and unable to care for the infant. As such, he will likely be placed in an orphanage until reaching the age of emancipation or perhaps adopted by a caring couple. Miss Schaeffer was a 1946 graduate of Lamar High School in Quincy and had been employed as a stenographer at the offices of Jefferson and Monroe Insurance Associates. Funeral arrangements are pending."

"Oh my God, Marcus. Why would someone kill Paula Schaeffer? Oh my God, that poor girl," Cassie blurted. "Marcus, I hate to say this, but do you think Cousin Judy could have done it?"

143

"No. At least I don't think so," Marcus was not thinking in those terms, but when Cassie asked him, he had to reconsider that possibility. "Cassie, we need to leave and get you home, but I'm coming back tomorrow afternoon to check out the rest of 1948 and maybe 1949 to see if there are news stories that describe the results of the investigation. I have to find out if Judy was involved or suspected in this."

New Information

After school on Wednesday, Marcus saw Cassie to her bus and then hightailed it back to the library for more research. He found it disheartening to accept that Judy had most likely lied to him about his past. And now, wondering if Judy could have been involved in the murder of Paula Schaeffer, Marcus was rapidly nearing the end of his proverbial rope. He immediately began scanning every news story the Journal had to offer, desperately searching for any information concerning the crime.

Marcus located a small news item in a September issue that reported on an unidentified Lewis County couple which had adopted an infant. The child had apparently been orphaned as a result of a heinous crime that had occurred earlier in the year. No names were mentioned, but Marcus drew a reasonable conclusion that the unidentified infant seemed to fit the profile of young Jude Urban Allensworth. He wished that more information was available on either the infant or the adopting couple, because it now seemed increasingly likely that he did indeed have a living relative. And even more enticing, that possible relative resided right here, somewhere in Lewis County.

After pausing to consider the likelihood that a new relative could exist and allowing himself the luxury of daydreaming about meeting the newfound cousin, Marcus brought himself back to earth. There was no conceivable way to know if the adopted infant could really be Cousin Judy's son, and if he were, it would be impossible to find out who he was or where he lived. No names were mentioned, no addresses given. There were no clues whatsoever for Marcus to pursue. It was obviously a road that would ultimately result in a dead end.

Refocusing his attention to the microfiche, Marcus continued through the end of 1948. Having no success finding other stories relating to Judy, Paula Schaeffer, or Jude Junior, Marcus commenced scouring the 1949 films.

It did not take long to find what he had been looking for. In March of 1949, a drifter by the name of Tobias Winslow had been arrested and charged with the murder of Paula Sue Schaeffer:

"Mr. Winslow had been reportedly seen in the vicinity of Lock and Dam No. 20 on numerous occasions leading up to and including the weekend of Miss Schaeffer's disappearance. Although Mr. Winslow and Miss Schaeffer could not be proven to have been in the company of one another, it became obvious through several items of evidence discovered by the Lewis County Sheriff's Department that they had crossed paths. Mr. Winslow is being held without bail pending commencement of trial, expected to be within ninety days."

Marcus immediately scrolled through the microfiche films, finally settling on an article dated July of 1949, describing the details of the trial. The article reported that the trial lasted a total of only two days. Although the evidence was basically all circumstantial, the jury of twelve men required only three hours of deliberation to return a verdict of guilty on the charge of murder in the first degree.

"Judge Leo Wilkins, following the recommendation of the jury, sentenced Winslow to the gas chamber at the Missouri State Penitentiary in Jefferson City. Sentence is scheduled to be carried out on Friday, November 18, 1949."

While the subject Marcus was researching was quite morbid and sad, he was certainly relieved to have not run across the name of Jude Allensworth in any of the stories he had studied. He was about to conclude his research when he stumbled across another report that described more intricate details of the trial. It was published just two weeks prior to the execution and included information that shook Marcus to the soul.

"While Mr. Winslow proclaimed his innocence steadfastly, and at times most belligerently, the facts of the case seemed to bear out his guilt. Although much of the evidence presented by the prosecution was admittedly circumstantial, there were still numerous facts that were undeniable. The investigation had revealed that a machete had been used to commit the crime, and Mr. Winslow had been previously observed using a machete on more than one occasion along the riverbank."

"A local witness, who had been fishing from the riverbank, observed the convicted man using a machete to clear an area adjacent to the river and testified that he assumed Mr. Winslow was clearing brush in preparation of a campsite for himself. Unfortunately, the machete in question has never been found and Mr. Winslow denied ever having been in possession of such a weapon. However, the good word of the local resident bore heavy credibility in the eyes of the jury."

"It is also interesting to note that when arrested, Mr. Winslow was in possession of two blue bandanas amongst his belongings. When the remains of Miss Schaeffer were discovered, there had been a blue bandana lying beneath her. The bandana was identical in size and color to the bandanas later discovered in the possession of Mr. Winslow, and in fact not just the size but also the material composition of the bandana matched those in the possession of Mr. Winslow at the time of his arrest. Although much of the evidence against him was circumstantial, Mr. Winslow's undoing most certainly was the ironclad and indisputable obvious match of all three bandanas."

Upon concluding the reading of this account, Marcus found himself physically shaking. Fifteen years had passed since this crime. The machete, according to this account, had never been found. He and Cassie had been threatened by someone holding a machete. A machete that now rested in the bottom of his old toy box in his very own bedroom. But even more chilling to Marcus was the discovery of the existence of the blue bandanas. Now, fifteen years later, it was his (technically his father's) red handkerchiefs that are popping up in questionable manner and very inopportune times. The harelipped dog putting one on his porch, bringing one to him and Cassie at the dam (along with the ski mask), and then the one left in the mausoleum, by whom Marcus had no idea.

Marcus replaced the microfiche in its proper cabinet and began the trek home. His mind was spinning like the tub on Mama's Maytag wringer washer. How he wished that Judy would stop by just one more time. Marcus had a million questions, but even if he could ask them, how could he know if he were getting truthful answers? All that Judy had told him apparently had been untrue. But why? Why would Judy make all of it up?

Marcus entered the apartment and headed directly to the kitchen. It was Wednesday and Margaret was working the dinner shift. She had left Marcus a peanut butter and jelly sandwich in the refrigerator for an afternoon snack. He checked a bowl covered in Saran Wrap to see what dinner Margaret had prepared for him. Marcus was pleased to discover two cheeseburgers. All he needed to do was warm them, place them on bread and add ketchup. Simple, yet delicious.

As he polished off the peanut butter and jelly sandwich and a half glass of milk, Marcus had an idea. He knew that in Margaret's bedroom closet there was a wooden World War II army footlocker that had belonged to his father. He had never had a reason to look inside it. Margaret had told him there were items in it that his father had planned to give Marcus when he was older, had become a man. Marcus had no idea what may have been in the footlocker, and until now, never was curious to find out. But, with everything that had been happening, with his world somewhat turned upside down, Marcus was now wondering. Maybe there were answers, perhaps there were clues, to the many mysteries that were piling up so fast it was difficult to keep everything straight in his mind.

With anticipation, Marcus opened the door to Margaret's closet. Squinting in the dark, he reached up for the drawstring and pulling it with a flick of the wrist turned on the dim forty-watt bulb. To the right, on the floor and buried beneath a comforter and several of Margaret's sweaters, lay the green painted footlocker. Marcus gingerly lifted the sweaters and comforter, carried them to the cedar chest at the foot of Margaret's bed, and deposited them carefully. He then returned to the closet and stood staring for a moment, wondering what kind of secrets could be hidden within the green box. He grabbed at the handle on the near side of the locker and pulled it out from the closet. Marcus drug it across the carpet and over near the cedar chest. It was not particularly heavy, and the footlocker probably far outweighed its contents. It was not until he had removed it from the closet that Marcus realized it was secured by a lock. Locating a key was not an issue, for it was secured by a combination lock. Dismayed, Marcus realized he would have to wait for Margaret to get home and ask her for the combination. The dilemma facing him was how to go about asking. He knew he was not supposed to see inside the locker for several more years. How could he possibly convince Margaret to let him open it now, at the age of twelve?

Marcus got up from the floor and returned to the kitchen where he poured himself a glass of orange Kool-Aid. He sat at the kitchen table, running through his mind any possible way that he could coax the combination out of Margaret without being forced to reveal any of the secrets he had stored away in his memory bank. He kept remembering that the harelipped dog had told Cassie not to tell anyone about anything and to trust themselves. If the dog was right (and why wouldn't he be after all that had happened?), then it was going to be up to Marcus and Cassie to solve the mysteries before them. Marcus concentrated and tried to convince himself he could somehow conjure up the combination. Numbers began coursing through his head, but nothing seemed to have any meaning. As he drained his glass of Kool-Aid and moved to set it back down upon the section of newspaper he had been using as a coaster to collect the condensation, Marcus noticed dark wet spots on the newspaper that had been left by the glass. A few of the spots were on the crossword puzzle that Margaret had been working to solve that morning. Three of the dark spots were on numbers on the crossword puzzle. Six, nineteen, and thirty-five were the numbers. "Impossible," Marcus muttered aloud. But nonetheless, he ran back into Margaret's bedroom and knelt before his father's footlocker. He briefly closed his eyes, took a deep breath and tried the combination 6-19-35. The lock opened easily.

James E. Anderson

Questions

Marcus removed the combination lock from the hasp and was about to raise the lid when he heard a knock on the door. He knew immediately it was not Denny's customary duh-duh-duh-duh-duh.... duh-duh knock. It was a firm, adult style knock. Not feminine, but masculine. A solid knock. Marcus stepped out of Margaret's bedroom, closing the door behind him, and walked the short distance to the front door. He unlocked and pulled open the door. Leaning against the door frame with a toothpick dangling from his smiling lips stood Cousin Judy.

"How you doing, Marc?" Cousin Judy asked, displaying a wide smile.

Marcus was taken back. The last person he expected to see at the front door on Wednesday afternoon was Judy. "I'm fine, Cousin Judy...I mean Judy." Marcus suddenly felt a bit uneasy. Considering everything he and Cassie had uncovered at the library, Marcus was not overly thrilled to be in the company of Judy, and especially alone with him. "Mama is at work at the diner."

"Figured as much, Marc. Do you want to go over there for dinner again?"

"No, Judy, I don't think so, not tonight. I've got a lot of homework to do and everything and...." Marcus was interrupted.

"Ah, come on, Marc. I saw the way you wolfed down that burger the other night. I do have to admit that guy Butch did make a good burger. Mine was a little overdone, but pretty darn good overall." Judy smiled his broadest, most charming smile.

"His name is Buster, the cook? His name is Buster, not Butch. And thanks for the offer, Judy, but Mama already made my dinner, and I can't let it go to waste," Marcus responded.

"Buster, right, right. So, what did Mags make for you, Marc?" Judy asked.

"Cheeseburgers," he answered, "Mama makes better cheeseburgers than Buster anyway."

"Well, tell you what Marc," Judy said. "When I leave tomorrow, I'll take those cheeseburgers with me for lunch on the road. I prefer a good, cold homemade cheeseburger over a drive-in burger any day. And besides, you can get another warm slice of pie with ice cream at the diner. You can't do that here, can you? You can bring your homework along with you, I'll help you with it if you'd like."

Marcus could tell that Judy was not going to take no for an answer. He had fibbed about having homework, he had finished it during the study time Mrs. Wolfe allotted the last thirty minutes of class each day. "Okay, Judy. I guess I can go with you. I just have reading to do, and I can do that at the diner if it's not too loud there."

The biggest concern was what to do about the footlocker he had pulled out of Margaret's closet. How was he going to explain it sitting on her bedroom floor, unlocked when they returned from the diner?

"Good choice, Marc. Let me just run to the facilities, it's been a long drive from Des Moines. I'll be right back," and Judy headed to the bathroom.

As soon as the door shut, Marcus ran into Margaret's bedroom, replaced the lock on the footlocker and slid it back into the closet. He hurriedly placed the comforter and sweaters back on the green locker and closed the door. He then ran to his bedroom, and as he was grabbing his social studies book and three-ring binder, could hear the toilet flush in the adjacent bathroom. As he quickly wrote 6-19-35 in his notebook, Marcus could hear water running in the sink. He was sitting on the couch when Judy emerged from the bathroom.

"Whew, long drive and too much coffee. You ready, Marc?" Judy asked as he strolled to the door.

Arriving at the diner, Marcus got out of the El Camino and walked around the back to meet Judy on the driver's side. As he circled the rear of the car, he made it a point to look down at the license plate. They entered the diner together and took up residence at the same booth they had used on Saturday evening. Margaret hadn't seen them come in and was mildly surprised when she approached their table. Pen and order book in hand she said, "Marcus, Judy, I wasn't expecting to see you two in here."

"Hi Mags, we thought we'd surprise you. And don't worry, Marcus told me you had made him cheeseburgers. I'll buy them from you, market price of course, and have them for lunch tomorrow," Judy explained.

"Don't be silly, Judy. You don't ever charge family for food. Help yourself to anything in our house," Margaret said.

"Why thank you, Mags, I'd be happy to."

"My only concern is your homework, Marcus. Did you finish it when you got home from school today?" she asked.

"Yes, Mama, I finished it at school," he replied, but then remembered what he had told Judy. "Except for a little bit of reading I need to do, but I brought it with me, see?" and he held up his social studies book as proof.

"You see what I was telling you, Judy? This boy is so responsible," Margaret bragged.

"Indeed, he is. I can certainly see it. I believe he has a lot of his father in him. I can tell he is also kind and generous, like you Mags. And gentle, wouldn't hurt a flea, I'm sure of it," Judy agreed and expounded to include kind words for Margaret.

Margaret took their orders and returned behind the counter to her duties.

Marcus was torn and troubled. The license plate on the El Camino was not from Georgia, but Illinois. JR9705, just as Cassie had told him. When he had last seen the license plate it had been a Georgia issue. Marcus still could remember it as if he had just now seen it. I-G-54713.

Marcus mustered his courage, looked across to Judy, who was in the process of licking the cigarette paper on a fresh smoke, and asked, "Judy, why does your car have an Illinois license plate if you live in Georgia?"

Judy stopped in mid-lick, stared at Marcus for a brief couple of seconds, then continued sealing the cigarette. Pulling his Zippo from the watch pocket of his jeans, and lighting the cigarette, Judy peered from behind a cloud of smoke, squinted and said, "Why do you ask, Marc?"

"I'm just kind of curious, Judy. Saturday, I noticed a Georgia license plate and today it is from Illinois. I was just kind of wondering, that's all."

"Well, if you really must know Sherlock Holmes, I found an Illinois plate at a rummage sale, and whenever I have to travel through Illinois, I put it on my car. The Illinois Highway Patrol are notorious all over the south for pulling cars over with southern license plates. You can be driving fifty miles per hour when the speed limit is seventy and they will pull you over and ticket you, saying you were doing eighty. I don't know why they do it, but they just do." Judy was obviously angered by the police behavior. "You can go to traffic court and try to fight the system, but it doesn't do any good. It's your word against a state trooper's word. Who do you think a judge is going to believe?"

"Wow, I didn't know that Judy," Marcus couldn't help but to sympathize.

"Putting on an Illinois plate and minding the traffic laws keeps me from having any run-ins with the cops, you understand what I'm saying, Marc? And besides, I had a couple of dustups with Illinois cops when I was young, and I don't need to wake up sleeping dogs." Judy snuffed out his cigarette, shook his head and said, "Where's the damn burgers?"

* * * *

It was almost nine-thirty when the doorbell rang at the Worthington residence on Fernwood Drive. Jack Worthington turned off the television and Debbie put down her needlepoint as he went to the front door. Looking through the peephole, Jack dropped his head and shook it disgustingly. Seeing his reaction, Debbie stood and with a concerned voice said, "Jack, who is it?"

"Marlowe and Evans," he replied as he opened the door.

They spoke for no more than three minutes, before Jack escorted them into the kitchen. Debbie followed them and asked the detectives if they'd care for a cup of coffee. When they accepted, she put on a fresh pot and was about to sit down while it brewed when 'Sticks' Marlowe raised his hand to stop her. "Ma'am, we've got it from here. We need to talk to your husband alone. This ain't nothing a lady should concern herself with."

Debbie Worthington returned to the living room, switched on the television and tried to immerse herself in The Danny Kaye Show, but was in no mood for comedy and flipped to the NBC affiliate and The Eleventh Hour.

155

Cassie had gone to bed at nine o'clock but had been lying awake wondering if Marcus had uncovered any more information at the library, when she heard the doorbell ring. No one ever visited this late, especially on a weeknight, so she went to her bedroom door, cracked it open and listened. As everyone entered the kitchen, the voices were somewhat muffled, but she could still understand some of what was being said. Somewhat, until her mother turned on the television. Cassie stole silently from her bedroom and down the hall, slipping unnoticed into the laundry room, located just off the kitchen and leading to the garage. From this location, she could hear just about word for word what was being discussed at the kitchen table.

Cassie was almost certain it was 'Sticks', the skinny one, whose voice she first heard. "So, Miss Carlson obviously was acquainted with you Jack, you don't mind I call you Jack, right Jack? Or she wouldn't of been with you at the Horseshoe, right?"

"Yes, detective, I suppose you're right. But we were just having an innocent drink. We weren't there, you know, together." Cassie could plainly hear her father's response. "I only knew her because she works at the store where we buy supplies for the office. So, when I saw her at the Horseshoe and recognized her from the store, I said hi. She was just an acquaintance. I was trying to be polite and bought her a cocktail."

"Fact remains, Jack. We got four witnesses that say they seen you there with the girl on Wednesday night and that you both left within five minutes of one another. That is a little suspicious. I mean, face it Jack, it looks like you two spaced your departures purposely so it wouldn't look like you left together," 'Sticks' was fairly adamant with his theory. "As far as we can tell Jack, you were the last person that saw Diane Carlson alive."

"I can assure you detectives, when that girl went out that door, I never saw her again. I had nothing to do with anything that happened to her." Jack Worthington was just as resolute. "And I haven't heard you say anything about fingerprints. When you came to my office Monday to obtain my fingerprints, and embarrass me in front of all my coworkers, I assumed you were going to try to match them. Well, did you have any luck?" This question was met by silence. "I didn't think so. I never touched the girl. There couldn't have been any matching fingerprints."

"You're right, Mr. Worthington, we weren't able to make a match in the Carlson case." 'Skip' Evans stopped taking notes and looked into Jack's eyes as he uttered the first words Cassie had heard him speak. "But your fingerprints do match in another investigation."

"What, what are you talking about?" Jack demanded to know.

"The polish girl, Wozniak, that was murdered over on the riverbank back around Memorial Day. Your fingerprints match prints in that case," 'Sticks' Marlowe chimed in. "That inquiry is not in our jurisdiction, but rest assured, you'll be hearing from somebody local on that."

Detective Marlowe stood and looked at his partner, "You got anything else?"

"Nah, I think we're done here.... for now," Detective Evans slipped his little notebook into his inside jacket pocket and put his fedora atop his head. "We'll be talking to you, Jack." He took two steps and turning back to Jack said, "Oh, thank the missus for the coffee. I like the way she makes coffee. You got a keeper there, Jack."

James E. Anderson

Thursday

When they returned from the diner, Marcus had made sure to do a bit of planning before going to sleep on the couch. With Cousin Judy once again spending the night in his bedroom, Marcus had gathered his next day's clothes, his schoolbooks and other small items from his room and brought them into the living room. Hopefully, he had remembered everything he would need on Thursday morning so as not to disturb Judy's sleep. While Marcus was rounding up his belongings, Margaret was in the kitchen putting on coffee and Judy lingered on the front porch having a couple of cigarettes. By the time he had entered the apartment, Marcus had already arranged his temporary bed and slipped beneath his blanket. Hearing the door opening, he had pretended to be asleep while Judy passed through the living room and archway into the kitchen.

Marcus would have liked to have stayed up with them. He had so many questions for Judy, and he honestly would like to have confronted him with at least some of what he now knew were contradictions to Judy's previous stories. But there were three main obstacles in his path. The first obstacle was Margaret. She would not have allowed Marcus to stay up late on a school night. School nights normally had a strict bedtime of nine o'clock. Occasionally, Margaret would allow Marcus the luxury of staying up until ten o'clock on Tuesday night to watch The Fugitive, but those exceptions were rare. The fact that Cousin Judy was there also presented an exception to her rule because he had brought Marcus to the diner and they didn't get back to the apartment until ten o'clock, so he was already forced into a later bedtime.

Obstacle number two was also Margaret. There was no way that Marcus could present any of his questions for Judy in the presence of Margaret. He was reasonably sure that Margaret knew none of Judy's history, at least as Marcus had discovered it. He was pretty sure that she had not met him prior to marrying Elijah, and with the uncertainties about him that Marcus was now aware of, he doubted that his father had told her much, if anything about him.

The third obstacle Marcus faced may have been the most daunting of them all. Fear. Marcus was quite certain that he could not muster the courage to ask Judy any of the questions that he wanted answered. It was easy for Marcus to envision grilling Judy with questions, presenting him with the evidence that he had a son, that his son had been adopted, his son's mother had been killed, and that he had not moved to Georgia after returning from the war. At least not for a couple of years. Yes, it seemed easy enough, but after tonight Marcus knew the truth about himself. He had asked Judy a simple question, thinking he had undoubtedly tripped him up and exposed the first lie of many. But he hadn't. Judy had deftly sidestepped the question, offered a reasonably simple and easy explanation, and had actually played on Marcus' sympathy by portraying himself as a victim. And the stare that Judy had exhibited through the haze of cigarette smoke had gone right through Marcus. If the intent behind the stare was to intimidate and instill fear in Marcus, it had succeeded. Marcus remembered too well all that he had read at the library, and he was not completely convinced that Judy was totally innocent in the death of Paula Sue Schaeffer. Yes, he had seen enough from Cousin Judy to have developed a healthy respect for the unknown side of the man. He could not deny that he was afraid to confront him.

Marcus awoke on Thursday morning anything but refreshed. It had been an uncomfortable night to say the least. Dreams were unkind and haunting. He even found himself dreaming of again finding the

160

young girl on the riverbank. They were the type of dreams he had not experienced since mid-summer. Marcus was brushing his teeth when he realized it was Thursday, and Margaret was working the breakfast/lunch shift at the diner. That meant she had already left for work. Leaving the bathroom and going toward the kitchen, Marcus also realized his bedroom door was open. Peeking inside, he saw that the bed was made, the room was totally in order as he had left it yesterday, and apparently Cousin Judy was gone.

As he reached to open the door to remove the milk from the Frigidaire, Marcus saw the note hanging. It was from Cousin Judy:

Hey Marc,

It was good to see you yesterday. Sorry to steal your bed from you again. I don't know when I'll get up this way on another business trip, but I'm sure we'll cross paths again one day. I feel like I've gotten to know you well. You're kind of like the son I never had. Tell your girl I said goodbye. Maybe one day I'll actually get to meet her face to face

Your pal,
Judy

Reading the note, Marcus wasn't sure what emotion he should be feeling. On the one hand, he was distrustful of Cousin Judy, but on the other, Judy was the only blood relative that he had. How could he not have some measure of love and compassion for him. He just wished he had more insight into Judy and could be more certain of what to believe.

* * * *

When Marcus saw Cassie stepping off the bus in front of Roosevelt Elementary, his heart lifted momentarily, but then seeing her eyes, it sank. He had been preparing to tell her about the evening with Cousin Judy, relate the revelation about the license plates. He had been rehearsing what to tell her during the entire walk to school. But one look at the puffy redness of her eyes told him that she was the one who needed the relief of talking to a willing listener.

"Cassie are you alright?" he asked sympathetically.

"I'm fine, Marcus, but I'm scared," she answered.

"What is it, what happened?"

"Marcus, remember those two detectives on Sunday? The skinny one and the short one? They came back last night, Marcus." Cassie looked as if she might start crying.

"For what?" Marcus asked.

"Marcus, I'm afraid they think my dad killed that girl up in Keokuk." She said softly, looking over her shoulder and hoping no one overhead her. "They came to our house last night; I was already in bed. They took my dad into the kitchen and started questioning him and accusing him of being with that girl the night she died."
Marcus pulled her even further from the sidewalk and into the grass, away from the other students. "But he wasn't Cassie, he didn't even know that girl."

"Yes, he did Marcus," Cassie shuddered, her arms were a cascade of goosebumps. "He admitted he knew her. And Marcus, he was with her that night in a bar called The Horseshoe."

Marcus was shocked. "How do you know this, Cassie? I don't believe it. It's just not true."

"It is true, Marcus. I was in the laundry room, next to the kitchen. I heard it all," now Cassie began sobbing. "Marcus, they said they have witnesses who saw them drinking together in the bar. And my dad admitted he was there with her."

"Cassie, we need to get to class or we're going to be late," Marcus said.

"I can't Marcus, I can't go to class like this," Cassie began crying in earnest.

"Come on Cassie, we're leaving. We'll walk back to my apartment; Mama is working until two o'clock. We'll leave before she gets home. We'll go by Randolph Park, kill some time and get you home about the time the bus would drop you off. If anyone asks any questions while we're walking, we'll just tell them you're sick and had to go home. Everything will be okay." Marcus had developed a sound plan and Cassie was grateful that he was there to help her.

As they walked, Cassie related more of what she had overhead, "Marcus, those detectives seemed convinced that my dad is involved with that girl's death. They even went to his office on Monday and got his fingerprints, right in front of the people he works with. My dad said it was embarrassing. Can you imagine how he felt?"

"No, Cassie, I cannot begin to imagine." Marcus was curious about the fingerprints. "So, Cassie, if they took his fingerprints on Monday and came to your house on Wednesday, they must have found fingerprints that matched your dad's. That's not good, is it?"

"No, Marcus, that's what is so stupid about everything. They want to accuse my dad because he was sitting with the girl, but his fingerprints don't match any that they found. He asked them last night if his fingerprints matched and they said no." Cassie's face suddenly froze. "Oh my gosh, I just remembered something. They said they didn't have a match for his prints, but his fingerprints were a match in another case. Oh my God."

"What, Cassie? What other case is there?" Marcus wanted to know what else was going on.

"The girl we found at the river. They said that his fingerprints matched in that case but that wasn't their case and someone else will be coming to see him about that." Cassie had blocked that part of last night's conversation out, or perhaps her mind had refused to accept it.

163

Marcus thought for a minute and said, "That's impossible, your dad has never even been to the river. He couldn't have been involved in that."

"That's true, Marcus," Cassie breathed a small sigh of relief. "I never told you, but my dad is afraid of the water. He can't even swim. He would never go anywhere near the river. I don't think he.....Marcus, look," Cassie pointed ahead.

Standing next to a tree stump thirty feet ahead was the harelipped dog. Marcus and Cassie continued walking and the dog fell in step. Ten minutes into the stroll, the dog opened up to Cassie. "Tell Marcus to check his room. Something strange has occurred there that he needs to correct. He also needs to open the locker. Answers lie within."

Cassie had stopped to listen to the dog, and Marcus realized the dog was in the midst of communicating with her again. "What is he saying Cassie?"

She held up one finger to Marcus to silence him while she listened. "He's going to ask again why I won't talk to him. Tell him to be patient. There are rules that must be followed. The truth will be revealed in due time."

"Cassie, this isn't fair," Marcus exclaimed, "He came to me first, why won't he talk to me, too?"

"He said you would ask, Marcus," Cassie was amazed that the dog knew he would ask. "He said be patient, there are rules. And you will know the truth soon."

The dog spoke once more, "Don't forget to tell him to check his room and open the locker. Elijah said to tell him he is old enough to know. Hurry, before Margaret gets home," the dog looked both ways, crossed the road and headed back in the opposite direction.

Discoveries

On the way to the apartment, Cassie told Marcus everything the dog had instructed her to pass along to him. Marcus was anxious to get home and examine his bedroom, and his thoughts were consumed by the mental inventory he was taking of its contents. But he was still disturbed, and perhaps jealous, that the dog would not communicate directly with him. "I just don't understand it, Cassie. That dog came to me long before you and I really even knew each another. He never even saw you until that day at the cemetery when he saved us from the snakes."

"I know, Marcus. I don't have an explanation for it. But you said he does say your name, right?" she asked.

"Yes, he says Marc. But that's all he says to me." Marcus thought back to the day with the snakes. "Except that one day at the cemetery with the copperheads, after he had killed them. I'm sure that I heard him say, 'it's okay, Marc' that day."

"He did say that. I heard him say it," Cassie remembered. "But does it really matter Marcus? He said there are rules that had to be followed. I certainly don't know what rules he is talking about, but obviously he does. And he said you would soon know the truth. You just have got to be patient and trust him, Marcus. I do. From what he has shown us so far, I think I would trust him with my life."

"You're right, Cassie. I do trust him. I sure wish I knew what this was all about though, and why he came into our lives. It's like something on the Twilight Zone, or that new show that just started a couple of weeks ago, The Outer Limits. Weird stories with people that are not normal or things happening that are not natural," Marcus considered the array of improbabilities portrayed on those supernatural fantasies.

Cassie saw the point Marcus was making, "Maybe you're right Marcus, maybe there are cameras hidden all around town and we are on an episode of The Twilight Zone. It's kind of like Candid Camera, except there isn't anything funny going on. Everything is dead serious and you and me are the patsies."

* * * *

With a degree of apprehension, Marcus unlocked the front door of the apartment and he and Cassie entered. Marcus had come through that front door literally hundreds of times after school, but for some reason it felt different today. He offered Cassie a glass of Kool-Aid, but she declined. She felt a bit uneasy this morning as well. Neither of them thought about it in these terms, but what they were doing was undoubtably dishonest and wrong. They had skipped out of school unbeknownst to their parents, they were alone together and unsupervised in Marcus' apartment and they were about to conduct a search of Marcus' bedroom based upon the advice of a mangy stray dog that any sane adult would conclude could not possibly have spoken to them. But, then again, there were no sane adults present when the dog spoke, were there?

They went into Marcus' bedroom. The bed was immaculately made, just as Cousin Judy had left it this morning. Everything certainly appeared to be in its proper place, knick-knacks on the small bookshelf apparently untouched, Marcus' baseball bat leaning against the corner wall, clothes still neatly hung in his closet, even the small Alfred E. Neuman bust on his dresser angled just perfectly so that Marcus would see his grinning face when the alarm clock next to it sounded in the mornings. Yes, everything seemed perfectly normal.

"Are you sure, Marcus? Are you positive nothing is out of place?" Cassie asked.

"Don't think so." Marcus replied. "Everything sure looks normal."

"I don't understand, Marcus. The dog said something had changed that you needed to correct," Cassie looked around the room, but having never been there, would not know if something had changed regardless of how obvious it may be.

"Check inside your dresser, Marcus. Do you keep anything in there besides clothes? Money, jewelry or anything else?"

Marcus was a little shy about opening the dresser drawers. His modesty was somewhat at stake. He was concerned about Cassie catching a glimpse of his tidy whiteys, so he quickly opened, looked inside, and closed the top drawer. He was more deliberate with the three other drawers and did look through them thoroughly for anything unusual. Concluding the search, he turned back to Cassie and said, "I don't know what he could have been talking about."

Cassie closed her eyes and concentrated, or at least tried to. She was interrupted by Marcus blowing his nose. She opened her eyes in time to see him fold the red handkerchief and slip it into his left back pocket. "Marcus, how many of those handkerchiefs do you have?"

"Six all together. Why?" he asked.

"Okay, one is in your pocket, where are the other five?" The tone of Cassie's question was quite serious.

"Two are in the laundry basket, the one that is from the river that was stained is hidden, and two are in my underwear drawer. Why?"

Cassie darted three steps to Marcus' dresser, pulled open the top drawer and peering inside said, "Where Marcus, where are those two?" she demanded.

"Cassie, that's my underwear drawer, do you mind?" Marcus couldn't believe she was looking at his skivvies.

"Where, Marcus? I don't see them."

"Next to my socks. Cassie…."

"Show me, Marcus, I don't see them. Everything in here is white, red handkerchiefs should be easy to see. I don't see them." Cassie had definitely taken charge.

"Let me see," Marcus gently edged Cassie to the side so he could check for himself. She was right. They were gone. "They're not here Cassie. They were here last night. When I got my clothes for school last night, I took a clean one out and put the old one in the laundry basket."
Cassie gave Marcus a sideways glance. "You take your clothes out the night before on school days? Why do you do that?"

"Cassie, I usually don't. But Cousin Judy was here again last night, so I slept in the living room, on the couch. I got my clothes out last night so I wouldn't disturb him this morning," Marcus explained.

"He was here again?" Cassie exclaimed. "What is going on Marcus? Why is he here all the time? You've never seen this Cousin Judy before and now, all of a sudden, he comes all the way from Georgia all the time!"

"That reminds me of something else I haven't had time to tell you, Cassie. We went to the diner last night and I looked at his license plate. Guess what? It was an Illinois license plate, like you said."

"I told you, Marcus. He doesn't live in Georgia. He lives in Illinois. I knew it," Cassie said gloatingly. She knew she had seen an Illinois plate.

"No, I don't think so, Cassie. I asked him about the plate, and he explained it all to me. He said the Illinois cops like to pull over people with southern license plates and give them tickets. He told me when he has to drive through Illinois, he puts on an Illinois license plate and follows the traffic laws carefully, so he doesn't get pulled over." Marcus tried to relate the conversation as he remembered it from last night. "Actually, I think he got angry that I asked him about it," Marcus had to stifle a giggle, "He even called me Sherlock Holmes," he said with a slight grin.

Cassie, however, did not see the humor. "And you believed him, Marcus? He was lying and you should have known it. How much trouble do you think he would be in if he did get stopped by the police or was involved in an accident and had a license plate that wasn't registered to his car? It's probably a stolen license plate, for God's sake." Cassie had become quite vocal in expressing her thoughts.

"I don't know, Cassie. His story was so convincing. I mean it makes sense, or at least it did last night. He even told me he didn't want problems with the police in Illinois because he had had what he called dustups with them before and wanted to let sleeping bears sleep, or something like that."
"Okay, Marcus, enough about Cousin Judy for now. What about the handkerchiefs in the laundry? Are they still there?" Cassie wanted to know.

Marcus checked the hamper in his closet. "Yes, they're here," he reported.

"What about the blood-stained one you have hidden?"

He knelt in front of his dresser and slid his hand underneath. It was still where he had relocated it from the closet, dead center and back near the wall.

"Okay, Marcus. I have one more question. Is the machete still in the toy box? You probably should check that, too," Cassie suggested.

169

Marcus opened the toy box lid and immediately knew the machete was probably gone. He distinctly remembered leaving the red teddy bear on top of the other toys. His father had won it at the county fair and given it to him when he was five years old. For that reason, it was his most prized possession, above all others. He used to keep it on his bed, but now it occupied a position of honor atop all the other toys his father, mother and Margaret had given him. Marcus could see it partially covered off to the left in the toy box.

Marcus removed toys until he could clearly see the bottom of the box and was certain that the machete was not there. He replaced all the toys, placing the teddy bear back in its customary position, and closed the lid. Marcus sat on the lid, leaning back against the drapes at the corner of the wall and windowsill just above his toy box.

Cassie sat on his bed facing him. They didn't speak for several moments, both deep in thought. They were both thinking the same thing, but Cassie was first to come right out and say that Cousin Judy had to have taken the machete and handkerchiefs. As they sat pondering how he could have removed the items from the apartment without being seen by neither Marcus nor his mother, Marcus was startled by the sound of bushes rattling outside the window he was leaned against. Turning swiftly to look out the window, Marcus banged his elbow sharply against the glass. The noise that Marcus created must have frightened whoever had been crawling through the hedge outside the window. All Marcus could see was the backside of a man with black hair, wearing a white tee shirt and blue jeans, running away. The stranger darted through the haphazardly spaced barbeque pits in the community picnic area and disappeared around the side of the building diagonally across from, and to the right of, the back of Marcus' building. As Marcus sat in a twisted position, straining to get a better look at the fleeing figure, he could see something red in the man's right hand. His immediate thought was of the missing two handkerchiefs. While sitting in that position, Marcus noticed the slight wisp of cool October air that was seeping through the slight opening below the window that was raised just ever so slightly. Looking up, he realized that the window lock that he religiously checked daily, had been moved to the unlocked position. Glancing back down, Marcus thought he saw a slight glint outside of the window, something reflecting the sunlight. He turned fully and opened the window. Lying on the ground was the machete. Two feet or less to the right of the machete, hanging from a tiny branch of the hedge, was one of Marcus' red handkerchiefs. The stranger had no doubt dropped it, or it had gotten snagged on the branch as he had squeezed through the hedge in making his escape. Marcus was fortunate that his elbow had banged the window, startling whomever had been crawling through the hedge, and forcing him to abort his thievery. It appeared that the intruder had initially managed to pick up both the handkerchiefs but panicked before he could grab the machete.

Marcus crawled through the open window, retrieved the handkerchief and picked up the machete. Cassie was watching intently as Marcus carefully laid the machete and handkerchief on the closed lid of the toy box. He then climbed back through the bedroom window, closed and securely locked it.

"Who was it, Marcus? Did you see who was running away? I could barely see from here. Was it your Cousin Judy? It was, wasn't it?" Cassie was certain that Cousin Judy had placed the items outside the window either during the night or early that morning and had returned for them just now. He would have been expecting no one to be home, certainly knowing that Margaret was at work and having no reason to believe that Marcus would not be at school.

"No, Cassie, it was not Cousin Judy," Marcus replied. "Not unless he grew his hair longer and dyed it black since I saw him last night."

"You didn't recognize him at all, Marcus?" Cassie asked.

"No, not at all." Marcus sighed in resignation.

* * * *

Marcus and Cassie entered Margaret's bedroom and as they approached the closet, Marcus prayed that Judy had not discovered and removed the footlocker. He opened the door, reached up and pulled the drawstring to turn on the light, and looked at the pile of sweaters and the comforter. They were just as he had left them yesterday – stacked atop the green footlocker. Marcus moved them to the cedar chest, and once again drug the footlocker out of the closet. He sat in front of it and Cassie sat cross-legged next to him. "I wonder what is in it?" she pondered aloud.

"I don't have any idea, Cassie," Marcus said.

"Marcus, if you remember, the dog said that answers lie within," Cassie reminded him.

"Let's hope so." Marcus dialed in the combination, 6-19-35. The lock did not open.

"Are you sure you got the combination right?" Cassie asked him.

"Of course I did, I'm positive. Numbers, remember? I don't forget numbers, Cassie. I probably slipped a little past one of the numbers or something, I'm a little bit nervous, here." Marcus' palms were damp. He was nervous. It had been an eventful day already and it wasn't even noon, yet. Marcus tried the combination again, and it still did not open. "I don't understand. It opened right up yesterday, on the first try."

"It's an old lock and it hasn't been opened in years until yesterday," Cassie said. She then suggested he try spinning the dial a few times before making another attempt.

Marcus spun the dial at least three full turns, and then dialed in 6-19-35. The lock opened smoothly. They smiled at each other and Cassie said, "See there, third time is a charm!" Without hesitation, but with a bit of anxiety, Marcus opened the lid. At the top of the contents was a sealed envelope with 'Marcus Twain Clemens' hand printed in blue ink. Below his name, Marcus read aloud the second line written in smaller print, "Welcome to adulthood, my fine son". Marcus picked up the envelope gently, and holding it in both hands, looked at Cassie and said, "The last time this envelope was touched by a person it was by the hands of my father."

"That's true, Marcus. From his hands to yours," Cassie was touched by the emotion of the moment. "You need to open it. Do you have a letter opener?"

"Yeah, we do," Marcus stood, and holding onto the envelope, ran into the kitchen and fetched the letter opener from a drawer. He returned, sat back down next to Cassie, and gently opened the envelope. He was extremely cautious to keep the envelope as intact as possible. Marcus nervously removed a single sheet of paper and read its hand printed contents aloud.

My dear son Marcus,

I suppose you are reading this on or near your eighteenth birthday. If I am there with you, you don't need to read on. I will be able to explain everything and answer any questions you may have, so you can disregard this letter. If I am there, destroy the letter now. If though, I somehow have not managed to survive to this day, you must read on and understand the information that is enclosed. It is all for your own good.

You will find newspaper clippings and handwritten notes that I have left for you. All should be self-explanatory. There is your mother's and my parent's obituaries, which may or may not have any bearing on your future. Only time will tell. There are a couple of documents that may prove to be of some value to you in the years to come. I'm sure you will wonder why you have had no relatives come to visit you, and the answer is quite simple. There are none. If I am gone, then you, Marcus, are the last surviving member of the Clemens family. Your mother's parents passed at a rather young age in a terrible tornado that occurred in Iowa even before I met your mother. My parents also died at young ages. To my knowledge, the only relative I had that may still possibly be alive is a cousin. I have not seen him in a few years, but knowing his lifestyle, I suspect that he too may no longer be alive. At any rate, he was a Clemens by blood, but not in name.

It will be your responsibility to carry on our proud name. I wish you nothing but the best in the coming years and hope the contents here are useful and fruitful.

Much love,

Your Dad

"Wow, Cassie. My father wrote this thinking I wouldn't be reading it until I was eighteen years old. I'm only twelve. Will I be able to comprehend whatever is in this footlocker?" He looked to Cassie for support and guidance.

"You'll be fine, Marcus. You're smart, I'm smart. Whatever is in there, we'll tackle it together and everything will be fine," she assured him. "As a matter of fact, let's get started. Let's see just what is in there."

Marcus gazed into the footlocker and, as his father had promised, there were envelopes containing the obituaries of his mother and his father's parents. He took the time to read them aloud to Cassie. His mother was only twenty-five when she succumbed to brain cancer. She had been an only child, and according to the obituary, survived only by her "loving husband Elijah and young son Marcus".

Evidently, Judy had told the truth about his grandfather, John Stuart Clemens, who "presumably drowned in the Mississippi River while working during the construction of the new dam". Just as Judy had told him, his grandfather was but thirty-one years old when he died in December of 1934. Quick math then revealed that his own father was only six years old at the time. His grandmother, Anna Claire Smith Clemens, had died of a massive and sudden heart attack just after Labor Day of 1947 at the young age of forty-one.

Marcus dug through more newspaper clippings, many of them relating to sports items that his father had no doubt planned to relive with Marcus when he had reached adulthood. He and Cassie were scanning and setting aside the clippings at a rapid rate, looking more intently for something that could relate more directly with the mysteries of today. There were several issues of The Quincy Herald-Whig and the Hannibal Courier-Post that attracted Marcus' attention. They had been bundled together with twine and had a small handwritten note wedged beneath the knot. Marcus loosened the knot, pulled out and unfolded the note.

In the event that I am not here with you, these newspapers contain accounts of the actions of my nefarious cousin. I learned long ago not to trust him. The last time I saw him was when he showed up at your stepmother's and my wedding, completely unannounced. I did not want to ruin the day for my lovely bride, so I treated Judy as my best friend in view of Mags and the guests. In private I asked him, in no uncertain terms, to kindly step out of our lives and to please never return. To this day, that request has been honored. If he is still alive and should ever attempt to involve himself in your life, be the man that I know you have become and keep him as far away from you and yours as possible.

Marcus began thumbing through the papers looking for items mentioning his father's cousin, Jude Allensworth. It did not take long. Both he and Cassie ran across stories detailing crimes committed by Jude Allensworth that seemed to begin as relatively petty but escalated through the years. The first accounts were a burglary in Hannibal, during which Judy was caught in the act, and a couple of minor offenses amounting to shoplifting. He then seemed to up the ante and changed the focus of his criminal intent to the state of Illinois, where he was arrested and accused, but not convicted, of committing an armed robbery of a liquor store in Quincy, and then another in Mount Sterling. In both cases, the robber had been wearing a thick ski mask and could not be positively identified. Judy had reportedly been seen in the vicinity of both crimes and witnesses described the robber's clothes as similar in color and style to that which he was wearing when arrested. However, without positive identification, police could not produce any evidence to warrant pressing charges against him. The next offense was the beating and robbery of an elderly man outside of a tavern in Camp Point in 1945. In this instance, witnesses were present and could have testified against him. However, Judy's sixth arrest between 1941 and 1945 did not get to trial as the proceedings were halted by his confession of guilt. His resulting punishment, however, was nothing more than a slap on the wrist as he was sentenced to just six months of unsupervised probation.

Through the bits of information preened from the articles, Judy was apparently still maintaining residence in Hannibal, Missouri. And despite his legal troubles, he continued to hold onto his job at the Hannibal Boat Works. Even though he remained a resident of Hannibal, Judy evidently spent a lot of time in the vicinity of Quincy, Illinois.

Quincy and the area to the east were the locations of three of his crimes spanning 1943 and 1945. The area must have held some attraction for Judy. Paula Sue Schaeffer graduated from a Quincy high school (Lamar, wasn't it?) and she appears to have drawn his attention at some point prior to or soon after her graduation in 1946. Enough attention, at the very least, to have brought about the birth of young Jude Allensworth in June of 1947.

Marcus continued perusing the contents of the footlocker. He found a few more notes that his father had apparently randomly written whenever the urge had developed. In the most interesting message, his father had scribbled a description of another cousin, a sister of Judy. In the note, Elijah had explained that he himself had just recently become aware of a cousin by the name of Elsie. He had not remembered ever seeing her or hearing her name mentioned. He had only found out about Elsie through a chance conversation during lunch with a coworker. As it turned out, the coworker – Arthur was his name - had casually mentioned that he had grown up in Monticello, Missouri. Elijah had told him he had relatives from Monticello. As fate so often does turn, when Arthur asked for names and Elijah told him Jude Allensworth, Arthur said he had grown up with Jude, known even then as Judy. Yes, he told Elijah, he went to school with Judy and his sister Elsie. He also was familiar with their father Jude, Senior.

Having not known anything about Elsie, Elijah had asked Arthur to elaborate. He learned that Elsie was a popular girl in school. She was a couple of years older than Judy, wore her red hair in pigtails and had cheeks splattered in freckles. She had quite obviously been the apple of her father's eye. Whenever her father had taken the carriage into town, usually to procure supplies from the general store, Elsie was always at his right elbow. Arthur even told Elijah he thought it odd that Jude did not bring Judy along to help with the heavier items. He had described Elsie as a real sweetheart who was so undeserving of the fate that befell her.

On a Sunday afternoon in the summer of 1933, she had taken six-year-old Judy to go swimming in Cutler's Creek, not a mile from their farm. Elsie loved swimming and fancied herself a modern Gertrude Ederle (the first woman to swim the English Channel, in 1926). Elsie had been practicing diving from a low hanging tree limb into a pooled area of the creek that was five or six feet deep. Judy claimed he was off investigating a turtle nest and did not immediately notice the stillness and quiet that had settled over the creek. He walked back to where Elsie had been diving to find her floating face down in the water. He had pulled her to the creek bank and seeing her bloodied face ran back to the house to alert his father.

No one could ever figure out exactly what had happened. The assumption was that Elsie had dived face first into a rock or tree limb and subsequently drowned. As the years went by and fellow students began to take note of Judy's strange and sometimes cruel behavior, rumors began to take foot that perhaps he had bashed his sister in the face with a rock or some other object and then left her to drown. The last sentence of Elijah's note expressed his feelings –

Having just learned these facts, and knowing what I do about my cousin, there is no doubt in my mind that Judy killed his very own sister in a fit of insane jealous rage.

Marcus and Cassie were in a state of near shock. Marcus, especially, was dumbfounded. It just did not seem possible that the Judy that he has just recently come to know could be such a Jekyll and Hyde personality. And yet the newspaper articles that he had read were indisputable and the note from his father, detailing the unbelievable story of his cousin Elsie, could not be discounted in the least.

"Marcus, that note is kind of freaky," Cassie nervously uttered.

"I know, Cassie." Marcus was thinking back to expressions on Judy's face, the look in his eyes as he peered at him through the haze of cigarette smoke. Then he thought about some of the references Judy had made about Cassie and her red hair.

"Did you notice how your father described his cousin Elsie's looks? Marcus, it sounded like he could have been describing me," Cassie said apprehensively, as if picking up on Marcus' thoughts.

"Oh, don't jump to conclusions, Cassie. He was only giving a secondhand description of her. He was just repeating how he

177

remembered his friend Arthur describing her. Keep in mind that my dad didn't even remember her at all. Heck, he didn't even know she existed until Arthur mentioned her name. She probably didn't even have red hair," Marcus said trying to calm Cassie's concern.

Marcus checked his watch. "Oh my gosh, Cassie, it's almost three-thirty already. We haven't even had lunch and we need to get to your house, pronto. Let's get this stuff back in the footlocker."

Marcus picked up a handful of newspapers and was about to deposit them back into the locker when he noticed the gun at the bottom. There was an ammo box sitting next to it. Setting the newspapers back down, he reached in the footlocker and carefully picked up the gun and ammo box. He examined the gun momentarily before placing it on the floor next to the footlocker. Peering once more into the footlocker he saw an old-fashioned, antique looking. brown leather document holder that had the name Clemens embossed on it. Marcus lifted it out and studied it carefully. It genuinely did appear old. It was sealed by a locking clasp that would require an extremely small key. Marcus looked again in the footlocker and saw a sealed letter sized envelope. Gently removing the envelope, Marcus noticed the faded old style cursive writing. Written were the words,

This envelope must be kept in tandem with the Clemens family document binder. This envelope and accompanying binder may only be legally opened by the last surviving or non-incarcerated member of the Clemens family and must be opened in the presence of a licensed and duly qualified attorney-at-law.

Signed and attested,

Malcolm J. Witherspoon, Esq.
December 14, 1909

"I wonder what that is," Cassie questioned.

"I don't have any idea," Marcus answered. "But I do know we have to get going really soon, or you will be late."

Marcus set the binder and envelope next to the gun and ammo. He ran into his bedroom, grabbed the machete and brought it back into Margaret's bedroom. He checked to see if it would fit in the footlocker and, when turned diagonally, it did. Marcus put the newspapers and all the other items (except for the gun, ammo, binder and envelope) carefully back into the footlocker. He closed it, replaced the combination lock, and hurriedly slid it back into his Mama's closet. Cassie helped him replace the sweaters and comforters. They returned to Marcus' room to hide the remaining items under his dresser next to the stained handkerchief. As he was placing the items under the dresser, Marcus noticed he had also grabbed a folded newspaper article, probably when he had removed the envelope containing Esquire Witherspoon's letter. Rather than putting it under the dresser, Marcus stuffed it into his back left pocket. Both he and Cassie knew they would have to figure out a more safe and secure hiding spot for these items, but they were in a hurry, and temporarily at least, the dresser would have to suffice.

Marcus locked the front door and sighed in relief. He looked at Cassie, who echoed his feelings. It had been an eventful day. Much had been discovered. Apparently, the dog had been right when he had promised that 'the truth would be known'. They began the walk toward Forest Park Estates, each lost in their own thoughts.

Cassie found herself wondering if she did resemble Cousin Judy's sister Elsie. The description Marcus' father had used could have just as certainly described her as well. She thought about the newspaper articles about Cousin Judy's arrests and wondered if there had been more in the years since Marcus' father had died. Apparently, from what Elijah had written, the trajectory of Judy's life had been spiraling drastically. He had expressed doubt that Judy would even have survived until Marcus had turned eighteen in 1969. Well, she knew positively that he was still alive here in 1963. Elijah's note had been written with the intention that Marcus would be reading it in his eighteenth year, so there were still six years remaining to learn if Marcus' father had made an accurate prophecy.

Marcus also thought about Cassie's apparent resemblance to his father's cousin Elsie. And he kept obsessing over Judy's comments about Cassie. He was sincerely worried that somehow Judy had been envisioning a projection of his sister when he saw or thought of Cassie.

179

He also remembered Arthur's comment that cited rumors amongst classmates suggesting that Judy could conceivably have killed his own sister. Surely no six-year-old child could be capable of committing such an indescribably brutal act. But Marcus' father's statement was even more severe, asserting beyond any doubt that he believed Judy, even at such a young age, was guilty. Marcus was also considering Judy's criminal history as an adult. It was obviously documented that he had been at least a suspect in all of the crimes reported in the newspaper articles.

They were just beyond Randolph Park when the harelipped dog appeared from nowhere, suddenly walking alongside Cassie's right leg. "You did well, you learned a lot," Cassie heard the voice before she noticed the dog walking next to her.

"Yes, we did," she responded. She turned to her left, "Marcus, your friend has returned."

Marcus looked down, saw the dog, and stepping in front of Cassie stopped, knelt and rubbed the dog's head. "You were right boy. Everything you told Cassie was right. We found the machete, the handkerchiefs – at least one of them – we read the newspaper articles in the footlocker, everything."

"Tell him, Cassie, not everything. There is still the article that was folded up under the envelope and that is now in Marcus' back pocket. Tell him to read it when he returns home," the dog instructed her. "It will offer clues that he should easily process."

"Marcus, did you put a newspaper article in your back pocket?" Cassie asked him.

"Yeah, I did, Cassie. I guess I missed it when I was putting everything away. Why do you ask?" Marcus replied.

"Because the dog says you should read it when you get home. It has more clues that he says you can figure out," she explained.

"Tell him to open the envelope. There is a key in it that will allow him to study the contents of the documents that are inside the binder. I do not believe he should unlock the binder at this time, but he should read the letter I placed in the envelope. Make certain to keep the key and binder in a safe hiding place," the dog began walking away, but stopped and waited while Cassie spoke.

"Marcus, he says to open the envelope and take out the key to the binder. Don't open it, just keep them both safely hidden. You are supposed to read the letter that is in the envelope."

The dog did not turn to face them, but Cassie could hear him clearly, "Cassie, keep an eye on your father. Right or wrong, he needs your support especially tonight." The dog began walking.

They continued the trek toward Cassie's house. As they strolled in silence, Marcus was considering something and decided to seek Cassie's opinion. "Cassie, do you think I should tell Mama about Cousin Judy? Maybe let her read some of the articles?"

"I wouldn't Marcus. At least not yet. Cousin Judy is supposed to be driving back to Georgia, as if he really is," she said sarcastically. "If he's going to continue with that stupid story, he shouldn't be coming back for a while."

"Yeah, you're probably right," Marcus answered.

Marcus checked his watch, it was 4:20 p.m. The school bus was just dropping students off at the corner of Driftwood and Fernwood as they were approaching the intersection. They were right on time. The students began scattering toward their homes, some running, some walking. Marcus was about to tell Cassie goodbye and let her walk the final half block alone so as not to chance being seen by her mother. At this stage of a long day, he did not want to arouse any unwanted suspicion. They took but a few steps past the corner street signs before Marcus stopped and pointed toward Cassie's house a half block ahead. There was a dark sedan parked on the wrong side of the street in front of Cassie's house. The license plate was visible, but unreadable from Marcus' vantage point. However, Marcus could clearly tell the design was not that of a Missouri plate, which would have been red with white numbers and lettering. The plate on the sedan was black with white lettering. "Cassie, that car, isn't that the car those detectives were driving?"

"I think so, Marcus."

The Plot Thickens

Marcus started back down the sidewalk, leaving Cassie to continue to her house alone. However, he only managed to return to the corner of Driftwood and Fernwood before he was overcome with curiosity. He stopped and looked back to see Cassie speaking through the open car window with one of the detectives. The conversation was brief, and as Cassie strolled through the expansive front yard, Marcus wondered what had been said. Just after Cassie had climbed the porch steps to enter the house, the dark sedan's engine started, and the car made an abrupt U-turn and came in Marcus' direction. For a brief instant, Marcus feared the detectives were coming to question him. Fortunately, the car rolled past him and neither of the occupants seemed to notice him at all.

Cassie had entered her house and gone immediately into the kitchen where her mother was no doubt in the early stages of dinner preparation. Just as she had expected, Debbie Worthington was busy slicing and dicing vegetables, preparing her delicious beef stew. Cuts of beef had been chopped and seared and were waiting in a skillet for the vegetables to be readied. The large stockpot was already on the burner in anticipation of the ingredients. Debbie was no stranger to the kitchen and impeccably timed her meal prep. Jack was due home at five-thirty, and a perfectly prepared stew would be served promptly at six o'clock.

However, Cassie was about to throw a wrench into Debbie's dinner plans. "Hi mother, I'm home," she said.

"Hello, sweetheart. I'm just about to put the stew on, would you like a carrot to snack on?" Debbie asked.

"No, mother, thank you. Mom, did you see the car that was parked outside a little bit ago?"

"No, I didn't. Is someone here, Cassie?" her mother started toward the front of the house to look out of the picture window.

"Not anymore, mom. They just left. It was those two detectives that were here over the weekend," Cassie paused and then continued, "They stopped me as I was coming up the sidewalk and asked what time daddy usually got home from work. I told them five-thirty. Is it alright that I told them that?"

"Why yes, that's fine dear. You should always be honest with a police officer. There is never a reason to not tell the truth to a policeman." Debbie thought long and hard about the detectives returning so soon, wondering what this visit could possibly be about. "Well, I suppose dinner will be kept on hold for a bit this evening. I wonder if I should prepare enough for two extra servings?" Debbie's nerves were beginning to frazzle. "I'm just not sure what Emily Post would suggest in such a situation." Debbie's mind was scrambling, 'do you offer dinner to two detectives who are here for the express purpose of harassing, or at least questioning your husband - or perhaps even to arrest him?' Debbie decided she would not offer, at least not until the purpose of the visit had been satisfactorily established.

* * * *

Marcus was nearing Randolph Park when a vehicle approached him from behind. The car slowed to a crawl and a voice from within called his name, "Marcus? Marcus Clemens, right?"

Marcus immediately realized the car, which had now come to a stop on the two-lane road, was a Lewis County Sheriff's cruiser. Adjusting his eyes while trying to look inside, he also quickly realized that the driver who had called his name was Deputy Daniels. Mitch Daniels.

"Yes sir, Deputy Daniels. It's Marcus Clemens, sir," Marcus responded. This was now the third time their paths had crossed.

"Where are you headed Marcus? I'd like to give you a ride, if it's alright with you," Deputy Daniels asked as he reached across and pushed open the passenger side door. Marcus felt a wee bit conflicted. While the ride was welcomed, he somehow had an inkling there was going to be more involved than a simple ride home. Deputy Daniels hadn't asked if Marcus would like a ride, he had said he'd like to give Marcus a ride. That choice of words seemed far more insistent than a simple request. And, he had pushed open the door before Marcus was even able to respond. Almost as if Marcus had no real choice in the matter. "Sure thing, Deputy Daniels," Marcus said as he climbed into the patrol car. "Thank you, sir."

Deputy Daniels checked his rear-view mirror and sped away. They did not travel far before the deputy engaged his left turn signal and turned into the playground parking lot of Randolph Park. He shut off the ignition, and raising his right arm to the seatback, faced Marcus and said, "You know, Marcus, I knew from the day I met you and your friend Cassandra that I liked the both of you. That was a very gruesome scene that you two had stumbled across at the riverbank. It was very responsible of you getting to a payphone and reporting what you had found. And your help in directing me to the scene was much appreciated. The statements that were recorded at the station were excellent, and very detailed. You both showed levels of responsibility that we frankly had not expected from kids your age."

"Thank you, Deputy Daniels," Marcus felt flattered by the deputy's words.

"With that being said, Marcus, now I have some questions I'd like to ask you. And let's keep this informal, shall we? Whenever it's just you and me, call me Mitch. I think it'll make you feel more comfortable, and you'll be able to relax and let the answers flow, okay?"

"Okay, Mitch," using the deputy's first name seemed to invite a little more intimacy, but Marcus was still apprehensive about the questions Mitch was planning to ask.

"Why don't we start with this one, Marcus? Why do you and Cassandra, and especially you alone, spend so much time at the Forest Park Cemetery? I've seen you entering the cemetery quite frequently." Marcus relaxed a little more, at least Mitch started with an easy one.

"Because my parents are buried there, Mitch. Cassie goes with me sometimes, but I go there a lot on my own to visit them," Marcus told him.

"Isn't that kind of scary for you, Marcus? That would be a hard thing for most kids your age to do."

"No. I've been going there a lot ever since my dad died in 1959. The only time I ever get nervous at all is after dark." Marcus gave a truthful response, but then had a question of his own, "Mitch, how did you know I go to the cemetery a lot?"

"Well, Marcus, we're still investigating that case, and since you and Cassandra are the closest thing we have to witnesses, we are sort of keeping loose tabs on you." Mitch seemed to be speaking honestly with Marcus. "Another question, Marcus. Jack Worthington, Cassandra's father, brought in a ski mask on the first of September. He said that you and Cassandra had found it over at the dam. Did you really find it there and where exactly was it when you found it?"

All of the tranquility that Deputy Daniels had instilled in Marcus suddenly flew out the window. Neither he nor Cassie had been asked where they had found the ski mask. They had merely told her father that they had found it. Whatever answer Marcus came up with, the odds against Cassie giving the exact same response were astronomical. But Marcus had to give an answer, and he certainly could not tell him that a talking, harelipped dog had brought it to them. "It was just beyond the

186

handrail, about halfway up the walkway leading to the guide wall, underneath some scrub brush."

"So, you found it walking up to the guide wall, when you first got there?" Deputy Daniels asked.

"No sir, Deputy...uh...Mitch," Marcus' palms were beginning to perspire. "It was on the way down the walkway, going to the parking lot, when we were getting ready to leave."

"That's pretty far from the scene of the crime, wouldn't you agree Marcus? How do you suppose it got there from where the girl's body was discovered?"

"I don't know, Mitch. Maybe a dog or squirrel or something picked it up and carried it there," at least Marcus felt he was telling some semblance of the truth.

"Seems unlikely to me, but it was three months later, a lot of time had passed, so I guess it could be possible," Deputy Daniels reasoned.

Deputy Daniels studied Marcus, attempting to determine his comfort level with the questions he was being asked, looking for signs of extreme stress or nervousness. He was also weighing how much information he should relate to him. Deputy Daniels had confidence in Marcus' maturity and ability to handle difficult situations and arrived at the conclusion that the young man should be able to cope with what he was about to be told.

"It was extremely difficult, Marcus, but the FBI lab was able to extract a set of fingerprints from the ski mask. The technology is brand new and probably won't even stand up in court, but we are hoping with the threat of that evidence, if we develop a suspect, that maybe that threat would convince him to confess to the crime." Marcus was surprised that Mitch was telling him so much information. "I may as well tell you too, because I guess there's a good chance that you will hear it from somewhere, but the prints found on the ski mask matched the fingerprint samples that were taken by Iowa authorities of your friend Cassandra's father."

"Oh no, that's impossible. Cassie's father couldn't have done that. There is no possible way. No, Mitch, I know he didn't do it," Marcus was incredulous. "The only way his fingerprints could be on the ski mask is because he was looking at it in the car after Cassie gave it to him. He was holding it up to the sunlight, I remember he turned it inside out, he was touching it all over. I touched it and Cassie touched it, too."

"Marcus, I understand what you're saying about the ski mask, and we've already considered that. We'll be talking to Mr. Worthington in the next day or so, possibly even this evening. Hopefully, he has an ironclad alibi," Deputy Daniels took a few moments before saying, "Marcus, I probably shouldn't have told you about Cassandra's father. You are quite mature for your age, so I'm trusting you to keep this between you and me. I'm counting on you not to tell Cassandra what I have told you."

"I won't, Mitch. I promise," Marcus gave his word.

"One more thing, Marcus. When you were here at Randolph Park, on Saturday, did you happen to see anyone dressed in camouflage clothing?" This question really shook Marcus. "We had several folks who told us they saw someone dressed in camouflage around the picnic table area of the playground, and also on the north side of the lake. There's no hunting allowed in the park, so it shouldn't have been a hunter. What makes it seem strange is that three witnesses claim this guy was less than six feet tall, mid-twenties with kind of long black hair. The two others saw him from a distance, near the lake and swear he was wearing a red ski mask. If they are right, it was awfully warm to be wearing a ski mask. And it's pretty coincidental that he was wearing a ski mask similar to the one you found."

Marcus fiercely wanted to tell Mitch about the camouflage wearing assailant in the mausoleum, but he was torn by his allegiance to the dog who had saved his life on at least two occasions. He wanted to keep his conscience clear and to do that, avoided a lie by saying, "No, Mitch. I didn't see anybody dressed in camouflage anywhere here in Randolph Park."

"Also, Marcus, did you happen to see anyone wearing camouflage that day in May at the riverbank?" Deputy Daniels asked Marcus. "We know now that the girl had died sometime the previous day. We have one person who has come forward and claimed to have seen someone dressed in a camouflage outfit on Saturday, the day before you found the girl's remains. I know it's unlikely, but did you see anyone like that on Sunday?"

"No, Mitch. There was no one at all on the riverbank where we were fishing. We didn't see anyone all day until you folks started arriving," Marcus responded with sincere honesty.

Deputy Daniels patted Marcus on the knee and said, "Okay, Marcus, let me get you home now. Thanks for talking with me."

Mitch fired up the cruiser and pulled out of the parking lot.

* * * *

Jack Worthington arrived home just after five-thirty and, as he pulled into his driveway, he spotted the dark sedan parked in front of his yard and was disappointed to realize that Marlowe and Evans had returned. Stepping out of his Jetfire, he saw that the detectives had already begun walking toward him.

'Skip' Evans spoke first, "Hello Jack. Good to see you again."

"Hello detectives. What disturbing news have you brought to ruin tonight's dinner?" Jack was obviously expecting the worse.

"Actually, we have good news Mr. Worthington," 'Sticks' Marlowe's statement brought a slight, if temporary, relief to the melancholy that had settled over Jack when he saw the two men approaching.

"Go on, I could certainly use something uplifting," Jack replied lacking conviction.

"No, he's not joshing you, Jack," said Detective Evans. "More witness canvassing has led us to the realization that, while you were seen sitting with the girl in the Horseshoe, she was spotted in the parking lot talking to some Elvis Presley looking guy in blue jeans and a motorcycle jacket. Witnesses stated they both got into her Chevy Corvair in the parking lot and left together. So, it looks like you're in the clear after all."

"Keep it in mind though, Mr. Worthington, that you still are going to have to explain your fingerprints in the Wozniak case eventually," 'Sticks' Marlowe reminded him.

"Yeah, good luck with that one, Jack. I just hope we don't have to drive down here to talk to you anymore. Good night, Jack," 'Skip' Evans said and headed toward the sedan.

'Sticks' hesitated a moment before leaving. "That's a nice little girl you got for a daughter, Mr. Worthington. I hope to hell for her sake you haven't done anything to tarnish her innocent life."

"Don't worry, detective. I wouldn't and I didn't," Jack answered solemnly.

* * * *

Marcus walked into his apartment to the glorious smell of frying chicken. He passed through the archway and sat at the kitchen table. "How was work today, Mama?" he asked, slightly surprising Margaret.

"Home so early, Marcus? I'm glad. Dinner will be a little early tonight. I wanted to go ahead and get these chicken breasts fried up before the fairy godmother showed up and took them back. Buster had them left over and wanted me to take them home before they went bad. He's a nice man, he'd rather give food to someone who will use it rather than throw it away. This would have cost 29 cents a pound at Dempsey's this week," Margaret was ecstatic to have gotten the chicken for free and saved herself nearly a dollar on the grocery bill this week.

"I can't wait, Mama. For some reason, I'm starving today," Marcus was getting hungrier by the moment, being tortured by the smell drifting from the scorching hot frying pan. It was no small wonder he was so hungry, as he hadn't eaten since breakfast this morning. "I'm going to go to my room and read my English assignment. What time will dinner be ready, Mama?"

"Plan on thirty minutes from now," Margaret told him.

"Okay, Mama, I'll be back at quarter after six." Marcus went to his room and immediately pulled the folded newspaper article from his back pocket. It was from the Quincy Herald-Whig and contained a synopsis of the Tobias Winslow murder trial. As he read on, Marcus uncovered information that the Lewis County Journal had not contained. The Journal account had mentioned a local witness to Tobias Winslow wielding a machete along the riverbank, but his name had not been revealed. However, the Herald-Whig did identify him as Oliver J. Compton of Monticello, Missouri. The name did not mean anything to Marcus, but he did sense suspicion in the fact that the witness was from the same small town as Cousin Judy. And there was an obvious connection between Cousin Judy and the victim, Paula Sue Schaeffer. Marcus lay back on his bed with one arm covering his eyes. He pondered a series of scenarios. Was it possible that Cousin Judy had killed Paula Sue Schaeffer and then had a friend from Monticello give false testimony in a courtroom? Could it be that they had collaborated to send an innocent man to his death? It was hard to fathom, but it was a very real possibility. If it were true, how could Cousin Judy sleep at night with the blood of two people on his hands?

Marcus was interrupted in his thoughts by Margaret calling him to dinner. He went to the bathroom, splashed water onto his face, washed his hands and took his seat at the kitchen table. Margaret's fried chicken was on a par with that of the Red Roof Lodge and, though her mashed potatoes were a tad on the lumpy side, Marcus preferred hers to the smooth creamy ones offered at the Red Roof. At the conclusion of the meal, when it became impossible for Marcus to even consider another bite, Marcus told Margaret, "Thank you, Mama. That meal was fit for a king. It would have passed brilliantly at any fine restaurant in the great cities of New York, Chicago or St. Louis." He stood, patting his stomach, which was stretched taut." Marcus excused himself and returned to his room, ostensibly for the purpose of completing his homework, but in fact to read the contents of the envelope left by Esquire Malcolm J. Witherspoon.

James E. Anderson

With much anticipation, Marcus extracted the envelope from beneath his dresser and retook his seat on his twin bed. Carefully, he opened the envelope and removed the folded handwritten letter. Turning the envelope over and shaking it gently over the center of his bed produced a small key which would serve to open the document binder in due time. But for now, Marcus was interested only in the letter.

My dear Marcus,

It will be very difficult for you to come to terms with the reality of the situation that you are about to encounter, but be brave in the face of any danger or hardship you may confront. Almost, and I must emphasize almost, everything is pre-ordained. But there are variables that can come into play and cause serious and irreparable harm.

The binder that you are now in possession of can only be opened with the key, which you also now have. There are documents inside the binder that are extremely valuable, but only if you have sole control of them on the eighteenth anniversary of your birth. Keep them safely, in a safe deposit box in a bank, perhaps. I cannot divulge the contents at this time, but you will be aware at the proper moment.

You no doubt noticed the date on the front of the envelope that contained the key and this letter. The envelope was sealed on that date by Esquire Witherspoon and at that time contained only the key to the document binder. This letter was added many years later. I cannot explain to you how it was inserted without breaking the seal, suffice it to say – and by now you and your friend also know - stranger things do occur. I volunteered, and was granted the power, to be your guardian angel. The rules of such arrangements are stringent, and I pray I have not broken them by revealing to you this letter. Guardian angels are not permitted to communicate with their subjects, however they are allowed communication with a surrogate, so to speak. To be considered an acceptable surrogate, both surrogate and subject are required to have demonstrated a life-lasting commitment to one another. After certification of this commitment, I was permitted to begin making small "involvements" in your life.

One last admonishment. There are some, perhaps only one, who will make any effort, any sacrifice, and would stop at absolutely nothing to obtain possession of the documents in the binder. Do not allow this to happen. I pledge all assistance I am capable of to provide safety and protection for you, my subject.

John Stuart Clemens

* * * *

Debbie watched the exchange in the driveway between her husband and the detectives. When Jack entered the front door, she was waiting with questions, demanding to know what they wanted, was he in further trouble, was there more on the investigation from the riverbank case? Jack told her all was fine and insisted they have dinner. He promised to talk more about it afterward, but for now, "I just want to relax and enjoy my family."

Despite Debbie's obvious tension, Jack was able to relax a bit knowing that he was no longer a suspect in the Diane Carlson investigation. He took the time to chop Charlie's vegetables into smaller bite-size morsels and even played a game with him from Charlie's toddler days, 'Airplane and Hanger'. Cassie felt a little more comfort by witnessing an improved mood in her father that had been missing as of late.

After dinner, Cassie took Charlie into the living room to play and left her parents the opportunity to talk. Still, Cassie made sure to keep herself as close to the kitchen as possible in order to hear every word she possibly could. She was able to make out most of what was said and was relieved to know that the girl had been seen leaving the bar with another man meaning that her father had apparently been exonerated.

Thirty minutes after Cassie and Charlie had gone into the living room to play, Jack and Debbie joined them. They had settled into the first twenty or so minutes of a one-hour episode of Rawhide when the doorbell rang. Jack went to the door, and after checking the peephole instructed Cassie to take Charlie to his room and play with him for a bit. He then opened the door and invited in his guests.

As the two deputies took seats on the sofa, Jack eased into his recliner and asked Debbie to please put on some fresh coffee.

Deputy Daniels broke the ice by reintroducing himself. "You'll remember me from the station when you picked the kids up that day.

And I'm sure you remember Helen Wilcox; she was the officer tending to your daughter that day."

Deputy Wilcox nodded and smiled.

"We don't want to make this difficult for you Mr. Worthington. We only have a few simple questions for you," Deputy Wilcox did her best to be pleasant.

"Mr. Worthington, had you known Miss Zofia Wozniak prior to her death? Had you ever met or seen her before?" Deputy Daniels started the questioning.

"No, I had no earthly idea who she was until you people informed us of her identity," Jack answered.

"Mr. Worthington, this may come as a shock to you, but the FBI lab was finally, here recently, able to lift some fingerprints from some of the materials found at or near the scene," Deputy Wilcox explained.

"Don't tell me, the ski mask, right?" Jack had already figured out how his fingerprints had been tied into the case. "I mean, that's the only place they could have been found. I never met the woman, never saw her, never touched her clothing or possessions, have never even been to the river other than to drop off and pick up Cassie and her friend Marcus at the dam on the day they found that ski mask."

"That is true, but your prints were found in abundance on the ski mask," Deputy Wilcox tried to explain.

"Because I handled it in my car, and in front of the kids. They could vouch for that. They both had handled it as well, I hope that doesn't make them suspects, too, does it? And besides that, they found it, what was it, two miles from the scene of the crime? How do you know it had anything to do with that poor girl's murder?" Jack was beginning to become annoyed that he was now being linked to this murder.

"We know it was connected because of the blood splatters on it," Deputy Daniels told him. "The blood type matched the girl's blood."

194

"Listen, I think we've asked enough questions for tonight, don't you Mitch?" said Deputy Wilcox as she started to stand.

"Yeah, I think so Helen. Listen, Mr. Worthington. Just because your fingerprints were on the ski mask, that does not make you a suspect. We understand how we think they got there, and believe it or not, our theory matches what you just said. So, relax, we mostly just wanted to confirm that you did not know the girl. Just because you frequented the bar at the Holiday Inn where she just so happened to have club meetings does not imply that your paths crossed. It could just be coincidence," Deputy Daniels stood as well.

"A lot of other people went to that bar," Jack said, a little more calmly.

"But yours are the only fingerprints we have," Helen Wilcox countered.

James E. Anderson

Flashback

Saturday, February 9, 1963, sometime after 9:00 p.m.

"I'm telling you, son, there is a fortune just waiting to be collected. My best friend's dad told me about it when I was helping them bale hay one day when I was about thirteen years old." The dark-haired man of nearly forty was sitting at his kitchen table, sipping a Schlitz beer and relating a tale from his youth, with his teenaged son devouring each delectable word. "He swore up and down that his wife's grandfather was Mark Twain's brother."

"Pop, that's an amazing story, but do you think it's really true?" the son asked, enraptured by the entire saga.

"Of course, I believe it. Look son, Mark Twain's real name was Samuel Langhorne Clemens, and his brother was Orion Clemens." The man went through the story again. "Samuel had a couple of daughters, but only one son and he died as a kid. Orion only had just the one daughter and she died before turning ten. The history books will tell you that with no male heirs, the Clemens family name stopped right there."

"So, all of Mark Twain's money and stuff should have gone to his daughters, right?" the boy asked.

"According to the man I was working for, that's where the story got interesting. You see, my buddy's dad swore that years after Orion's daughter died, Orion fathered a child with his wife's dressmaker, and his wife supposedly never found out. That child was born around 1872 and his name was David Clemens. And David grew up to be the father of this guy's wife and her brother." The boy's head was spinning, the Clemens family history seemed so complicated.

"Okay, let me get this straight," the boy said. "Your best friend's mother and her brother were the children of David Clemens. And David Clemens' father was Orion Clemens, right?"

"Right son. And Orion's brother was Samuel – Mark Twain. Even though Orion's wife never knew about David, Samuel did. And he knew that David was the last of the Clemens family line. Do you understand now?" he asked.

"Yes, I understand what you're saying dad. So that's why you think Samuel prepared the special will, for David right?" the boy was getting the picture.

"That would make perfect sense, except for one thing," the father looked his son steadily in the eye and continued, "he didn't want to leave his money to someone who would end up hiding from society. David was a recluse because he had been born with a harelip, couldn't talk very plain, and was ashamed of it. Samuel had love for David but hated seeing him afflicted like that. Anyway, he insisted that the inheritance go to the next surviving Clemens male that was born without a harelip."

"So, dad, did David have a son that was normal?"

"No. His only son John was also born with a harelip. At that point, right after the turn of the century, Samuel had the will rewritten and added the stipulation that it not be opened until the eighteenth birthday of the first grandson of John Clemens. I suppose he thought the malady would phase out of the family by then, I don't know. Some lawyer by the name of Witherspoon in Connecticut drew it all up. I don't know what was supposed to happen if John's son or grandson had been born with a harelip." The man lit a cigarette, inhaled a few drags, and told his son, "But, we now know that neither one was born that way, don't we?"

"That is some tale, dad. So, this kid Marcus Clemens who is John's grandson, he's going to inherit all this money when he turns eighteen, is that right?" the son asked.

"He's supposed to yes, but here's the rub – he's not going to inherit anything. I've been thinking this over for years, and I think I've come up with some scenarios that will prevent that boy from getting any of the inheritance. And to make matters even sweeter, I think I've come up with some ideas that will legally prove you are the rightful heir, son. But for all this to work according to plan, I'm going to need your help."

* * * *

The young man surveyed the situation and determined it could not have presented itself any more ideally. 'This is exactly what dad has been waiting for', he thought. It was the first Saturday in May and the teenager had been waiting months for the prime opportunity that now presented itself. The chubby young kid he had been stalking for these many weeks was at the magazine rack at Franklin's Five and Dime, sampling a MAD magazine along with his buddy. He had just been approached from behind by a cute little red-headed girl that the teen himself was starting to feel a strong attraction toward. While the three of them were distracted by conversation, he snatched the red handkerchief that had been carelessly left behind on the soda counter and stuffed it into the pocket of his jeans.

A few long and tormenting hours later the teen ran to his car. Barely old enough to drive, and bubbling with excitement, he was fortunate to not receive a ticket. He had violated just about every speed limit in his haste to propel the 1949 Ford back home to Monticello. After haphazardly parking in the gravel driveway, he ran to the front door, fumbling with his key ring. Upon entering the house, the young man didn't immediately see his father. The television had been left on and was set at a ridiculously high volume. He crossed the living room and shut it off. With the empty house suddenly a deathly quiet, the slight hum of a bench grinder permeated the walls from the garage workshop. He knew by that hum that his dad was busy cutting and cleaning someone's house or car keys.

Stepping into the informal office and workshop of Lewis County Locksmith Service, he waited quietly until his father flipped off the switch and the grinding wheel began to slow enough that he could be clearly heard. "Dad, look what I found today." He held up the red handkerchief, extremely pleased to see the smile on his father's face.

"Let me have a look, but be careful not to touch it too much," said his father. The boy held it up by the corners and then reversed it to display the other side.

"Oh, this is absolutely perfect. Fingerprints probably won't matter anyway. It will be easily identified, with his father's initials sewn onto it. There will be no doubt who the owner is. Indisputable evidence." The plan was unfolding.

The father had decided on a date that the victim would be abducted from the Alexandria Holiday Inn. He had picked out his mark back in April, making it a point to cross paths with her regularly. As expected, the familiarity had penetrated her defense and he had gained her confidence sufficiently that they were on a first name basis. He could confidently call her Zofia and know she would respond in kind, calling him "Jackie".

On the night of May 25, just as he had planned and rehearsed several times, "Jackie" encountered Zofia as she was crossing the Holiday Inn parking lot after the conclusion of her weekly polka dance club meeting. He called out her name as she approached her car. Seeing that it was "Jackie", she dropped her guard and turned to smile and wave to him. That was when the hand reached around from behind and pressed a rag soaked in a bleach and alcohol solution tightly over her mouth and nose. Less than an hour later, Zofia Wozniak's body was deposited next to a huge fallen oak tree on the banks of the mighty Mississippi River.

They were careful to leave no evidence behind. Gloves were worn to eliminate the possibility of fingerprints, and they made doubly sure there were no weapons, no personal effects, nothing incriminating left behind. Except for one damning piece of evidence which would be quite easy for the police to track and identify. One red handkerchief with the embroidered initials E.C.

* * * *

Many weeks – too many weeks - had passed and there had been no public announcement of the discovery of the red handkerchief at the scene. No suspects had been identified and no arrests had been made. The plan to eliminate Marcus Clemens from the equation by framing him had not come to fruition. To make matters worse, "Jackie's" son had taken his ski mask off when the body was staged on the riverbank, and apparently dropped it somewhere in the vicinity. Several clandestine trips had been made to search the area and its perimeter, but they had no luck locating it. If the police had found it, they were keeping mum about its existence.

"Jackie" needed an alternate plan, and quickly developed one. With minimal effort he discovered where Marcus and his stepmother lived. Choosing a day when Marcus was hanging out with his friends and his stepmother was at work, "Jackie" carried his locksmith tools to the Clemens' apartment and proceeded to pick the front door lock. He not only picked the lock, but was able to also produce a mold which, when he returned to his workshop, would allow him to create his own key to Marcus' apartment. After developing the mold, and before leaving, "Jackie" took a mental photograph of Marcus' bedroom. And after discovering where Marcus stored them, he took one of the handkerchiefs. It would be used in a second attempt to frame Marcus for murder.

* * * *

James E. Anderson

Saturday morning, September 28, 1963

They cautiously followed Marcus in their '49 Ford, intermittently passing him as he walked, sometimes laying back, sometimes parking the Ford sedan and just watching until he was practically out of sight, and then following again. Ultimately, he reached Cassie's front door, and in a short while they left the house and were walking again. Judging by the direction they were going, and with it being a Saturday, the two observers decided the youngsters were no doubt going to Randolph Park. They found a parking space about two hundred yards from the playground. One of them went to the picnic benches near the playground, while the other took up a position on the dock at the lake. From that vantage point, a pair of inexpensive binoculars would allow a complete and unobstructed view of the goings on.

In less than twenty minutes, Marcus and Cassie came strolling across the parking lot and entered the playground. It was not long until other, mostly smaller, children and their parents began arriving at the playground. After perhaps an hour, Marcus and Cassie left the playground and started toward the lake. Recognizing where they were headed, the observer with the binoculars left the dock and began circling the lake, ultimately taking up another position at the northeast end of the lake. He was joined moments later by the second onlooker. From the cover of thick marsh, they intently tracked every movement of their subjects.

Eventually, Marcus and Cassie were again up and on the move. This time, the two decided to leave the car in the parking lot and follow along on foot. Wisely, they had chosen to wear camouflage clothing which allowed them the ability to remain inconspicuous. They were able to tail Marcus and Cassie unnoticed all the way to the cemetery and right up to the moment that the youngsters decided to enter the mausoleum. The situation could not have been choreographed more ideally. The younger one donned a ski mask and gloves to ensure his identity was secured. He went around to the north entrance to the mausoleum, and after silently entering, quietly made his way to the west alcove at about the midway point of the building. The other one waited patiently at the edge of the forest, just northwest of the mausoleum.

202

The camouflaged figure in the alcove stepped further back into the shadows as Marcus and Cassie made their way along the east wall, playing some type of game as they went. As he waited, the predatory figure felt a fleeting moment of guilt and remorse over what he was about to do. The little girl in the red ponytails was at the cusp of blossoming into young womanhood, with so much life still ahead of her. It seemed such a pitiful shame to snuff out that burgeoning flame. He took two steps forward, slowly raising the machete with his right hand. However, he was startled by Marcus and Cassie suddenly turning to face him just as he was about to charge at them. In a split second, Cassie ran toward the south entry, and before he could refocus his attack on Marcus, a savage dog leapt, seemingly from nowhere, viciously latching onto his right forearm. He dropped the machete as he was knocked to the floor. The dog continued fiercely applying pressure, twisting its head from side to side. It seemed to relax its bite for an instant, probably in anticipation of readjusting the grasp on his arm, but that was all the intruder needed to desperately shake his arm enough to escape the death grip. He jumped up and ran frightfully for the north entry, continuing to run with extreme urgency toward the forest.

Meeting up with his partner, they made their way back to the Ford and then raced home. Even though the dog's victim was in obvious pain, his counterpart was angry with him. "You failed again. Do you still have the handkerchief?"

"No, I dropped it."

James E. Anderson

Sharing the News

Marcus was waiting for her when Cassie descended from her school bus. They hurried to a bench located several feet away from the steps leading into the school. They both had news to convey, and Cassie was bursting to tell Marcus the good news concerning her father. Sensing her anxiety and before she could even spill a word, Marcus asked her, "What did the detectives want yesterday?"

"It was good news, Marcus. They told him he was no longer being considered a suspect in the case of the girl in Iowa. They said they have witnesses that saw her leaving that place with some other guy in a motorcycle jacket." Cassie excitedly gushed her response.

"That sure is good to hear, Cassie," Marcus replied.

"I'll say. Marcus, I have got to admit, I was a little bit worried. I know my dad couldn't have done anything so hideous, but I was scared. You know, you see those television shows where people get accused of things they didn't do, and then can't prove that they are innocent. I was really worried. Thank God those people saw her with that guy in the parking lot." Cassie's relief was not feigned. The news obviously reassured her faith in her father and justified her belief in his innocence.

Cassie continued, "And then, later last night, Deputy Daniels and Deputy Wilcox came to see my dad. You remember them from the river, back in May, don't you? He was the officer that responded, and she was the one that took us to the station."

"Yes, I remember them. What did they want?" Marcus was sure he knew the answer but wanted to hear it from Cassie.

"They said they found his fingerprints on that ski mask that we found. Well, the one that dog brought to us, really." Before Cassie could say more, the first bell sounded, indicating they had five minutes until classes officially started.

"Did you get a note, Cassie, for your absence?" Marcus asked her as they climbed the steps.

"Yeah, I wrote one," she laughed, "I have my mother's signature down pat. Her trick is instead of dotting the i in Worthington, she puts a small circle to make it unique. What about you, Marcus, did you forge one, too?"

"No, I couldn't possibly copy Mama's signature. I'll just tell Mrs. Wolfe that I forgot it on the kitchen table. I'll figure something out over the weekend and bring it Monday." They had just gotten through the classroom door and were approaching their seats when the final bell rang.

When lunch break arrived, Cassie finished explaining to Marcus that it sounded like Deputies Daniels and Wilcox believed her father's explanation for his fingerprints being on the ski mask. After all, he had his hands all over it in the car before turning it in at the police station. "They told him they had thought the same thing," she said. "But they did remind him that they had not found anyone else's fingerprints, that his were the only ones they had."

"Yeah, that's kind of what I thought they would say." Marcus agreed.

"What do you mean, that's what you thought they would say?" Cassie asked. "You said that like you knew they were there. Marcus, did you know they were at my house? How did you know that?" Marcus was amazed by Cassie's perceptiveness. He did not realize he had given anything away, but she had picked up on his choice of words like a hawk on a field mouse. She had zeroed right in.

"Okay, Cassie. It's not a big deal, but on the way home from your house yesterday, Deputy Daniels stopped and gave me a ride home. He parked at Randolph Park, by the playground and asked me some questions about that case." Marcus had a lot to tell Cassie, now that she had revealed her news.

"What kind of questions, Marcus? He told you about my dad's fingerprints? Why didn't you call and tell me?" Cassie was hurt that Marcus had not given her a heads up that the deputies were coming to her house.

"First of all, Cassie, I didn't know they were coming last night. Deputy Daniels said they were going to talk to your dad in the next couple of days, and maybe last night. He didn't say anything definite. And secondly, he specifically told me not to tell you." Marcus tried to emphasize that he was following the orders of Deputy Daniels. "He asked me a bunch of questions. Cassie, did you have any idea that they have been keeping an eye on us?"

"No Marcus, why would they be watching us? Do you think that they believe we could have done that?" Cassie could not comprehend how they could be suspects, they were just kids.

"Deputy Daniels said they were keeping up with us because we were the only witnesses they had. He wanted to know why you and I go to the cemetery so often." Marcus suddenly remembered the most important part, "Oh, and remember when we were at Randolph Park, before the craziness at the mausoleum? He asked me if we saw anyone dressed in camouflage at the park."

"What did you tell him, Marcus? You didn't tell him about what happened at the mausoleum did you? The dog said not to tell, remember?" Cassie reminded him.

"No, I didn't tell him, Cassie. I didn't lie to him, though. I told him I did not see anyone dressed in camouflage at the park. He also asked me exactly where we found the ski mask."

"But we didn't find it, Marcus. The dog brought it to us. What did you tell him? I know you didn't tell him about the dog, did you?" She was sure he had not mentioned the dog.

"No, I told him it was halfway up the walkway and underneath some scrub brush. He asked how I thought it ended up so far from the crime scene, and I told him I had no idea. I suggested maybe a dog had picked it up and brought it there," Marcus smiled with the realization that he had unintentionally, in a roundabout way, told the truth. "I'm glad I was able to tell you what I told Mitch, so if they ask you, your story will match mine."

"Mitch? Who is Mitch?" Cassie wanted to know.

"Oh, sorry. Mitch is Deputy Daniels' first name. He said that when it's just him and me, to call him Mitch." Marcus paused momentarily before asking, "So, Cassie, are you ready for debate club today? We haven't talked about it at all today."

"Yeah, I think so, Marcus. I haven't thought much about it. I did remember though, because I reminded my mother this morning that you were walking me home this afternoon."

* * * *

The debate club meeting was brief and touched on the basic concepts and rules of debate. Mr. Bowman, the club coach, promised they would have a great time learning the fine art of structured argument. He suggested they do a bit of research on the topic of women's suffrage, because that would be their first subject and they would begin preparations right away the following Friday.

On the walk home, initial conversation centered on the club meeting. Marcus and Cassie agreed they had both heard the terms women's suffrage but had no real idea what it was. They were obviously more interested in things that were occurring in their own lives opposed to occurrences from decades past.

"Marcus, I forgot to ask you about the newspaper you had in your pocket. The dog told you to read it, did you?" Cassie had wanted to ask at lunch, but there hadn't been sufficient time.

"Yeah, I did. It was from the Quincy Herald-Whig. Remember the guy that was executed for killing Paula Sue Schaeffer? Tobias Winslow was his name. Well, the article was about his trial." Marcus went on to share the details, "Remember the research we did at the library only told us there was a witness that saw him with a machete, it didn't tell his name? Well, the Herald-Whig identified him. His name isn't that important, I think it was Oliver Compton, but what caught my eye was that he was from Monticello. You know who else was from Monticello?"

"I don't think I know anybody from there. Who, Marcus?"

"Cousin Judy, that's who." Marcus decided to run his theory by Cassie, "You remember all the things we read about Cousin Judy from the footlocker, don't you? Cassie, what if Cousin Judy killed that girl? What if she wouldn't let him see Jude Junior and it made him so mad that he decided to get rid of her? And what if him and that guy Compton were friends, and Compton lied in court about Winslow and his machete just to cover up for Cousin Judy. What if Winslow was innocent and they conspired to get him convicted and he got executed?"

"I would say that's a lot of what ifs, Marcus. Don't you think you're grasping at straws?" Now Cassie wanted to be the voice of reason. "You don't even know if your Cousin Judy and this Compton even knew each other, much less would get together to frame some innocent man for a crime that one of them had committed."

"Maybe you're right, Cassie. Maybe I'm jumping to conclusions. But it sure seems like it could fit, doesn't it?" Marcus thought about

209

another important discovery he had made. "Cassie, I opened the envelope that was with the document binder."

"The envelope that the dog told us contained the key to unlock the document binder? He said there was a letter in the envelope, too. Was there?" She asked.

"Yes, Cassie, the key was in there, and so was the letter. Cassie, I remember what you told me, but I need to know exactly what the dog said to you. I have to know one thing for sure." If Cassie told him what he thought she would, this whole affair was going to take a remarkable turn. "Cassie, you said the dog told you to read the letter that he put in the envelope."

"Yes, Marcus. I hadn't thought of it, but that's precisely what he said. The letter that I put in the envelope. A dog couldn't have written a letter."

"And a dog can't speak either, Cassie, not even telepathically," Marcus could not himself believe what he was about to tell Cassie, how could he expect her to accept it? "Cassie, listen very carefully. The letter was written to me, but I have a feeling it was probably written before I was even born. Anyway, it warned that someone or some people would do anything to get the contents of that document binder. It said what was inside was very valuable, but only to me on my eighteenth birthday. It said to keep the binder in a safe deposit box in a bank, but I can't do that, I don't have any money."

"Marcus, we'll hide it at my house, no one would ever think to look there for it, what do you think?" Cassie's suggestion was a logical solution.

"Yeah, okay Cassie, that sounds good. There are some other things, Cassie. That envelope was sealed in 1909. The person who wrote it was only born in 1903 and it certainly wasn't written by a six-year-old. It says in the letter that it was placed in the envelope after the letter had been sealed. It said it could not tell me how it was done, only that it was put in the envelope years after the envelope was sealed. It specifically said that you and I were aware that strange things can and do happen. Such

210

as the signature on the letter," Marcus paused for a couple of seconds, and Cassie couldn't contain her curiosity.

"Who signed it, Marcus? Who was it?"

"It was my grandfather, John Stuart Clemens. And here is the most amazing part of all. He says in the letter that he is my guardian angel, but he cannot communicate directly with me. He can only communicate through a surrogate."

"A surrogate, what is that Marcus," she asked.

"I didn't know either, Cassie, I had to look it up. It's basically a substitute," Marcus admitted to her.

"So, when do you think your grandfather will contact me? Did the letter tell you or give any clues?"

"Cassie, have you been listening?" Marcus was surprised he had to spell it out for her, "My grandfather had a harelip, this dog that has been such a part of our lives has a harelip. The dog has been talking to me through you and...."

"Oh my God, Marcus, that dog is your grandfather, he is your guardian angel!" Cassie was far beyond excited. "Oh my God, he saved us from those snakes. Marcus, he saved us in the mausoleum! He saved you from that truck on the first day of school. I can't believe this. I can't wait to see him again; I want to hug him!"

"It is hard to believe isn't it, Cassie?" Marcus was amazed as well.

As they reached Cassie's house, Marcus was thinking ahead to Saturday. "Do you want to go down to Main Street tomorrow, Cassie? I'll spring for a milkshake."

"I'd love to Marcus. Pick me up about eleven o'clock?" she asked.

"Eleven it is."

As he made his way out of Forest Park Estates on his way home, Marcus was thinking of something else about the letter that he had not mentioned to Cassie. In the letter, his grandfather had specifically told him that as a guardian angel, that he was unable to communicate with Cassie until it had been certified that both surrogate and subject had a 'life-lasting commitment' to one another. Marcus was unsure if Cassie shared the same types of feelings for him as those he felt for her, but he was quite certain that he was beginning to understand the concept of love.

* * * *

For the second consecutive day, Marcus sensed a vehicle approaching from behind and could almost feel the eyes upon him. In fact, he was very nearly at the same location, about a half of a mile or so, north of Randolph Park. This time the voice that called his name was immediately recognizable. As the car stopped and the passenger door was flung open, Marcus greeted the driver, "Hello, Mitch. Thank you for the ride," and climbed inside.

"How are you today, Marcus?" Deputy Daniels asked.

"I'm fine, Mitch." Marcus silently wondered if Deputy Daniels had more questions for him, or if it was just coincidence that he was passing by and saw him walking alongside the road. The answer became glaringly clear moments later.

"Marcus, I was a little bit curious why you and Cassandra skipped school yesterday. You know, I told you we have been keeping tabs on you two. And from our observations, it clearly is unusual for either of you to miss school without just cause. And especially both of you on the same day." Deputy Daniels slowed the cruiser, taking his eyes off the road just long enough to give a small but intense stare into Marcus' eyes. "Marcus, I don't want it to seem that I'm making any accusations, but I somehow feel that you have not been totally honest with me. It is part of my job, and I am trained to read people, to assess their reactions and try to ascertain their motives. Young people like you, according to textbooks, are supposed to be simpler to read than adults. Your defense mechanisms have not been developed as keenly as those of an adult, especially an adult who has become accustomed to facing tough and accusing questions.

212

You though, you're a different bird. You and Cassandra, you both are. You two are mature beyond your years. Hell, how many kids your age would dare walk through a cemetery, even in broad daylight?"

"I don't know, Mitch. I've been doing it so long; it doesn't bother me at all."

"What about the girl, Marcus? It doesn't cause any doubt or fear to her to be there with you?" he asked.

"At first, maybe it was a little tough for Cassie." Marcus answered. "But I think when I gave her the advice that Mama gave me, it calmed her down and made her realize everything was okay."

"What advice was that, Marcus?" Deputy Daniels was curious what Marcus had told her that could have been so profound as to allay her fears.

"Mama always told me that dead people can't hurt you, it's the live ones you have to worry about."

Mitch let the words sink in before saying, "That's quite true Marcus. I've never had to arrest a dead person in my entire career. Every criminal I've cuffed has been as alive as me."

"Mitch, there is something I have to tell you," Marcus knew he had to be cautious with what and how much he said. "Maybe I haven't been a hundred per cent honest with you."

"How so, Marcus? I had a feeling this might be coming," Mitch waited for Marcus' confession.

Marcus could not mention his guardian angel - the dog, and he was not ready to talk about the encounter at the mausoleum. "I have two items at my apartment that may be something you would like to have." He went on to describe the blood-stained handkerchief that was found along with the ski mask. He told Deputy Daniels that he knew it was his handkerchief, but that it had been missing since the first Saturday in May, the day he and Cassie had essentially met at Franklin's Five and Dime.

He also described the machete. Marcus had to stretch the truth a bit, there was no way he could tell Mitch about the encounter with the camouflage wearing assailant in the mausoleum and the resulting attack by the dog. He did, however, admit that he found it in the mausoleum, near the west alcove in the center of the building. At least he felt he was offering some semblance of the truth.

"Can we go get those items, Marcus? I'd like to check them for possible fingerprints and pull blood samples from the handkerchief to see if they are a match along with the ski mask," the deputy asked. "I'd also like to ask your stepmother a few questions, if she is home."

"I can get the machete and handkerchief for you, and Mama should be home, I'm pretty sure she left work at two this afternoon," Marcus told him.

Arriving at Marcus' apartment, Deputy Daniels waited on the porch while Marcus went in to ask Margaret to come out to the front. "There is a deputy that wants to talk to you for a minute, Mama. And don't worry, I'm not in any trouble." He then went to fetch the items he had promised Mitch that he would surrender.

Drying her hands as she walked out to the front porch, Margaret smiled when she saw Deputy Daniels waiting patiently, hat in hand. "Hello, Mitchell. I haven't seen you since Elijah's funeral."

Marcus was just crossing the living room when he overheard Margaret's greeting through the open front door. He immediately sat down on the couch. It never occurred to him that Margaret might already know Mitch. He decided to utilize Cassie's proven method of gaining information, and remained where he was, eavesdropping.

"Yes, I know Margaret. It's been several years, hasn't it? I hope you have been well," the deputy was being very cordial, but the tone of both their voices indicated to Marcus that their connection may have been, at one time or another, more than just casual.

"Everything has been good. I stay busy, I work part-time, and having Marcus here gives me reason enough to smile every day. Speaking of Marcus, he said you wanted to talk to me about something. He hasn't done anything wrong, has he? I cannot imagine that he would or could have, he is such a well-mannered and conscientious young man, so much like Elijah." Marcus felt a bit of pride at being spoken of so highly and being compared so favorably to his father.

"Oh no, no, no, Margaret. Marcus is a fine young man. Actually, the department is still actively investigating the death of the young girl that Marcus found back in May, and Marcus has been extremely helpful in acquiring evidence in that case. Although, we have yet to identify a suspect, we are still diligently working all the avenues we possibly can," Mitchell, as Margaret apparently knew him, said. "Which brings me to the reason that I wanted to speak to you. We have noticed the presence of Jude Allensworth's vehicle in front of your apartment over the past month or so and were more than a little curious about the purpose of his visits."

"Oh, yes. Well, he has had a couple of business trips, uh, one to Chicago and another to Iowa. I guess perhaps he was feeling a bit homesick since he's been living, oh what is it, a thousand miles or so away from here and hasn't been home in quite a while." Margaret had no real idea how far away Savannah, Georgia was, but her estimate was quite accurate. "But anyway, yes, he has spent a couple of nights here, sleeping in Marcus' bedroom. Marcus stays on the couch of course, and in a short time Marcus and Judy have become remarkably close. Judy thinks the world of Marcus, swears he is the second coming of Elijah." With all the doubt that Marcus had been developing about Judy, he was not sure how to feel about Margaret's assessment of his and Judy's relationship.

"Well, I must admit, Margaret, I was a little bit leery. I know it's been what fourteen, fifteen years since his old girlfriend was killed, and with his roughneck history before that, I guess I'm just not confident that he ever changed, or even grew up for that matter." Mitch shook his head and said to Margaret, "You'll remember, there were plenty of people that blamed Judy for Paula's death. If it hadn't of been for his buddy Ollie's testimony, that drifter would never have been arrested and convicted, and who knows, it might have been Judy that ended up being accused."

215

"I never believed any of that Mitchell. I know Elijah didn't trust him as far as he could throw him, and he always thought that as a kid he had killed his sister Elsie, but I never bought any of that. I've always been a good judge of character, and I honestly feel that I always saw the soft and decent side of Judy." Margaret was convincingly supportive of Judy. "I think he got all of the rogue out of his system before the baby was even born. I know from what I remember of him, that he never got over her taking the baby to Illinois to raise him and shutting Judy out like she did. I still believe that when the baby went up for adoption, that that was what drove him to move away. He couldn't stand the idea that someone else, right here in his backyard, was going to raise his son and he would have no part or say in it."

"Maybe you are right about Judy, in fact I hope you are, but as a lawman, I will always have my doubts." It sounded to Marcus like the conversation was winding down. Picking up the machete and handkerchief, he walked out to the front porch and handed them to Deputy Daniels.

"Thank you, Marcus. I guess better late than not at all, right?"

"My goodness, Marcus, where did you get that huge knife, and is that one of your father's handkerchiefs?" Margaret practically squealed. "Where did that knife come from, Marcus?"

"It's okay, Margaret," Deputy Daniels intervened. "These are items that Marcus found and wanted to turn in to me just in case they might contain evidence for our investigation. He didn't want to upset you or cause you any undo worry. That's why he came directly to me about it. Everything is okay, Marcus did the right and responsible thing with these items, and I commend him for not bothering you with it."

"He's right, Mama. I didn't want to worry you, so I told Deputy Daniels that I had found these things over by the river and wanted to give them to him."

"What about your father's handkerchief. Why was it at the river?" Margaret asked.

"Marcus had lost it, Margaret," the deputy explained. "He lost it a month before the girl died, and when he found it, it had blood splatters on it. We just want to check it to make sure the blood type doesn't match the victim. It might just be from an animal, who knows? And the machete he found was abandoned.

We want to check it for fingerprints. Somebody probably was using it and just left it laying. I'm sure it's nothing, but we have to check these things out."

Deputy Daniels thanked Marcus for his citizenly duty and told Margaret he had enjoyed speaking with her. As he carried the items to his cruiser, Margaret went into the apartment to continue preparing dinner, but not before scolding Marcus, "Don't you ever keep anything like this from me. Ever. Ever. Again."

"Yes ma'am. I'm sorry Mama." Marcus wondered to himself how he was ever going to explain to Margaret everything else he was keeping from her, from the newspaper clippings to microfiche stories, to letters and notes written by his father, to the letter written by his grandfather, to the document binder, to the mausoleum, to the harelipped dog – his guardian angel. Oh brother, what a conundrum.

James E. Anderson

The Most Perfect Day

As promised, Marcus rang Cassie's doorbell at eleven on Saturday morning. She met him at the door, wearing a pink blouse and blue skirt with shoulder straps. Along with her shoulder bag, she carried a milky white sweater, for it had chilled a bit. It was October 12, and a frigid northern Missouri winter was just around the corner. Marcus took her hand as they began walking down Fernwood Drive. They laughed and giggled while walking, enjoying the lovely fall weather. There were some clouds in the sky, but nothing ominous. The weather forecast had not predicted rain, and while it was in the mid sixty-degree range, Marcus had hoped that the sun would soon penetrate the cloud cover and they would enjoy a relatively warm and comfortable afternoon.

Marcus and Cassie had come to really enjoy their walks, although they both did look forward to the day that Marcus was old enough to afford a car and they could drive to their destinations. It would be nice also to expand their horizons, perhaps venture as far as La Grange or perhaps even Quincy, on the Illinois side of the river. Although Cassie was originally from Illinois, Marcus had rarely been there. He and Margaret had been to Quincy a handful of times with friends of Margaret,

219

but the bulk of his excursions to Illinois had come the previous January, when he and Denny had braved the frozen over Mississippi River and made the trek across ice to the eastern side of the waterway. He and Denny had often wondered aloud how many times a young Mark Twain had made the same venture in his youth down in Hannibal.

Passing before Walt's Tire and Auto Repair, they decided to slip over to the soda vending machine and take a quick break. Marcus dropped a pair of dimes into the machine and secured two 6-ounce bottles of ice-cold Coca-Cola. They sat in the metal chairs in front of the plate glass office window and discussed again Mr. Bowman and the debate club. They wondered just how effective a debater Denny was going to be. While Marcus had been promoted to Cassie's 'A' level class, Denny had remained in the 'B' class. Fortunately for him, there were not enough students at Roosevelt to warrant a 'C' level. Academics just were not of interest to Denny. If life were only dependent on sports, Denny would no doubt be ranked at the top of the class. He was a good baseball player and an extremely fast runner. He was just a natural athlete, but academically, not so much. Marcus knew Denny's competitive nature and based solely on that quality was sure that he would hold his own in the debate club.

As he and Cassie finished their Coca-Colas and stood, Marcus noticed their reflections in the office picture window. He hadn't thought a lot about it, in fact he could never even remember seeing a reflection of them together, but he was probably six full inches taller than Cassie and also twice as wide. Over the summer he had gained some height while his weight had basically remained unchanged. Marcus thought it a bit odd that things like that are often not consciously recognized. Sometimes it takes the subconscious to bring reality to the forefront. Sometimes the subconscious can bring out the good, but sometimes the subconscious can bring out the bad. Sometimes the happy, sometimes the sad. Sometimes the grandest of dreams, sometimes the darkest of nightmares. 'Whoa,' Marcus thought, 'this is getting too philosophical.'

Marcus took the used bottles to the empty bottle case next to the vending machine. From there, Walt would collect a two cent per bottle refund from the Coca-Cola driver. If a customer was going to leave with an unfinished bottle of soda, he would be expected to go to the counter and pay the two-cent deposit, to cover Walt's cost. As Marcus was returning from the machine to Cassie, he took the time to really notice how pretty she truly was. Her red hair, which she uncharacteristically had worn down today rather than in her customary pigtails, appeared exceptionally shiny and had an almost angelic glowing aura. Marcus always had known how pretty she was, he had thought since the third grade that she was the prettiest girl of all at Roosevelt, but today especially she looked exquisite.

They continued down White Street and got to the A&W just past noon. Marcus felt especially hungry today and thus ordered a Papa Burger. Cassie had her usual Coney Island Hot Dog and they split a large order of Cheese Fries. The feast was washed down by two medium root beers. They had to sit at the picnic bench for a little while to let the delicious meal settle before moving on down the street. They continued, hand in hand, until reaching Franklin's Five and Dime. They entered and decided to check out the toy and game section. Nothing seemed very new or unusual, Barbie dolls, plastic cars, the usual board games such as Monopoly, Chutes and Ladders, and Life. They did notice one new game that had just become available. Marcus remembered it from an ad in one of Margaret's magazines. It was called Mouse Trap Game and Cassie was enamored by it. She told Marcus, "That game is going on my Christmas list, and Santa had better make sure to bring it on Christmas Eve!"

From the toy section, they meandered to the magazine rack. They each had their own favorite section to sample, and they spent over half an hour thumbing through their respective favorites. Marcus preferred Mad and Cracked, while Cassie honed in on teenage inspired magazines such as Teen Scene, Teen Wardrobe and Teen Life. Becoming bored with the magazines, they retired to the soda fountain where Marcus ordered a chocolate malt, while Cassie opted for the strawberry. As usual, they enjoyed the show Ellis, the soda jerk, put on flirting with the girls a couple years younger than himself. They thought his antics were funny until he turned his attention toward Cassie and began commenting on her lovely red hair. Marcus did not find humor in his flirting with Cassie, and especially with him sitting right next to her. Fortunately, Ellis' attention span was short, and he soon was averted to another young girl, this one with blond curls.

Leaving the Five and Dime and walking back up White Street, Cassie sensed Marcus' aggravation with the soda jerk. Realizing he had not taken her hand as he had all day to that point, Cassie took his and leaned into him. "Thank you for being jealous, Marcus. That kind of makes me feel special."

"I wasn't jealous, Cassie," he said.

"Yes, you were in there, and you still are, Marcus. Thank you," Cassie felt touched that Marcus cared.

"Okay. Yes, I was, and I still am. I really care a lot for you Cassie. I've never felt anything like this before. I know we're only twelve, but I have to tell you, I think we are going to be together for a really long time," Marcus envisioned the 'life-lasting commitment' portion of the letter. Although he had yet to reveal those words to Cassie, he knew it was a mutual commitment. That letter could not lie.

"I know Marcus, I feel the same way," Cassie's words went straight to his heart.
As they approached Forest Park Cemetery, Marcus had the urge to talk to his parents. "Cassie, how do you feel about stopping by my parent's graves?"

"Sure, Marcus, whatever makes you happy. Afterward can we go to Randolph Park and sit by the lake? I feel like just kind of mellowing out. The sun doesn't look like it's going to shine much today, but it has still been wonderful being with you all day. This has been the most perfect day," Cassie's mood seemed unusually laid back today, she had not been nearly as hyper as normal. Just very at ease, peaceful and serene.

"That would be great Cassie," Marcus said, "You know, the sun hasn't been shining today, but you sure have been a brilliant ray of sunshine to me. I can't tell you how happy I am that you came to me in Franklin's that day. You're the best thing that has ever happened to me." Marcus leaned over and kissed Cassie at the top of her forehead, sending shivers throughout her body.

As they were passing through the cemetery, it seemed the temperature had dropped ten degrees since leaving White Street. Marcus wished he'd brought a light jacket or flannel shirt. Cassie had donned her milky white sweater and was no longer holding Marcus' hand. She had her left arm and hand beneath his right bicep against his body, her right hand was on the outside of his bicep and her head leaned against his shoulder as they walked silently.

Marcus did not hear or feel any premonitory sound or movement, he was just suddenly knocked off balance by a force to his right. There was a brief gulping type sound and before he had any idea of what might have happened, he felt Cassie slumping and saw red cascading across the front of her beautiful white sweater. All he could do was try to ease her fall to the ground, and just before she landed, he saw the machete imbedded between the base of her neck and right shoulder, buried at least two to three inches. As he did his best to gently place her on the ground, he realized the machete had penetrated nearly halfway across her neck. A quick glance over his shoulder revealed someone with black hair, dressed in camouflaged clothing running toward White Street. Looking back at Cassie's beautiful face, with her beautiful blues eyes staring at him lifelessly, Marcus could do nothing but scream, "Noooooooooooo…."

James E. Anderson

Now, Who's the Fool?

The Westclox alarm clock could just as well have been the sirens at the firehouse. It seemed the hammering bells would fracture his skull, his head pounded to an extent he had never before felt, his pajamas were soaking wet, his bedsheets were soaked with sweat, and his hair was drenching with perspiration. He immediately jumped from the bed and ran to the kitchen, praying Margaret was home. Thankfully, she was whisking pancake batter for breakfast. Marcus felt like he had just run five miles as he breathlessly asked, "Mama, what day is it?"

"Relax, Marcus, you're not late for school, it's Saturday," she answered.

"Is it October 12th?" he asked.

"Yes, Marcus. What are you so worked up about?" Margaret asked.

Marcus didn't answer her. He ran to the living room and dialed Cassie's number. Debbie Worthington answered the phone and Marcus, breathlessly asked, "Hi, Mrs. Worthington, this is Marcus. Is Cassie there?"

"She's still sleeping, Marcus. I can have her call you when she wakes up," Cassie's mother offered.

"No, please Mrs. Worthington, would you please wake her, I really need to talk to her," he pleaded.

"Just a minute, Marcus. I'll see if she wants to come to the phone." Debbie Worthington laid the receiver down and went to wake Cassie.

Margaret came into the living room, concerned by Marcus' behavior. "Marcus are you alright?" She raised the back of her hand to his forehead and asked, "Do you have a fever? You're soaking wet, are you sure you're alright?"
"Yes, I'm fine, Mama. I just have to talk to Cassie, that's all," he said.

Cassie's groggy voice came on the line, "Hello? Marcus, is that you? Are you okay? Are you sick? You're still coming over this morning, right?"

Marcus had never been so relieved in his brief lifetime. "Oh, Cassie. I had the absolute worst dream. You have no idea how wonderful it is to hear your beautiful voice."

Cassie's brow furrowed as she asked again, "Are you okay, Marcus?"

* * * *

For the entire journey to Cassie's house, Marcus' mind was consumed by the horrific nightmare he had experienced last night. He mentally kept replaying all the events of the envisioned day, and while his efforts were to focus on the many happy, peaceful and tranquil moments, those thoughts were callously interrupted by the tragic final seconds of the dream. He still could not shake the terror he felt upon waking up and not realizing that what he remembered had been nothing more than a dastardly nightmare. His panic had been severe and his worst possible fear, that Cassie might actually be dead, would have been validated if Margaret had informed him that today was Sunday rather than Saturday. Even though his worst fears had been quashed, Marcus still had a severe case of anxiety. His overall feeling was that of apprehension and anguish. The entire episode had left him feeling restless and his spirits in a state of turmoil. He wished for the uneasiness to subside before he reached Cassie's house. He had already convinced himself that Cassie would never be told the truth of the tragedy that was the final, and much too realistic, scene of the movie that his mind had cruelly given him a role in.

Approaching Cassie's front porch, with the aura of gloom still hanging over him like a shroud, Marcus steadied himself. He was determined not to deter Cassie from having a remarkable day with him. As he reached to ring the doorbell, Marcus reminded himself just how beautiful he thought Cassie had been when, in one of the happiest moments of the dream, she was standing in front of the office window at Walt's Tire and Auto Repair.

As the front door swung open and Cassie stood smiling before him, Marcus realized that her beauty in the dream was not exaggerated, it was here right in front of him, and in the flesh. Even prior to the door opening, Marcus had managed to replace his burdened facial expression with one of happiness and anticipation. Seeing Cassie's smile only served to enhance his improved mood. Cassie grabbed her shoulder bag, and together they raced down the steps, breaking into a gallop across the front lawn before slowing and turning right onto the sidewalk adjacent to Fernwood Drive.

As they walked, Marcus realized that the cloud cover appeared to have gotten heavier, and although the temperature was probably in the low sixties, a bit of breeze had started to gently blow from the east. As he had walked from his apartment to Cassie's house, there had been extended periods of sunshine. But now, with the thickening clouds, the sunlight had diminished. The lack of sunshine, combined with the slight breeze, had resulted in slightly cooler temperatures. By the time they had reached Walt's Tire and Auto Repair, it had gotten noticeably cooler. Cassie was wearing a relatively short skirt, and even though she had on knee-length socks with her saddle oxfords, she had a fair amount of skin exposed. "Marcus, can we stop and go into Walt's shop waiting room for a few minutes, I feel a little chilly."

"Sure, Cassie." With Marcus opening the door to allow Cassie in first, they entered the waiting room. After sitting on a pair of straight back wooden chairs, Marcus asked, "Would you like a Coca-Cola from the vending machine?"

"No thank you, Marcus. I don't think I want anything cold to drink right now. I'm tempted to get a cup of coffee from that pot over there, but I don't like coffee. And besides, that handle looks awfully greasy. What I wish I had was some hot chocolate," Cassie said.

"Well, maybe later we can stop at the diner and have Buster fix us a couple of mugs," Marcus suggested.

"Yeah, maybe," Cassie was in the process of letting down her pigtails and fluffing out her hair. Marcus figured she was just trying to cover her neck to counteract the breeze a bit. As she used both hands to fluff her hair, he marveled at how pretty it was when she allowed it to flow unfettered. Unfortunately, having her hair down revived memory of the dream. And with that memory the realization of something that thus far had escaped Marcus' eye. Cassie was wearing a pink blouse and blue skirt with shoulder straps. Now, with her hair down, she looked almost identical to the way she had appeared in his dream. The only difference Marcus could see was in the shade of blue in her skirt. It seemed a darker blue today than what he recalled from the dream. At least today she was not carrying that white sweater.

After a few moments' respite, Cassie pronounced herself ready to proceed to A&W and they continued their stroll down White Street. As they made their way the small talk returned to the debate club, and just as it had in his dream, it became centered on his friend Denny. The conversation played out almost identically to the way Marcus remembered it. When they eventually reached the A&W, it occurred to Marcus that he wasn't very hungry. With the degree of stress and anguish the nightmare had thrust upon him, it was no small surprise that his appetite was diminished. Cassie, on the other seemed famished. She ordered a Mama Burger and fries. The roles seemed reversed as Marcus asked only for a

Coney Island Dog and had no interest in a side item. Both decided on medium root beers for their drinks.

Next stop on the excursion was Franklin's Five and Dime and, according to the established script, their first destination inside was the toy and game section. Before relocating to the magazine rack, and not to Marcus' surprise, Cassie announced that the Mouse Trap Game would be on her Christmas list and that "Santa had better make sure to bring it on Christmas Eve." In Marcus' eyes, this was definitely evolving into a 'déjà vu' type of afternoon. As they started examining and replacing magazines, Marcus could have made a small fortune predicting exactly which magazines Cassie would choose to look through. He would have gotten the correct order in which she chose them, as well. Teen Scene, Teen Wardrobe and Teen Life. A perfect trifecta.

Following the magazine rack came the soda fountain. Marcus' choice of refreshment was obvious, he always opted for the chocolate malt. He could also have placed Cassie's order, if he had so chosen, as she asked for a strawberry malt just as she had in the dream. It was as the malts were delivered that Marcus was alerted to the first thing that seemed off script. The same soda jerk, Ellis Compton, had been there all summer long. He was the self-imagined local version of Elvis Presley who loved playing it up to the young girls at the counter. He brought Cassie's malt in his left hand and Marcus' in his right. He set Marcus' malt down first, without a word. He set Cassie's down with a smile, a wink, and "How is your day going, my red-headed sweetheart? I never see you in here alone anymore." Tilting his head in Marcus' direction, he said to her, "What are you doing? Are you baby-sitting this big lump of clay next to you here, are you?"

Cassie was taken back by the insulting words. She was used to seeing him flirting with all the girls, herself occasionally included, but this seemed completely different. It did not sound good natured at all, and most definitely was an insult directed toward Marcus. "No, he's my boyfriend," was the only response she could muster. Ellis laughed heartily and walked to the far side of the counter. Cassie looked over at Marcus, unsure what type of reaction he might counter with. To her surprise, his face was devoid of any visible emotion.

229

"Don't pay him any mind, Marcus. He's just a soda jerk, emphasis on the word jerk." She said, hoping to diffuse any anger that may have been festering.

"Oh, it's okay Cassie. He's just a smart aleck."

Marcus continued watching Ellis at the far end of the counter. Cassie redirected her attention to him as well, wondering what Marcus was looking at with such intent.

"Cassie, do you see the bandage on his right forearm?"

"No, Marcus I don't." She tried to train her eyes a little more strongly, and said, "Yes, now I do. It's hard to see."

Ellis was wearing a long sleeve white shirt. Both sleeves were rolled up to just below his elbows, about a quarter of the way down the forearms. And high up on the right forearm was a pad of white gauze about 2" x 2" in size, secured with white medical tape, and partially covered by the folded sleeve. Aware now of what had caught Marcus' attention, Cassie said, "I wonder why he has the bandage? Marcus, do you think it's possible that he...."

"I don't know what to think. But when he comes down here, I'm going to ask him about it," Marcus promised. As they continued watching Ellis toy and flirt with the girls, Marcus saw something else that elevated his heart rate several beats. Ellis had moved a few feet closer to them, improving their perspective a great deal. He had reached into his back pocket, pulled out a handkerchief and wiped his forehead. What sparked Marcus' interest and caused his pulse rate to increase was the fact that it was red. Marcus raised his right hand calling out, "Ellis, can I get a couple of napkins, please?"

The soda jerk heard Marcus and started toward him, grabbing some napkins on the way. He set them in front of Cassie, and turned away, but Marcus reached across the narrow counter and fleetingly touched Ellis' elbow before saying, "I've got a question for you."

Ellis turned back, looking at Marcus with disgust. He leaned forward with both fists on the counter and in a low, but threatening voice said, "Listen kid, don't you ever put your hands on me. I'm working right now, but if you ever touch me again, you'll be lucky to ever see another sunrise, do you understand what I'm saying?"

"Yes, I understand Ellis, but I was concerned for you. What did you do to your arm?" Marcus asked trying to sound sincere.

"Neighbor's dog bit me, as if it's any of your business."

While Ellis had been threatening Marcus with both of his fists on the counter, Marcus had been studying the handkerchief tightly gripped in his right hand. "Can I ask one more question?"

"What?"

Pointing to the red handkerchief, Marcus was thankful to be able to ask, "Why do you have my handkerchief?"

"Listen punk, what makes you think it's yours?" Ellis demanded as he held the handkerchief up at about chest height.

"It has my dad's initials embroidered on it, E.C. for Elijah Clemens," Marcus knew he had tripped him up with that question. Now he was sure who had stolen the handkerchiefs, who had left one with the girl's body, and who had dropped one in the mausoleum. Yes, Marcus felt smug.

Ellis looked at Marcus, more indignant than ever, "You are really stupid aren't you, kid? It is my handkerchief and I have several of them. They were gifts from my mother. You little dumbass, my name is Ellis Compton. E.C., you idiot."

* * * *

As they stood outside Franklin's Five and Dime, Marcus felt like an absolute fool. He thought he had trapped Ellis in an inescapable quandary. Upon seeing the handkerchief with the embroidered initials,

Marcus was so overcome with emotion and the conviction that it was his, that the obvious had completely evaded his tunnel vision. He was perfectly cognizant of Ellis' last name, and before making a bold accusation should have realized that his initials were also E.C. With his eyes squarely on the sidewalk, an embarrassed Marcus said, "Cassie, I'm sorry I made a fool of myself in there with Ellis."

"It's okay, Marcus. I would have said the same thing that you did." Cassie was sympathetic, for she too had noticed the initials on the handkerchief and was also convinced it was the one that had been taken from Marcus' dresser. "I thought it was yours, too. And, you know what? I still believe it is. I think Ellis is lying. I just wish I could prove it."

"Me, too," Marcus mused. They stood quietly for a few more minutes, Marcus continuing to stare down at the pavement.

It was Cassie who ultimately broke the stillness, "Marcus, I don't want to let that jerk Ellis ruin an otherwise perfect day. I have some dimes in my coin purse. How about we go over to Lorenzo's Pizza and play the 'Swing Along' pinball machine for a while, okay," Cassie suggested as she reached into her shoulder bag.

"Good idea, Cassie," Marcus said, assuming Cassie was getting her coin purse out of her bag. He was about to tell her to save her dimes because he still had a pocketful of change. But his thought processes were abruptly altered when he saw that Cassie was pulling a milky white sweater from her shoulder bag.

As she was putting her arm into the sweater, Marcus was moved to say, "I didn't know you brought that sweater, Cassie." He was stricken by the fact that her ensemble now almost perfectly matched what she had been wearing in his dream. Only the blue shade of her skirt varied, and that difference was only minor. She looked almost identically as he had dreamed, even down to the detail of her hair not being in pigtails, but rather flowing freely. Seeing her wearing the white sweater now caused his heart to sink. He knew perfectly well there was no possible way that the events of that nightmare could be replicated in real life, but the coincidental elements were impossible for him to dismiss.

The Trials of Marcus Clemens

"Yes, the weatherman on the radio this morning said the temperatures would drop a little this afternoon, so I came prepared." Cassie took Marcus' arm and smiled, "Ready Marcus?" They began the three-block journey to Lorenzo's.

The aroma of freshly baked pizza was delightful. Larry Schmidt, the owner of Lorenzo's did not have a drop of Italian blood in him. In fact, all of his grandparents, both paternal and maternal were from the German/Austrian region of Europe. He had learned from a roommate in college the secret of preparing an authentic Italian pizza sauce and had managed, through trial and error, to improve upon the recipe. When he had decided to open his own pizza shop, he felt it prudent to settle upon a name that sounded decidedly Italian. Thus, Lorenzo's Pizza was born rather than a much more mundane 'Larry Schmidt's Pizza'.

Marcus popped in two dimes and pressed the two-player button. Cassie took the lead as Player One. Marcus studied the high score total, which was 9,370. The scoreboard maxed out at 9,999, meaning that the high score was very nearly perfection. He only wished he had the ability to score in the vicinity of that lofty stratosphere. His own personal best score had barely edged over 7,000. He and Cassie had only played the game together twice before. When he had scored his 7,140, Cassie had miscalculated her timing with the right flipper on her third and final ball, ending her game at 6,990. One more 150-point bumper would have tied her with Marcus, and she probably could easily have beaten him if not for her poor timing at a critical moment. To this day, about three months later, Marcus was still convinced that Cassie's faux pas with the flipper was intentional.

On the third game of the afternoon, Marcus managed to earn two free games by posting a new personal best with a score of 8,260. On the fifth game of the afternoon, Cassie produced a score of 8,200, earning two more free plays in the process. By the time they had burned through six dimes and all their free games, they were exhausted, and it was past three o'clock. They decided to head toward Cassie's house, but planned a detour to stop at the lake at Randolph Park to make sure the ducks had begun their migration southward.

* * * *

At just past four in the afternoon the lake at Randolph Park was quiet. All the waterfowl had made their way toward their winter homes, and the water was smooth as glass. With the lone exception of an occasional unsuspecting water bug being gulped down by a predatory bass, there was absolutely no discernable activity on the surface. Marcus and Cassie had started across the playground parking lot to continue their way north on Highway 457, when they realized a car was parked near the parking lot entrance. The fact that a car was parked near the entrance was only unusual in that all the other vehicles had parked nearer to the playground, where children and parents were winding down their Saturday afternoon excursions. The lone automobile parked at the lot entrance was a black, somewhat older Ford sedan. Marcus estimated it to be a 1949 or 1950 model. The other unusual circumstance was the man with arms folded across his chest and leaning against the trunk, one foot on the back bumper.

As they drew within 150 feet or so of the Ford, Cassie said, "Marcus, it's the soda jerk, Ellis Compton."

"Yeah, I see that" Marcus replied, "I wonder what he's doing here."

Marcus deliberately steered Cassie in a wide arc, attempting to keep a safe buffer from Ellis and his car. However, Ellis seemed to have a purpose for being exactly where he was. "Hi, sweetheart." Ellis called out to Cassie, raising one hand in a small wave. He started walking toward them, and turned his attention to Marcus, "How you doing, kid? You two kind of skipped out quick on me at the fountain a while ago. Kid, you didn't even wait for your change when you paid. You had forty-five cents in change due. At first, I thought you left it as a tip, but then I realized that even with a ten percent tip, it was still about thirty cents too much. So, I figured I'd square up with you and I brought you a quarter and a nickel."

"That's nice of you Ellis, but just keep the thirty cents for your trouble of driving over here," Marcus suggested. He didn't want to have any reason to be in close contact with Ellis, he just did not trust him.

"Well thanks, Marcus. That's real nice of you. So, tell me kid, are you planning on taking the shortcut through the cemetery on your way back to Little Red Riding Hood's house?" Ellis' eyes seemed penetrating as he waited for a response from Marcus.

"How do you know we take a shortcut through the cemetery?" Cassie's question was almost in a demanding tone.

Ellis smiled, "Oh I know a lot about you little girl, and your boyfriend here. Although I know more about him than you."

"What are you talking about Ellis? How do you know anything about me, and why would you want to, anyway?" Marcus' ire was beginning to rise.

The smile faded from Ellis' lips, "Let's just say I know you come here a lot, I know you like to fish, I even know your skinny little friend Denny Wallace. But, most of all I know you've got something I want, that belongs to me. And I intend to have it, whatever it takes, and despite whoever gets in my way." Marcus glanced at Cassie, wondering if she was thinking what he was. Ellis picked up on their eyes meeting and said, "Yeah take a good look at her Marcus. Maybe she's what I'm talking about, but then, maybe not."

"I don't have any idea what you're talking about, Ellis. I don't have anything that you would want. And if you're referring to Cassie, you can forget that right now. She wouldn't give a creep like you the time of day," Marcus wished he had not mentioned Cassie. He didn't want her involved in any of this, and here he was blabbing about how he hoped she felt.

"Don't worry about Little Red Riding Hood, kid. Not interested, she's too young. I like them old enough to drink liquor, or at least jump up and do the polka or jitterbug, get my drift?" Ellis paused, and then smiling said, "I've got you all figured out, kid. And I'm going to bury you.........oh yeah, and the handkerchief?" Ellis started laughing, "you were right, it is yours."

Ellis continued laughing as he opened the car door and climbed in. After firing the engine, he started backing up. Shifting into low gear and turning toward the exit to highway 457, Ellis rolled down his window and said, "By the way, if you take the shortcut, I'd stay out of the mausoleum if I was you." He threw up gravel as he popped the clutch and sped from the parking lot.

"Marcus, we have to call Deputy Daniels. That idiot just about admitted to everything. Did you hear all that he said?" Cassie was beside herself.

"Yes, Cassie, I heard everything he said. But Cassie, it would be our word against his, he would deny everything."

"Marcus, he kept saying you have something that he wants. Do you think he's talking about your 'What Me Worry?' bust of Alfred E. Neuman? Marcus, don't ask me how, but he knows about the footlocker and the document or the will or whatever it is that is in that binder."

"You are probably right Cassie. But how could he know? Nobody knows about that footlocker but us and Mama. And I know she didn't tell him," Marcus reasoned.

It only took a few seconds of thought before Cassie said, "But there is someone who she might have told, or maybe he could even have found it himself. He has certainly had opportunities."

"What are you talking about Cassie?"

"Cousin Judy, Marcus. Cousin Judy might have been who told him," Cassie was beginning to lay it all out in her mind. "Oh my God, Marcus. Remember Jude Junior? Marcus, what if Ellis is Jude Junior? He said the red handkerchief he had at the soda fountain was yours. And how could he get it? From Judy!"

"I think you're right, Cassie." It was all falling into place for Marcus. "When the machete and handkerchiefs were outside my bedroom window, the window was unlocked. Those things were put there from inside my room and who spent that night in my room? Judy, that's who!"

"Marcus, who does Ellis brag that he looks like?" Cassie asked pointedly.

"Elvis Presley,"

"Right, and the girl that died in Keokuk, the one that Evans and Marlowe tried to pin on my dad, how was the guy described that was seen in the parking lot with her?"

"Elvis Presley, with a motorcycle jacket," Marcus remembered Cassie telling him that. "Cassie, do you think Ellis killed that girl?"

"I don't know, Marcus, maybe. He also said he likes girls old enough to drink and dance. Well, she had been in the Horeshoe drinking."

"And Cassie, he didn't say dance, he said jitterbug and polka. Specific dances, and the girl we found was a polka dancer," Marcus was linking the dots.

"And he said he was going to bury you! I think that's a threat, don't you?"

"Cassie. He said when I go to the cemetery, if he was me, he'd stay out of the mausoleum. How does he know about the mausoleum unless that was him there that day? And he admitted he had a dog bite on his arm," Marcus remembered.

"Cousin Judy had his arm bandaged, too," Cassie reminded him. Maybe that was him in the mausoleum and he told Ellis about it."

"I just don't know, Cassie. I can't believe Cousin Judy is involved in this."

"One more thing Marcus, Missouri tag 3BK.491." Cassie had it memorized.

James E. Anderson

Sunday, the 13th

Reverend Drummond had delivered a fine sermon in church, and it had been a fine lunch at the Red Roof Lodge. But both Marcus and Cassie were restless. Anticipation and anxiety ran high for each of them. Marcus had held onto one of Deputy Daniels' business cards on which Mitch had added his personal home telephone number. Marcus and Cassie had agreed that matters had reached a boiling point, and that the deputy's expertise was now required. Upon arriving at home on Saturday, Marcus had called Mitch to arrange a meeting, along with Cassie, at Randolph Park for three o'clock on Sunday afternoon. They had decided that it was time to inform Mitch of their suspicions concerning Ellis Compton.

Arriving back at Cassie's house a little late, but still ahead of two o'clock, Marcus and Cassie set sail for Randolph Park. On the way, they went back and forth on exactly how much information to divulge. Of course, any mention of the dog, or guardian angel, was out of the question. They could not reasonably expect Deputy Daniels to seriously consider anything that they had to say if they came across as two little kids spouting some science fiction fantasy. They arrived at the parking lot expecting to see the deputy's Lewis County cruiser awaiting them, so they were a little bit disappointed to see only a handful of family style sedans in the area. However, as they approached the bench at the south end of the lake where the meeting was to take place, Marcus recognized the figure already seated there and smoking an old-fashioned corn cob style pipe. Out of uniform, in blue jeans and sport shirt, Deputy Daniels appeared several years younger than Marcus thought him to be. He also felt a twinge of guilt when he realized that it was Sunday and Mitch was off duty. He immediately offered an apology, "I'm sorry, Mitch. I didn't think to ask if you were working today. I guess I thought you policemen never took a day off."

"That's okay, Marcus. A lot of the time we don't get days off. We are public servants, you know. Here to serve and protect and all of that."

"Hi, Deputy Daniels, I'm Cassie Worthington, if you don't remember me," Cassie introduced herself, unsure if Mitch did indeed remember her.

"Of course, I remember you, Cassie. You kids were great assets that day on the riverbank, how could I forget? And, like I told Marcus, when it's just us, please just call me Mitch, okay?" Greetings and informalities out of the way, Mitch was ready to get right to brass tacks, "Now, shall we get down to it? Marcus, you said yesterday that you had some important information for me, would you like to share?"

"It's kind of hard to figure out where to start, Mitch. I guess it all begins with the ski mask that we found," Marcus was nervous, and couldn't help but think in the back of his mind that this was probably good practice for the debating he would be doing on Friday afternoons, after school. Meanwhile, Cassie held her breath waiting for Marcus to continue, somewhat worried that he might let something slip. "We both know that you guys found Cassie's father's fingerprints on it, but if you checked, you would also find ours. We all three touched it that day, but especially Mr. Worthington. And of course, I gave you the machete and handkerchief the other day. Did you find anything on them, Mitch?"

"I don't know yet, Marcus. It will only take a couple of days to find out about the machete, but the handkerchief will take a little longer. It had to go to an FBI lab for analysis," he explained. "But, while we're on that subject, I need to contact both your stepmother Marcus, and your parents Cassie, to get you two to the station to get your fingerprints. Not that we think you could be involved, but purely to be used for comparison and to eliminate any of yours from our consideration. Any unidentified fingerprints only add to the difficulty of the case. So, what else do you have, Marcus? Or you, Cassie. Do you have anything to add?"

"Oh yes, there is more Deputy Daniels," Cassie replied. "Go ahead, Marcus."

"Mitch, there is something I wasn't completely honest about with you."

Deputy Daniels felt a bit of perspiration trickle down the back of his neck. These were precisely the types of words he had not wanted to hear today but was nevertheless prepared for them. He had been somewhat expecting them and reminded himself that although they were mentally mature for their ages, he was, after all, dealing with children. "Okay, go on, Marcus."

"Mitch, I told you that I found the machete in the alcove at the mausoleum, and while that is true, it's not completely true."

Deputy Daniels gazed at Marcus with steely blue eyes, "Would you care to correct your story, Marcus?"

"Yes sir. Cassie and I were walking through the mausoleum, playing a game that I made up, where we would look at the dates on the crypts and...."

"I don't care about the rules of your game, Marcus. Please get to the point," Deputy Daniels said impatiently.

"Okay, Mitch. We went to turn around and leave, by the alcove, and some guy dressed in camouflage and wearing a red ski mask raised the machete like he was going to hit us with it and..."

"Wait, wait, wait, Marcus. The guy was wearing a red ski mask? Like the one you gave me? And you didn't tell me this before?" Mitch

Daniels was more than miffed. "Why haven't you told me this Marcus? Or you, Cassie? How could you keep this to yourselves?"

"Well, Mitch we were told...." Marcus was interrupted by Cassie.

"We were sure that if we told anybody that they would either think we were stupid kids fantasizing or that we were making it up for attention. I mean, it does sound a little far-fetched, doesn't it?" Cassie interjected. She thought for sure Marcus was about to bring the dog into the story, and if he did, they would lose any credibility.

"Perhaps you're right, Cassie," Mitch reasoned. "But if this guy had raised the machete in a threatening manner, how did you kids disarm him and recover the machete?" the deputy could not see either of them overpowering an armed adult in this scenario.

Cassie resumed the narrative, "Marcus pushed me back and told me to run, and so I did, back to the mausoleum entrance. When I got to the big doorway, I turned around to see Marcus tackle the guy, just like a football player would. The guy dropped the machete and then jumped up and ran out the other doorway."

Marcus was glad Cassie was there. He was sure he would have buckled and admitted that the dog had attacked the man.

"You did that, Marcus?" Deputy Daniels asked. It seemed a little bit unlikely, but what other explanation could there have been?

Marcus hated to be dishonest with Mitch, but really had no choice. "Yes, Mitch. It happened so fast, it was like in a dream, like it never really happened."

"If the perp was wearing a ski mask similar to the one you found at the riverfront, it certainly raises the possibility that it could have been the same person who committed that crime. But, unless we are able to pull prints from that machete or handkerchief, I don't know. And I really don't understand why your handkerchiefs keep turning up, Marcus." The deputy mused.

"I have a theory on that Mitch," Cassie offered.

"I'm anxious to hear young lady, continue."

"Mitch, I know Marcus doesn't want to tell anybody about this, but he found a footlocker that his father had left for him," Cassie began.

"No, Cassie, you shouldn't tell him," Marcus said. Mitch looked from Cassie to Marcus and then back to Cassie, expectantly.

"Marcus is the last surviving member of the Clemens family, and there is stuff in the footlocker that he wasn't supposed to see until he turns eighteen years old."

"Okay, Cassie," Marcus thought it best to continue the story himself. "The important part is that there is a document binder that I can't legally open until I am eighteen years old. I don't know what is in it, but I suspect it is a will or something. And we think someone else is after it."

"No, Marcus, we don't think, we know!" Cassie was anxious to get it all out in the open. "Mitch, when Marcus knocked the machete out of that guy's hand, it must have hit him on the right arm and cut him. So ever since then we've been noticing people with bandages on their right arms."

"She's getting ahead of herself, Mitch. Before I gave you that machete and handkerchief, I had them hidden in my room. Somebody found them and opened my bedroom window and placed them outside the window Wednesday night or early Thursday morning. When Cassie and I skipped school on Thursday, we went back to my apartment to open the footlocker," Marcus was having a hard time containing the excitement as he told the story. "The timing was perfect, because we found the machete was missing from where I had hidden it. And just then I heard noises outside my bedroom window. When I turned to look out the window, someone was running away with one of my handkerchiefs. There was another handkerchief and the machete laying on the ground outside the window."

"Did you get a good look at the person running away, Marcus." Mitch asked.

"No, but I could tell he had black hair and was wearing a white tee shirt and blue jeans."

"So, no good ID, then?"

"Not then, but later," Cassie interjected.

"What do you mean Cassie?" the deputy asked.

"Yesterday, we went to Franklin's Five and Dime, and we ran into the soda jerk that works there. Have you ever seen him? His name is Ellis Compton," Cassie told him. Even mentioning Ellis' name now left a bad taste in her mouth.

"Yeah, I know of him," Mitch had a bit of knowledge concerning Ellis. "Got a bit of a lead foot, a real smartass I've heard. Yeah, I know of his dad Ollie, he's a locksmith over in Monticello. So, what does this kid have to do with it?"
"First, Marcus noticed he had a bandage on his right arm. Then he saw Ellis wiping his brow with a red handkerchief," she continued.

"Then when he came closer to us, I saw the initials E.C. on the handkerchief," Marcus picked up the story. "I asked him why he had my handkerchief."

Mitch couldn't contain a bit of a smile as he asked, "And how did he respond to your question?"

"He said it was his, called me a stupid kid, and reminded me his initials were E.C."

"Until later when he told Marcus the truth and said it was Marcus' handkerchief," Cassie went on.

"What do you mean later, Cassie?" the deputy asked.

"A couple of hours later, here at Randolph Park. We were leaving to go back to my house, and he had parked his car over by the lot entrance and was waiting for us when we were walking out to highway 457." Cassie was glad they were finally able to tell someone what they had experienced. "I don't remember exactly what he said, but he was a real jerk. I know he said he would bury Marcus."

"Really, he used the word bury, Marcus?" Mitch asked him.

"Yeah, he did Mitch. He said I have something he wants and that it belongs to him and he'll get it no matter who gets in his way. We think he's talking about what is in the footlocker," Marcus tried to remember it all.

Yes," Cassie said, "and that's when he told Marcus he was right, that it was Marcus' handkerchief. And he also said he knows all about us, especially Marcus. He even knew about the shortcut we use leaving the north end of the cemetery when we visit Marcus' parents."

"Oh yeah, and you know what else he said, Mitch?" Marcus couldn't possibly leave out what was no doubt the kicker, "He said if we went to the cemetery, we should stay out of the mausoleum."
Mitch Daniels could not believe that the dumb kid had told them to stay out of the mausoleum. How much more obvious could he have been, other than admitting that he was the one who had attempted to attack them? "He told you to stay out of the mausoleum?"

Cassie corrected the narrative, "Actually, I think his words were, if I were you, I'd stay out of the mausoleum."

"I believe that I just might start looking into our friend Ellis Compton tomorrow morning," Deputy Daniels said as he scribbled a few notes into his pad. "Anything else you need to tell me kids?"

"Just one more thing deputy," Cassie answered. "Marcus doesn't want me to mention this, but I think it's important. Marcus' father had a cousin named Judy...."

"Yes, I know Judy," Mitch said. "And I know he has spent the night at your apartment a few times lately," Mitch said, directing his comments toward Marcus.

"Including the night that the machete and handkerchiefs went missing," Cassie added.

"Cassie, that doesn't mean that he took them and put them outside the window," Marcus tried to explain, hating to cast suspicion on Judy.

"Marcus, we've discussed this. Judy had a son that got adopted by someone in this area. That boy is now Ellis Compton's age. He could have been the one who gave Ellis all of his information about the footlocker. Heck, it could have been him in the mausoleum, he had a bandage on his right forearm, too!"

"Cassie, he is my dad's cousin. Why would he want to harm me?"

"To help his son, maybe? I don't know Marcus." Cassie turned to Mitch, "What do you think Deputy Daniels?"

"I don't know either Cassie. I knew Judy when he was a teenager and in his very early twenties. And yes, he was a rabble-rouser and generally an unsavory character," Mitch explained what he remembered. "But he's an adult now, has a responsible job, so who knows. Yes, he did have a son, but I have no idea if Ellis Compton could be him. Ollie and his wife are divorced, and I honestly don't know if Ellis is their kid, or maybe he was adopted. I just don't know."

"He doesn't look anything like Judy, Mitch." Marcus practically pleaded on Judy's behalf. "Ellis is about the same height, but they don't look alike at all. Their hair isn't even the same color."

"I don't know, Marcus." Deputy Daniels closed his notebook. "Is there anything else that you need to tell me? I need to get on home. We always have an early dinner on Sunday so we can watch Walt Disney's Wonderful World of Color at 6:30."

"His car, Mitch," Cassie remembered, "it's a Ford and the license number is 3BK.491."

"You're sure of that number?" Mitch asked.

"Cassie is never wrong with a number." Marcus was certain she remembered it correctly.

"Okay then," Mitch added the tag number to his notes and asked, "Do you kids want a lift somewhere?"

"No thanks, Mitch," Marcus replied. "I think we're going to visit my parents on the way back to Cassie's house."

"Well, in that case I'll get moving. Thanks for the information kids," Mitch said standing up from the bench and stretching. "I'll get on this first thing in the morning. Especially this character Ellis."

"Goodbye Mitch," said Marcus and Cassie, not in unison, but close.

* * * *

"Do you think we left anything out, Marcus?" Cassie asked as they walked toward Forest Park Cemetery.
"I don't think so, Cassie," Marcus answered. "Although I did almost slip up and mention the dog."

"I noticed that." There was a lull in the conversation before Cassie continued, "There is one thing that I wonder about, though."

"What is it, Cassie?"

"I kind of wonder what is going to happen when they do catch the guy from the mausoleum and he tells them that a dog attacked him that day, that it wasn't a machete cut on his arm," Cassie had a valid point about the conflicting stories that would be presented.

"If it came to that, we would just have to lie and admit that some strange dog had come to our rescue and bitten the 'perp', as Mitch called him. Some dog we had never seen before or since. We can never admit the existence of my grandfather in the form of that dog," Marcus suggested.

"Yep, guess so," Cassie concurred.

The Missouri weather was unpredictable in mid-October. Sometimes it could be unseasonably warm, reaching into the seventies. At other times, like today, it could reach into the mid-sixties, and suddenly this late in the afternoon, approaching five o'clock, dip into the fifties on the way to an overnight low in the forties. Just before entering the cemetery, Cassie reached into her shoulder bag, removed and began putting on her white sweater. Marcus' heart sank when he saw the sweater. In a way, he wished he had told Cassie about his dream. Perhaps then she would not have brought the white sweater and would have opted for an alternate color. Marcus knew he could never again see Cassie in a white sweater without reliving the horror of that nightmare.

As they walked along the roadway, approaching the mausoleum, Cassie asked Marcus for the time. Checking his Timex, Marcus told her, "About ten of five."

"Good," she said. "Let's cut through the mausoleum. We have a little over an hour until I have to be home."

"I don't know if that's a good idea, Cassie," Marcus felt uneasy about going back into the mausoleum. It still wasn't the idea of dead people that bothered him, it was the live ones that he was leery of. He remembered Ellis' warning about entering it and was unsure he wanted to tempt fate.

"Don't be silly, Marcus. It's like falling off a bicycle. You just have to get back on and ride it again. Come on," and Cassie began skipping toward the entrance.

Marcus had to jog to catch up with her. "Wait, Cassie. We don't have to prove anything to anybody by going back in there."

"Yes, we do Marcus," Cassie seemed defiant. "We have to prove to Marcus and to Cassie that we are not scared, that we are two brave young kids that are just about ready to face whatever the world might throw at us. We are invincible, Marcus!"

Cassie was obviously going to be the strongest member of the debate club.

They entered the mausoleum, and with dusk less than an hour away, the lighting was meager. "Okay, Cassie. We came in, now we can leave, alright?"

"No, Marcus. I want to walk all the way through to the other doorway. I've never been to that side. Come on, let's go."

Marcus looked at Cassie in her milky white sweater and could not shake the foreboding feeling he was experiencing. As she defiantly started through the mausoleum, Marcus couldn't suppress a small smile at the pluckiness Cassie was displaying. He didn't know if she was doing this to satisfy her own needs or if it was to show him how brave she was. Or maybe it was designed for the express purpose of helping to quell Marcus' own feelings of insecurity. Regardless of her reasoning, whether it was for her benefit or for his, Marcus knew it made him proud to have her at his side. He certainly hoped his grandfather had been right when he had written that they had shown a life-lasting commitment to one another.

Nearing the halfway point, and with the light diminishing, Marcus asked Cassie, "Are you sure we need to go all the way through, Cassie? We could turn around and head back, you know."

"No, you can't." A voice came from behind.

Before either of them could turn around to face the voice, a burlap sack was thrown over each of their heads and a drawstring pulled tight. Each sack contained two rags soaked in a bleach and alcohol solution. Within moments both Marcus and Cassie had passed out.

Marcus awoke to extreme cold and darkness, only a small amount of moonlight filtering into the mausoleum. Next to him, on his haunches sat the harelipped dog. "Grandpa, is that you?" Marcus had a hard time speaking, his throat dry and sore, his nose burning. "Is that you? You're my guardian angel, right? What happened, where is Cassie?" Marcus looked around, his head pounding. He couldn't see much, but there was no sign of Cassie. "I know you're not supposed to talk to me, but you have to tell me what happened to Cassie!"

The dog sat, not moving, but sadness pouring from tearful eyes. "Please tell me," Marcus began crying. "You are my guardian angel! You're supposed to look out for me!"

Marcus realized a voice was making itself known inside his brain. "She is alive, but they took her. I wanted to help her, but I couldn't. I am your guardian angel. I can only look out for you, but if I can help her at the same time.... I did all I was capable of. I managed to mark both of them. They will be easy for you to identify. I pulled the sack from both your heads, lest you both would have died. They took her, but she lives. Go now, get help. I may have broken too many rules and as a result, I may be recalled. But you are strong, and you can survive without me. Go now, Marcus." The dog left Marcus' side and proceeded out the north doorway of the mausoleum and into the forest. Marcus wondered if he would ever be seen again. He had saved Marcus once again, and Marcus was sure he had saved Cassie as well. He had to find her. He looked toward the north doorway, whispering the words for the first time in his life said, "I love you grandpa."

Marcus ran nonstop to the payphone at Walt's Tire and Auto Repair and as quickly as possible dialed Mitch Daniels' home telephone number.

Late Night

The ringing startled Mitch Daniels from a restless sleep. He had been dreaming of Jude Allensworth, reliving the first time he had placed his hand over the top of a drunken Judy's head to protect him from injury as he was guided into the back passenger seat of a county cruiser. Reaching for the bedside telephone's receiver, Mitch noted the time on his alarm clock. It was half past eleven. Answering the phone with a dry mouthed and groggy "Hello, Deputy Daniels here," Mitch immediately recognized Marcus Clemens's excited voice. Marcus sounded desperate and fearful and spoke tearfully. Mitch immediately broke from his disoriented, half-asleep state. "Marcus, slow down and speak clearly. Repeat what you just said."

"They took her Mitch. There were two of them and they took Cassie. They tried to kill us, but a dog came out of nowhere and attacked them."

"Who was 'they'? Marcus, did you see them? Can you identify them?" Mitch was wide awake now and in full police mode.

251

"No, Mitch. I never saw them. They put a sack over my head, it smelled like bleach or something and I guess I passed out. I just woke up a couple of minutes ago," Marcus tried to hurriedly explain, he wanted Mitch to start searching for Cassie immediately.

"And Cassie was with you? And I assume that now she is gone?" Mitch asked.

"Yes, exactly. We were together in the mausoleum when we were attacked. When I woke up, Cassie was gone. But the burlap sack they had put over her head was still laying there. Please, Mitch, you have to find her," Marcus pleaded.

"Okay, Marcus. I'm going to hang up and call dispatch. We'll get cars on the lookout for Cassie, then I'll come and get you. Where are you calling from?" Mitch asked him.

"I'm at Walt's, on White Street, at the payphone. Please hurry, Mitch."

"I'll be there in fifteen minutes, Marcus. Stay calm and try to stay out of sight in case they come back looking for you. I'll have my red lights on, so you'll know when I pull up. I'll see you in a few minutes, Marcus." Mitch hung up from Marcus, called dispatch with the information Marcus had given him, and raced to get into uniform.

Ending the call with Deputy Daniels, Marcus immediately called his home number. His watch had been stolen and he had no idea of the time, but it was obviously well past sundown. Knowing how meticulous Margaret was about dinner time, Marcus had no doubt she was beside herself with either anger or worry, dependent upon how late it really was. He tried calling twice, but the phone rang endlessly. That was not a good sign. It must be quite late, and the fact that the telephone was not being answered, lead Marcus to believe that Margaret had gone out looking for him. His immediate urge was to call Cassie's parents but the realization that they were no doubt worried sick over her failure to come home made him think twice about the wisdom of placing that call. He would be unable to give them any information or explanation concerning her disappearance. Marcus elected to leave that responsibility to Mitch and

252

the other officers. He walked over to the office picture window and looked up at the righthand wall. A Bardahl Oil wall clock with illuminated hands and numbers told Marcus it was later than he would have guessed. It was nearly midnight.

'Well, I guess I won't need that note for Thursday's absence tomorrow, will I?' Marcus thought to himself.

Marcus was partially hidden behind a stack of used tires when Deputy Daniels, with red lights blinking as promised, pulled into the parking lot of Walt's Tire and Auto Repair. Seeing the lights approaching, Marcus had emerged from his hiding spot and moved toward the cruiser. Taking a seat on the passenger side, Marcus was somewhat taken back a bit by the number of lights and colors visible on the interior of the car. He had been in this seat two or three times previously, but never at night, so the relative light show was a new experience for him. "Marcus," the deputy was all business and wasted no time getting down to the matter at hand, "are you sure you did not get a look at the two men who accosted you? Are you positive you couldn't identify them?"

"I'm positive, Mitch. I never saw them at all," Marcus responded honestly.

"Then how do you know there were two of them, Marcus?"

Marcus was painfully aware that it was going to take a lot of self-discipline to keep the dog, his grandfather, out of this. He paused for three or four seconds before formulating an answer. "I guess because there were two burlap sacks on the floor when I woke up, Mitch. If there was only one person, he couldn't put a sack on both of our heads at the same time. There had to be a second person putting the other sack on Cassie's head."

"How do you know for a fact that there was a sack on Cassie's head if your own head was covered and you couldn't see her?" Mitch asked.

"I could hear her, Mitch. Her voice was muffled because someone was holding the sack with the rags tight against her face, just like someone was doing to me. That's another reason I'm sure there were two of them," Marcus reasoned.

"You say you could hear Cassie's muffled voice. Did you hear any other voices, Marcus? Did either of the attackers say anything at all that you could hear?" Mitch was hoping Marcus might have remembered recognizing a voice he had overhead or perhaps a few key words that could offer a clue to their identity or plans.

"No, Mitch. I did not hear a single word from anyone other than Cassie. I do remember a dog barking though. Maybe after I passed out, maybe the dog did something to help Cassie. Maybe, I hope." Marcus was trying to plant a seed that might lead to the discovery of physical damage to the attackers, just as his grandfather had told him. He had told Marcus that he had marked them.

"Marcus, the kid from Franklin's. You said he had threatened you at the park. Do you think it could have been him and one of his friends?" Mitch asked.

"I think it's possible. He said I had something he wanted, and he would get it from me. And he told us that if he was us, he wouldn't go in the mausoleum. Because of him saying that, I resisted going in there. But Cassie thought it was important that we put that behind us and the best way was to go back in there, and I suppose she was right. But I guess we were being followed." In retrospect, Marcus certainly wished he had been adamant about not going into the mausoleum.

"If you were being followed, Marcus, it probably wouldn't have mattered if you had entered the mausoleum or not. They had come prepared to do what they were going to do, and they could have done it just about anywhere. It was late on a Sunday afternoon. Shops and stores were all closed, most people were home with their families, there weren't many folks out that could have served as witnesses." Mitch Daniels made a compelling argument to convince Marcus that avoiding the mausoleum most likely wouldn't have made any difference. No matter what they might have done differently, Cassie would still be missing right now.

A call came in for Deputy Daniels from dispatch. Apparently, Mitch had acted upon the information Marcus and Cassie had given him earlier in the day. Word had been sent to the Clark County Sheriff's

Department and a deputy had just visited the home of Alicia Compton, the ex-wife of Oliver Compton and mother of Ellis. Now that he drove a car, Ellis Compton lived with his mother most of the time, but his official residence was still with his father in Monticello. When his parents had divorced, he had wanted to remain in the Lewis County School District and attend Lewis and Clark Senior High School. The report from dispatch indicated that Ellis' vehicle was not at the residence, and when a Clark County Deputy questioned Mrs. Compton, she reported that she had not seen Ellis since Thursday evening. Although she had appeared concerned that a deputy was asking about her son's whereabouts at midnight on a Sunday, she commented that Ellis kept strange hours for a teenager, and she was not always sure if he was staying with her or his father.

Deputy Daniels left the parking lot at Walt's and headed to the west, in the direction of Monticello. "Mitch, have you talked to Mama? I tried to call her a couple of times from the payphone, but I didn't get an answer. I'm sure she is worried about me."

"No, I haven't Marcus. Let's take a detour by your apartment and see if she is home," he suggested.

"What about Cassie's parents, Mitch? Have you spoken to them?"

"Actually, Deputy Wilcox went to see them. She said they were not at home, but another deputy spotted their car over near the lock and dam and pulled them over. They were out looking for Cassie and were frantic. They said they had been driving all over the county searching. They knew you two frequented the park, the playground, the cemetery and the dam and riverfront. They told Deputy Bizelli that they had been all over the areas where they knew you liked to hang out but had not found a single clue. Deputy Bizelli had them come down to the station and Deputy Wilcox is no doubt talking to them right now, explaining that Cassie has probably been kidnapped." Mitch told Marcus everything he knew, and Marcus' heart sank with the sadness he felt toward Jack and Debbie.

No one was at home when they arrived at Marcus' apartment. Using his key, which was fortunately still in his pocket, Marcus and

Deputy Daniels entered the apartment. Turning on lights as he made his way into the kitchen, with Deputy Daniels in tow, Marcus was surprised to notice a familiar suitcase resting in front of the couch. Cousin Judy had obviously returned, yet again.

Pointing toward the suitcase, the deputy asked Marcus, "Does that belong to who I think it might belong to?"

"Yes, I think so. I've seen Cousin Judy's suitcase enough times lately to recognize it for sure."

"Seems to be convenient timing doesn't it Marcus? I wonder what time he arrived?" Mitch looked at Marcus, knowing that Marcus had to agree that the timing was suspicious.

Marcus jotted a note to Margaret, telling her that he was with Deputy Daniels and that he was safe and okay. He explained that there had been an incident, that Cassie had disappeared and that he was with Deputy Daniels looking for her. He put the note on the kitchen table and left the ceiling light over the table turned on so Margaret would be sure to see it.

Marcus locked the front door and they returned to the Sheriff's Department Cruiser. As Marcus opened the door to get in, he was struck by high beam headlights that made the note he had left unnecessary. Judy's light blue El Camino pulled in and parked behind the deputy's car. The car had not even come to a complete stop before Margaret had jumped out and began running toward Marcus. She grabbed him in a bearhug and then, while firmly holding his shoulders, pushed him back at arm's length to examine him in the pale light of the solitary streetlamp on her block. "Marcus, are you alright? Where in God's name have you been?"

"He's fine, Margaret," Deputy Daniels responded for Marcus. "He's good, but his friend Cassie is missing. I'm going to keep Marcus with me for a bit while we look for her, if you don't mind."

"Seeing Marcus and not Cassie, I was afraid of that, Mitchell. Her father called me a few hours ago, about six-thirty in fact, concerned that

256

she hadn't arrived home for dinner. He said she and Marcus had spent the day together after church and he had no idea where they were, wanted to know if I had known where they were going." Margaret had not yet realized anything was wrong until Jack Worthington had called, because she had dinner planned for seven and Marcus often didn't come home until just before seven, especially on a Sunday.

"And were you able to help him, Margaret?" Deputy Daniels asked.

"No, not really. I told him all the usual places that I know they go, the playground and lake at Randolph Park, the cemetery, that is practically Marcus' second home. He likes to fish at the river, goes to the A&W. You know Mitchell, the usual places kids go these days."

"And you, Judy. Good to see you again. What brings you back around?" Mitch Daniels had his suspicions.

"Things weren't going well at the Des Moines plant, so they are sending me there to take over as production manager," Judy sensed Mitchell's doubt, and realized it probably did look a little strange to intermittently be back in town after such a long absence. "It was a quick decision, they just decided Thursday evening at a board meeting and told me Friday. They could only give me until Tuesday to get there."
"What time did you roll in Judy?" Mitch asked.

"What am I, a suspect or something? Come on Mitchell, you know perfectly well that I'm not the same guy I was as a teenager," Judy immediately took a defensive stance. "That was a long time ago. I've changed a lot since those days, which I would be the first to admit, were reckless. I got to Margaret's just after six-thirty or so, why?"

"Just curious. I'm a cop, that's what I do is ask questions." Mitchell tried to ease Judy's ruffled feathers. "I'm not accusing you of anything, Judy."

"Okay Mitchell, I understand. I was just here to try to help Margaret find Marc. And now we know he's safely in your hands, so I'm ready to get some sleep, if you're good with that." Judy was ready to end the conversation with Mitch.

257

"Sure, we're good Judy." Mitchell turned his attention to Margaret. "I have one more stop that I need to make before I bring Marcus back home. Are you okay with that, Margaret? As late as it is, I would recommend he take tomorrow off from school anyway. I can even write the excuse if you'd like."

"I can handle that, Mitchell. Just get him back as soon as possible will you please?" Margaret asked him.

Judy put his hand on Marcus' shoulder and said, "Marc, I hope you find her."

Redemption

As Deputy Daniels sped west along Missouri Highway 16, a mere fourteen miles from his destination in Monticello, he was mentally preparing the line of questioning he would utilize. He had never met the teenaged soda jerk, but knew he would easily recognize him, based upon the detailed description Marcus had hurriedly provided on the drive. He remembered Ellis' father from back in their days at Lewis and Clark Senior High School but had not seen him in the past several years. However, he was confident the man would still look essentially the same, with perhaps a few gray hairs thrown in. He could not be sure that either of them had any involvement in Cassie's disappearance, but in view of the threatening behavior displayed by the teen toward Marcus, the possibility certainly existed.

Pulling into the gravel driveway of the split-level ranch style home, Deputy Daniels noted the sign on the pass-through pedestrian door to the left of the roll-up garage door – Lewis County Locksmith Service. The deputy couldn't help but wonder how Oliver Compton managed to muster enough income in the sparsely populated area he serviced with his business to afford such a spacious abode. How much demand could there be for keys and other locksmith activities in Lewis County? Turning off the ignition and headlights and removing his keys, Mitch turned to Marcus to offer explicit instructions. "Marcus, there are lights on in the house, so it appears someone is still awake. I'm going to go to the door and ask them a few questions. I want you to stay right here in the car. If I need you to positively identify this Ellis kid, I will come and get you, or bring him out here. Do not get out of the car unless I specifically tell you to. Understood?"

"Yes, Mitch. I understand. I'll stay in the car, I promise."

Mitch stepped out of the cruiser, pocketed his keys and adjusted his utility belt and holster. Flashlight in hand, he strode through the darkness toward the front door. As he was reaching up to knock, the door suddenly opened. Standing inside the screen door in pajama bottoms and undershirt stood Oliver Compton. He was roughly six feet two inches tall and from inside the house was several inches taller than the five feet ten Mitch Daniels. "Mitchell, I didn't know you grew up to be a deputy," he said.

"Ollie. Long time no see," Mitch replied.

"Just curious Mitch, are you here to tell me a relative has been in an accident or something? I mean, it's nearly one in the morning. I really don't think this is a social visit, is it?"

"No Ollie, it's not. I'm glad you were still up," Mitch explained. "I would have hated to have to awaken you, but I needed to ask you a few questions. And I also need to talk to your son. He is here, isn't he?"

"Yeah, he's here Mitchell, but he's asleep. Can't this wait until another day?" Oliver asked. "You are aware that tomorrow is a school day, aren't you? I don't know what could be so important."

"I wouldn't be bothering you this late if it wasn't necessary, Ollie."

"Well, it better be important. I was about to go to bed myself when I happened to catch your headlights through the front window."

"Ollie, how long has Ellis been here today? Rumor has it that although this is his official address, he spends most of his time at his mother's house in Alexandria. Has he been here the whole weekend?" Mitch asked.

Annoyed at being questioned, Ollie answered reluctantly, "He spends every weekend here and most weeknights as well. He visits his mother occasionally, but only if I don't need the car that night. What does it matter? We have joint custody of him."

Mitch sensed the aggravation in Ollie's voice and also saw a slight opening to pursue more information. "Ollie, is that '49 Ford in the driveway the only vehicle you own? If Ellis takes it to his mother's house, doesn't that put a crimp in your business activities? I mean, what if someone is locked out of their house in the middle of the night, how do you respond to their need?"

"I don't Mitchell. If I don't have the car, it's a little tough to satisfy a customer."

"So, you just pass on the call, is that right, Ollie?" Mitch asked him.

"That's right," Ollie said confidently.

"Then where does the Chevy panel truck in your garage come into the equation? It looks like an early '40's model. Does it still run?" Mitch always tried to stay one step ahead.

"Yeah, it runs, but it ain't registered and don't have tags." He admitted. "How did you even know it was out there?"

"You have windows in your garage door, Ollie. And I have a flashlight," Mitch explained the fairly obvious. "I looked on my way to your door."

Mitch continued, "Let's get back to my original question, how long has Ellis been here today? When did he show up?"

261

James E. Anderson

"He didn't show up, Mitchell. He's been here since he left work at the Five and Dime yesterday." Even in the shadowy light, Ollie's face was showing a bit of red, as his anger was beginning to swell.

Mitch decided it was time to push a little harder, "That's not what I hear, Ollie. I am under the impression that he was seen driving on White Street today, in the vicinity of Forest Park Cemetery. And my information indicates that you were with him in the car. Can you deny that Ollie? Has Ellis really been here all day today?"

"He's been here all day, I swear Mitchell."

Deputy Mitchell Daniels was not convinced that Oliver was involved in the abduction of Cassie Worthington. The only thing he had been able to trip Ollie with was the admission of the Chevy panel truck in the garage. Why he had wanted to lie about that was a question unto itself. It is certainly not a crime to own a vehicle that is not properly registered and tagged. Chances were good that he used it on public roads when Ellis was gone with the Ford sedan, but that was not a serious offense, and he was surprised that Ollie had tried to hide its existence.

"Ollie, why don't you go get Ellis for me so that I can ask him a few simple questions. Then we can all get to bed and put this behind us." Mitch was tired and truly was ready to get Ellis out here and finish up for the night. Ollie left to get Ellis and Mitch looked out to his cruiser, wondering if Marcus was still awake, and rethinking the wisdom of bringing him along. He doubted he would really need him to verify anything and wished he had left him with Margaret and Judy.

A few minutes passed before Ellis came to the door, his father behind him. Ellis was wearing blue jeans, a white tee shirt and had taken the time to put on and lace up his Keds sneakers. The first thing Mitch noticed, aside from the fact that he taken the time to fully dress, were the scratches on his left cheek and bandages on his left hand and right forearm. "Hello, Ellis," Mitch began. "I just wanted to ask you a couple of things and I'll try to be brief."

Aided by the porch and foyer lights, Marcus was able to tell, even from at least thirty feet away, that Ellis had new bandages on his left hand

262

and had scratches on his left cheek. Thinking back a few minutes, he remembered that Oliver Compton also had a bandage on his right hand. Marcus realized that his grandfather, or guardian angel, had been right when he said that he had marked them. He was one hundred per cent sure they were the attackers from the mausoleum and that they had kidnapped Cassie. The problem was that he could not tell Mitch how he knew they were the ones. No one would believe that proof had been provided by his guardian angel.

"Ellis, were you in the vicinity of Forest Park Cemetery today?" Mitch asked straight away.

"No, I was not. I don't know anybody buried there, why would I have any reason to be there?" Ellis responded as straightforward as possible.

"Your car was seen there, on White Street, that's why I had to ask. I wanted to see how honest you would be with me." Mitch decided to keep the pressure on, "Do you ever hang out in Alexandria, Ellis? Specifically at the Holiday Inn?"

"No, I don't hang out there. I live there most of the time, with my mother. But I spend a lot of my time here, with Pop. He's training me to join the family business when I get out of high school." Ellis seemed sincere enough about his living arrangements, but the family business remark was a little tougher to swallow. Mitch found it hard to believe Ollie could earn a decent living as a locksmith in Lewis County, it was an even steeper task to think two people could draw livable salaries by basically doing nothing but making keys.

"Ellis, do you know a young boy by the name of Marcus Clemens?" Mitch asked, anxious to see if Ellis would admit to knowing him.

"Yeah, he comes in the Five and Dime sometimes on Saturdays when I'm running the fountain. Chubby, kind of goofy kid," Ellis had no problem fessing up on that question.

263

James E. Anderson

"Marcus has told me that you have red handkerchiefs that are identical to some that he owns," Mitch began digging a little deeper. "Would you mind showing me one of them?"

"Sure," and Ellis turned, heading down the hallway toward his bedroom.   He returned a few moments later with one of the handkerchiefs (the only one he was in possession of).

Marcus saw Ellis turn to go toward his room and seeing him from behind immediately knew he was looking at the same person with long black hair, and wearing a white tee shirt and blue jeans, that he had seen running away from his bedroom window on the day of the machete and handkerchief attempted theft.   He was making mental notes of every incriminating detail he detected.

"Yep, you are correct Ellis, it sure does have your initials on it doesn't?" Mitch said.   "If you contend that this is your handkerchief Ellis, why did you admit to Marcus yesterday that it was indeed his?"

"I was just messing with him."

"Were you 'just messing with him' when you told him that you would bury him?" Mitch asked.   He followed that question by asking, "Were you 'just messing with him' when you told him he had something you wanted, and no one could stand in your way of getting it?"

Ellis denied the accusation, "I never said that.   He's a fat liar."

Mitch went on, "Were you 'messing with him' when you told him if you were him, you would stay away from the mausoleum?"

"Never said that either."

"What about when you attacked him and Cassie in the mausoleum?"

"I didn't do that."

The Trials of Marcus Clemens

"What about when you killed that girl in Alexandria and dumped her body on the riverbank back in the spring? Were you 'just messing with her' when you did that?"

"That wasn't me deputy. I didn't even have a license back then," Ellis said with defiance. "Pop! You hear what he's asking?"

Mitchell Daniels heard the hammer click back on the revolver and froze. He looked beyond Ellis and saw the barrel of a .45 pointed at his face.

"Get the car, son," Oliver ordered. "But take his gun out of the holster first and put it in the trunk, in the tackle box."

Ellis did as he was told, removing Mitch's service revolver from its holster and then ran to the car. He opened the trunk, leaned in, moved some blankets out of the way and opened an old tackle box. He placed the deputy's service revolver in the tackle box and just as he secured the box by throwing a blanket over it, the trunk lid smashed into the back of his head. He slumped, bleeding from the impact and unconscious to the ground. Marcus pulled the tackle box out of the trunk, set it on the ground and futilely attempted to lift the now motionless Ellis. His effort was suddenly taken over by someone a good foot taller and far stronger. Judy lifted Ellis up and into the trunk and after pulling the car keys from Ellis' pocket, whispered instructions to Marcus. Marcus ran to the driver's side door with Judy crab walking behind him to avoid being seen. Marcus opened the door and scurried across the bench seat and down to the passenger side floorboard. Judy slipped into the driver's seat, pulled the revolver from the tackle box and started the car.

"What the hell is taking so long, Ellis?" Oliver Compton shouted while keeping his gun aimed toward the face of Mitch Daniels.

As the Ford slowly eased toward the front door of the house, Mitch said, "Ollie, this doesn't have to end like this. I only came here looking for the little girl."

"That's bull, Mitchell. You were on to me. You tried to confuse me by throwing it onto the boy, but he didn't do anything really. He was

265

just helping his dad. How did you know I killed that girl in Alexandria? Did you know about the one in Keokuk, too?"

"I didn't even know about the one in Alexandria, Ollie. All I knew was your tag number had been spotted in the Holiday Inn parking lot. I just assumed it was Ellis hanging out, maybe getting someone to buy him a beer." Mitch didn't see a way out of his predicament and told Oliver the truth. "I just threw that out there to see his reaction."

"Don't matter now, Mitchell. Tomorrow morning you'll be catfish and snapping turtle dinner while you're resting at the bottom of the Mighty Mississippi. Ellis!" Oliver yelled to his son, "Get out of the car and open the trunk. Get the blankets out so we can roll Mitchell up in them after I put a slug in his brain."

With the Ford's high beam headlights in his face, it was hard for Oliver to see past the front of the car. When the driver side door opened and Judy stepped out behind it, Oliver at first did not realize he wasn't Ellis. While Judy held Mitch's service revolver in his left hand and rested it on the top of the door frame, he reached in with his right and turned off the headlights. It took a few seconds for Oliver's eyes to adjust, and when he realized that Judy had a revolver pointed at him, he swung his gun in Judy's direction firing off a shot. Mitch immediately took advantage of Oliver's distraction by grabbing his right arm and raising it. The second and third shots went up harmlessly into neighboring trees. A well-placed knee to the groin, followed by an elbow that shattered Oliver's nose resulted in a loosened grip that allowed Mitch to pry Oliver's gun from his hand. Mitch quickly pulled out and applied his handcuffs to a dazed and disoriented psycho, locking both hands behind his back.

As Mitch was leading Oliver Compton to the backseat of his cruiser, he glanced over at the Ford to see Marcus and Judy embracing. There was blood trailing from a wound to Judy's upper left arm. Mitch secured Oliver in the back seat and then returned to Marcus and Judy. A quick examination revealed the wound to be superficial, it had not penetrated Judy's arm and the damage was minimal.

"Come on," Mitch said, "we have to get into the shop". Taking the keys from the ignition, Mitch ran to the garage, fumbled for the correct key, and unlocked the pass-through pedestrian door. With Judy and Marcus close behind, Mitch ran to the Chevy panel truck and fished through the keys again until he located the proper key and unlocked the rear cargo door. Upon pulling the door open, Mitch immediately caught sight of what he feared was a lifeless twelve-year-old, red-haired girl, lying on her right side, back facing him. With uncontrolled emotion and tears building, Mitch jumped into the back of the panel truck and turned Cassie from her right side to her back and placed his fingers at the side of her neck to check for a pulse. Just as his fingers made contact, her eyes opened. To his relief, Mitch saw that she had only been sleeping. Recognizing Mitch, a tearful Cassie threw her arms around his neck and pulled herself up to him in a hug. Easing her back down, Mitch said, "I'm not the only one here, Cassie."

Cassie crawled back to the doorway, jumped out and without hesitation ran to Marcus, throwing her arms around him. "Marcus, I knew you and your grandpa would save me," she whispered before kissing his cheek and beginning to sob.

"Ah, Cassie, I didn't do nothing. We would have all been in a mess of trouble, but for Judy. He's the real-life hero." Marcus smiled at Judy and Cassie ran to him arms wide open, burying her head in his chest as she squeezed him.

James E. Anderson

Judy Comes Clean

It was a long night at the Lewis County Sheriff's Department for Mitch Daniels. A multitude of reports had to be filed, details that could not wait until morning had to be tended to. The facts of what had occurred, both tonight and all the back to May had to be recorded. And then some.

When backup had been called, Mitch commandeered Oliver Compton's telephone line to call Cassie's parents with the good news that she was alive and well and would soon be brought home by a deputy. She was placed on the phone, allowed to tearfully talk with her parents and explain the occurrences of the day. Judy made the call to Margaret, and Marcus was also afforded the opportunity to talk with her. When Deputy Wilcox arrived, she would take the responsibility for reuniting Cassie with her family. Waiting for reinforcements to arrive, along with an ambulance to treat the wound to Judy and the cut to the back of the head of a still unconscious Ellis, Mitch Daniels approached Judy to thank him for his heroism. Without his unexpected arrival, Mitch knew he would have been killed and didn't dare consider the fate that would have faced Marcus and

Cassie. Following the thank you and handshake, Mitch had to ask, "Judy, why did you follow us out here?"

"Because I know Ollie Compton, that's why," he explained. "I've always known he was crazy, since I was a little kid. I never told anyone, but I'm almost certain he killed my sister Elsie. The day she died; I had seen him lurking in the woods next to Cutler's Creek. I was off messing with a turtle nest when I heard her scream, and when I ran back, she was floating face down in the water, bleeding. No one really believed she had hit her head diving; she was too good. A lot of folks thought I did it to her. I was only six years old for Christ's sake. Ollie was the same age as her and had a crush on her. He loved her red hair, but she hated him. She always said he was a dirty kid. Anyway, my dad hired him one summer to help us bale hay. He must have been about thirteen years old, and my dad filled his head with some story about us being related to Mark Twain. I guess it impressed him, because after that I couldn't keep him away. Even though he was a couple of years older, he wanted to be my best friend. So, I put up with him hanging around for a few years."

Mitch found the story strange. "So, even though you suspected Ollie of killing your sister, you became his best friend?"

"I didn't say that, Mitch." Judy went on, "He clung to me, he bullied me, and I went through my teenage years intimidated by him. I felt I couldn't escape his grasp. Eventually, I met Paula, you remember her, I'm sure. Well, she got pregnant, and we had a son, Jude Junior. I wanted to get married, but she wasn't keen on the idea, and beside that, Ollie was always around, and she hated him, was always rude to him. If you recall, she had red hair and he was always infatuated with girls that had red hair. Didn't matter how she treated him; he drove her crazy with his flirting."

"Judy, are you telling me that you think Ollie might have killed Paula?" From what Mitch remembered of the case, it seemed to be falling into place. "He was the witness that fingered that drifter Winslow for killing her."

"Exactly, Mitch. There was no evidence, couldn't prove anything. Then he suddenly got married, before that trial even started. And when

Jude Junior went up for adoption - I was in no position to raise him mind you - guess who the couple was that claimed him? Yep, Ollie and Alicia Compton. I believe he had everything planned to a t."

"Amazing, absolutely amazing. Don't tell me, Alicia has red hair?"

"Of course, she does," Judy replied.

"Judy, Compton admitted to me that he killed that girl from Alexandria, the one Marcus and Cassie found, although that confession wouldn't hold up in court. But, that girl, Wozniak was her name, she had red hair with pigtails, the day Marcus took me to her body." Mitch thought for a moment and then added, "I'd bet a dollar to a doughnut that girl up in Keokuk, I think her name was Carlson, I bet she had red hair, too. What a sick psycho."

"Well, anyway Mitch, that's why I followed you out here. I thought about it for about ten minutes after you left, and I was worried about Marc. I think he's the son I never had."

* * * *

Additional deputies arrived, along with an ambulance. Deputy Wilcox took Cassie home to her parents and after receiving four stitches in his left bicep area, Judy drove Marcus back home to an anxious Margaret. Ellis took stitches to the back of his head as well and was transported in a car separate from Ollie to the county jail where they were housed in separate cells far enough apart that they could not see or hear one another.

Mitch and two county detectives searched the house, garage and workshop areas for evidence, spending two hours on the task before Mitch was sent back to the station to begin the arduous task of compiling reports and preparing for statements. The stash of marijuana that Ollie possessed and apparently had been dealing along the banks of the Mississippi River from Iowa to St. Louis provided an explanation for the comfortable residence and lifestyle of a simple locksmith.

And the Carlson girl from the Horseshoe in Keokuk? Red hair.

271

James E. Anderson

Epilogue

Mother's Day, Sunday May 10, 1964

It seemed like a perfect day for a celebratory get together. Jack and Debbie Worthington, Margaret Clemens, Judy Allensworth, Deputy Mitch Daniels and Mrs. Daniels, and their respective families had all gathered at the Red Roof Lodge for a festive dining experience. They were gathered to celebrate Mother's Day and the pending graduation of Marcus and Cassie from Roosevelt Elementary and their resultant promotion into junior high school. Unspoken, but felt by all six adults along with Marcus and Cassie, was the celebration of the conclusion of the trial for Oliver and Ellis Compton two weeks prior.

Oliver Compton had been convicted of first degree, pre-meditated murder in the case of Zofia Wozniak. Everyone was obviously pleased with that result. The case against Ellis, however, was a little bit tougher for many to stomach. Although he had not raised him and never known him as he had grown up, Ellis was nevertheless, Judy's son, and therefore he had heartfelt concern for Ellis' well-being. As only a sixteen-year-old,

273

Ellis had been tried in a juvenile court, charged with aiding and abetting in a capital crime. His court appointed attorney had successfully argued that Ellis had been subjected to undo and psychotic influence by his adoptive father and as a result was handed a relatively light sentence. He was ordered to serve in a juvenile detention center until reaching the age of eighteen, at which time he would serve two years of supervised probation. In addition, he was to be required to undergo psychiatric evaluation and treatment for the entirety of his incarceration in juvenile detention. Judy was troubled by the sentence, but ultimately relieved by the leniency, and vowed to develop a relationship with Ellis during his time in the detention center. Judy looked forward to the day of his release in 1966, when hopefully they could begin a father-son relationship.

As for Marcus and Cassie, everything had pretty much returned to normal. They were back to trips to Randolph Park, lunch at the A & W, and spent time on Saturdays skimming the magazines at Franklin's Five and Dime. Of course, the milkshakes were not quite as good with Denny Wallace's brother Billy prepping them in his position as the new soda jerk. But he would learn his customer's preferences and the little tricks of the trade with experience. The young female clientele seemed just as happy with Billy. He was no Elvis, but with his perfectly coiffed hair, he bore a meager resemblance to singing and television heartthrob Fabian. There were still regular visits to Marcus' parents in Forest Park Cemetery. The only thing that had changed was the lack of occasional meetings with the harelipped dog. Cassie had never gotten the opportunity to give him the hug she had promised, and Marcus truly did miss seeing the dog that he now knew was his grandfather.

Cassie's father had found another job, this one as an accountant in Hannibal. The drive was a little longer, but the pay and hours were an improvement, plus there were no security duties on the weekends.

Judy was doing well in his new production manager position in Des Moines and was able to drive down and visit Marcus and Margaret one or two weekends a month. Marcus sometimes wondered if there might be a budding romance in the offing. It seemed that Margaret would let down the bun in her hair a little more often nowadays, especially on the weekends that Judy would visit.

Deputy Daniels had made it a point to stay in touch with Marcus and Cassie as well as their parents, and the families had all become close friends.

With the meal concluded, everyone gathered belongings, gifts and flowers (and their respective children) and began making their way to the parking lot. Goodbyes and hugs were exchanged, and the families separated to load and climb into their vehicles. Margaret and Judy headed for the El Camino with Marcus and Cassie tagging along. After their goodbyes, Marcus and Cassie had begun walking toward the Worthington's Jetfire when they were stopped in their tracks. Looking into one another's eyes, an elated smile decorated both their faces as an eerie but welcomingly familiar voice emanated from the nearby shrubbery.... "Marc ...."

James E. Anderson